A TIME FOR DYING

Jonathan Ross

St. M
New York

Library of Congress Cataloging-in-Publication Data

Ross, Jonathan.
        A time for dying / Jonathan Ross.
              p.   cm.
        ISBN 0-312-03441-5
        I. Title.
    PR6068.0835T56   1989
    823'.914—dc20   89-33021
                                                            CIP

First published in Great Britain by Constable & Company Limited.

First U.S. Edition

10 9 8 7 6 5 4 3 2 1

1

It was an autumnal evening appropriate to dying, its sounds muffled by a cold mist that, condensed into its minute water droplets on the heights of the dark moor behind the town, had drifted down to lie trapped in the blanketed quietness of its streets. Overcoated against the chill, his hair glistening with moisture, the tall man walked along the footpath of a street deserted but for a scattering of parked cars.

Entering between gateless stone pillars, he climbed steps to the door of the high terraced building. Unseen, silent as a night-flying moth in its feathered thrust through the air, the missile hit the back of the man's neck, its metal head tearing into skin and muscle to pass through its thickness and emerge from his throat. There was shock at the sudden pain, then numbness and the disintegration of thought. A hoarse whistling noise came from a mouth opened to shout, his hands reaching up to the embedded missile and dropping as his legs folded, his face hitting and sliding down the door he had been about to open. With his head twisted grotesquely against a cement step, blood spilled from his mouth and from the torn flesh where the metal head protruded from his throat. With the failure of the brain and heart, he passed unknowingly into the darkness of death.

Blood congealing and heat decreasing rapidly, the body lay unnoticed by passersby. When the door against which it lay was opened from the inside by the woman, she screamed, running back to her apartment to dial with a shaking finger the telephone emergency number.

Detective Superintendent George Rogers, the appointed senior investigator of murder committed within his bailiwick, in his flat and streets away from the man choking in his own blood, was off duty and unaware of the burden with which he was soon to be saddled.

5

He was not without other burdens, cerebral and physical, divorced as he was from a wife on the perhaps justifiable grounds of his neglect of her in preference to the irregular commitments of constabulary duty, an incompatibility of temperament and, definitely unjustifiably, his alleged refusal to restore her conjugal rights. It had left him free, hung-up and still sexually viable with access to only half his salary and with no option but to live alone in a town flat undoubtedly designed for a bachelor dwarf.

No dwarf himself, he was six feet and a couple of inches of masculine robustness with black hair, a flat stomach, a full complement of teeth unstained by his pipe-smoking, and what he sometimes called his Australian-type nose: his beak-shaped pride, thrusting, interrogative and a sniffer-out of other peoples' misdeeds. While he had his soft side, his job limited the giving out of a natural amiability to small infrequent doses, his expression rather more comfortable in impassivity, using a heavy-browed sternness when in a mood to disapprove.

Though – as he himself would sardonically put it – he was no butterfly flitting from flower to flower, there were women who were attracted to him; usually, and happily, on a short-term basis. Despite his largely unwarranted fear of a permanent involvement and his somewhat prudish fastidiousness, he gave way at appropriate intervals to what Police Discipline Regulations could quite easily construe as 'discreditable conduct by a serving officer'. While on call for the twenty-four hours of day and night, he should, he considered, be allowed occasionally the uninterrupted and civilizing influence of a woman's company in his bed.

Waiting in his shoe-box-sized sitting-room and drinking from a tumbler of undiluted whisky, he was worrying out the problems likely to be raised by the uninhibited attentions of his lower flat neighbour. Unforthcoming about her background, the name she had printed on the doorplate of her flat was shown as Nanoushka Moth, and that, although a surname he hadn't encountered before, sounded English, suggesting the complication somewhere of a husband.

Believing a knocking on forty Rogers to be a neglected and helpless male, she was now, unasked, in his kitchen and cooking him a late meal. Though regarding her with affection and being grateful, he was apprehensive that it could be her first step towards a permanent take-over. At least a generous ten years older than himself and far from being the worse for that, she had allegedly been a ballet dancer and, later, a not too successful actress. Tall with a slender gracefulness touched only lightly with angularity, she had clearly chosen that evening to leave off her bra from breasts that had never needed its support, and to put on a particularly disturbing scent. Rogers, having cut his adolescent teeth on a girl student's *Soir de Paris* scent, found that perfumes could still disturb him. That and her tightly drawn-back glossy black hair, her pale skin, her luminously deep-green eyes and her over-lipsticked mouth showing a warming kindness, made her still a dangerous woman to have in too close a proximity. Her speech possessed a foreigner's grammatical correctness, made appealing by what Rogers accepted to be a Russian accent, and, behind her undeniable attractiveness and vivacity, he thought he detected bleak loneliness and an inner sadness.

In some sort of a female renaissance of sexuality, or because of loneliness, she had made plain to him that she wanted him as a lover. Ambivalent in any need for her, he was reluctant to add to her sadness by a rejection that would, however he phrased it, be brutal. At her age she might accept it as a confirmation that she was no longer sexually desirable to a man, and that he couldn't do.

He was coming to the conclusion – not too unhappily – that he should stop acting like an elderly maiden lady hung up on the local vicar and try to show that he found her unbearably tempting and to succumb or whatever one did in the circumstances, when his telephone bell rang. A call out – which it was – to a violently dead body was an imperative, and he had been so far mentally committed to being seduced that he muttered, 'Bugger and blast it!', frustrated and bloody-minded in his perversity.

2

Disraeli Street, lined with lofty late-Victorian buildings and situated in a backwater adjacent to a recently developed industrial estate, had lost the status it once had of being desirably residential. Not improving it, darkness and a dense mist diffused the stone solidness of its houses to a closed-in and murky mysteriousness, diminishing the street lamps on their tall concrete standards to strips of smouldering orange light that died to a muddy brown on reaching the pavements below.

Rogers, having recovered in the cold night air from what he now considered to be an uncharacteristic aberration of intent and turning his car into the street, pulled up short of a police patrol car parked with its front wheels across the pavement, its engine running and its headlights burning bright holes through the mist and onto the house it faced. Beyond it stood one of the unmarked cars used by his department, its supposed anonymity to the town's villains only weakly believed in by the detectives using it. The uniformed driver of the patrol car and a helmeted constable, neither to Rogers doing more than standing upright in a trance, saluted him as he climbed from his car. He glimpsed a pale face behind the fogged glass window of the patrol car and heard angry words coming from its interior, recognizably those of Detective Inspector Hagbourne. Plainly defensive answers to them were squawking from the radio he was using. For Rogers, the scene should have been active with hurrying and purposeful detectives doing investigative things with the department's equipment; and it wasn't.

Close to rasping his irritation at the nearest animate object, Rogers positioned himself tight-lipped behind the beams of the headlights and took in what they showed him. The house, semi-detached and ill-weathered by time, its upper structure invisible in the mist, showed an occupancy only by a red glow coming from behind a ground floor curtained window. A short flight of cement steps with ornamental stone pillars at their entrance led up to a white panelled door with 27 on it in tarnished brass numerals. The body that had made him miss a meal and, probably, much else lay across the upper two steps in a foetus-like hunching that did not disguise what must have been its living tallness. The dead man's dark-blue overcoat with its velvet collar had been forced up to the buttocks, dragging with it a trouser leg that exposed a sock and an inch of pallid flesh. Away from the street lighting and in the night's darkness, the body could appear to passersby as a tipped-over black plastic rubbish bag.

Passing through the pillars and climbing the steps to its side, he studied the clever-looking face with its half-closed eyes, its high cheekbones, the bloodied mouth opened as if about to yell, and the prominent nose that now nuzzled crookedly against a step. The hair was dark and tightly ridged – a womanizer's hair in the opinion of the straight-haired detective – the skin olive despite death's draining of blood from its capillaries. Unusually, and for a reason he couldn't put into words, he wasn't feeling too much pity for the violently dead subject of his investigation; certain that he would have disliked him in life. Embedded in the back of the neck, two inches from the left of the vertebrae, was the yellow-feathered butt of an aluminium crossbow bolt. Its bloodstained and bullet-shaped head protruded from the centre of the throat, a finger's-breadth above the knot of what had been a grey-coloured tie. Some of the blood that the wounds had shed freely on the steps was smeared thinly down the lower half of the door. Stooping and stifling his repugnance at touching dead flesh, Rogers put the back of his hand against the face. Difficult for him to judge, it felt cool and damp. He slid his hand carefully between the lapels of the coat and felt for body heat through the shirt. A lukewarmness there that, because of the chilliness of the night, told him little more than that death had occurred fairly recently.

He was using the skirt of his overcoat to rub the contact with dead flesh from his hand, and scowling about it, when he heard the slamming of a car's door and Hagbourne joined him. 'What the bloody hell's going on?' Rogers snapped angrily, his eyebrows down. 'Or isn't going on! Where's everybody, or are you expecting me to do the calling out?'

Hagbourne, heavily married with enough children to keep him hard-up for money and awake at nights, showed it in his pouched hangdog eyes, his down-turned moustache and in the too many creases that gave him a look of permanent melancholy. Because he had been found numerately better than average, he had been weaned from the bloodier aspects of criminality and detailed to work on the department's input of fraudulent villainy committed with computer, typewriter and forged signatures. It neither insulated him against an emergency call out, nor from standing in for absent colleagues. Being taken away from his stacks of documents, print-outs and account books rarely pleased him, and he wasn't cheerful about it now.

'Sir,' he said, choking with outraged emotion at Rogers's rasping, 'I've been working my backside off trying to get somebody here. I've been through the list and they're all supposed to be on their way. Well, most of them I could get hold of. We traced Dr Twite to the Provençal and he said that he'd be here when he'd finished his dinner, that he was buggered if he would get indigestion for the sake of a dead body that wasn't going anywhere. His words, sir, not mine. Sergeant Magnus was home and had to collect his cameras from Headquarters; the Coroner's Officer is out on a sudden death and he'll be here later. Nobody can find Mr Lingard who seems to be out for the evening, and the only two men in the office are dealing with a couple of prisoners. They'll be along with the screens and floods as soon as they've bunged them back in the cells. I,' he added feelingly, 'happened to be the only bugger available.'

'And who better, Thomas,' Rogers said mollifyingly, close to being amiable now that his initial irritation was soothed by something having been done. 'Apart from all that, you've some information for me? Who he is? Why was he killed? Things like that?' He smiled, taking a pipe from his coat pocket and beginning to stuff tobacco into it from a pouch. It had been a long half an hour since the last.

Hagbourne, straight-faced and back to being only morose, said, 'It's just a suggestion, but perhaps somebody didn't like him very much. According to the woman who nearly trod on him coming out, his name's Stephanakis.' He nodded in the direction of the lighted window near them. 'A Miss Whicher, and she's in there waiting. She's a bit shaken and difficult to get on with, so I haven't had the time to get much out of her, but she says he lives in the apartment above her. And there's a woman who isn't his wife and isn't there anyway. I banged on her door to check and couldn't see a light from any of the windows, so she's obviously out.'

With the street not wholly dead, Rogers noticed that the occasional car driver and pedestrian were being chivvied along by the constable against their understandable wishes to pause and see what was going on. Dead bodies and their manipulation by the police weren't supposed to be the subjects of a public interest or its emotional discomfort and his irritation returned. He growled, 'It's about time we had those screens here, Thomas. I feel as if we're up here on a bloody stage. Does this Miss Whicher know what he does?'

'I didn't ask her and she didn't say. I don't think she knows much about him at all.'

Rogers crouched over the body and again slid a reluctant hand between the lapels of the overcoat, feeling inside the jacket and withdrawing a wallet. He straightened himself upright and examined it, an expensive soft leather one with the gold-coloured initials SS impressed on it. Opening it, he went through the contents. 'His bank card agrees that he's Stephanakis,' he told Hagbourne. 'Solon Stephanakis.' He sniffed at the dankness of the mist. 'Not quite the sort of climate for a Greek to die in, I feel. A well-breeched one, too. He's got all the credit cards you need to flap around in five-star restaurants and roughly . . . ' – he riffled £10 and £5 notes with his fingers – ' . . . about two hundred and fifty pounds in used notes and not a sign of a drachma. A bit on the heavy side for loose cash, isn't it? When you've credit cards as well?' He frowned his uncertainty, refolding the wallet and passing it to Hagbourne. 'Hold it with anything you find on him after he's been photographed and . . . '

He stopped, hearing vehicles turning into the street, then seeing the large dipped headlights of what he recognized as the major incident coach emerging from the mist. It was followed by a red car he knew to be used by Detective Sergeant Magnus. 'Right, Thomas,' he said sardonically, 'now that somebody's decided to come, get them organized while I contact the Chief Constable. I'll try and convince him that we're about to do something positive, although I expect he'll be out somewhere as well.'

Spending a little more time in the patrol car than that demanded, he thought things out, although not very productively, while he filled it almost to suffocation with tobacco smoke. He climbed out only when the concealing canvas screens had been erected around the body, the flood lamps illuminating it and

11

the photographer busy with his electronic flashes. He had heard Hagbourne sending off the two newly-arrived detectives on house-to-house enquiries, though it was doubtful that anybody being more than a few yards from the scene could have seen or heard anything in the clogging mist.

Walking along the pavement away from the floods that flared a milky white cave to surround the steps, he crossed to the opposite side and, standing midway between two of the overhead street lights, checked the limits of visibility. Returning to where Hagbourne waited, he said, as if continuing an uninterrupted conversation, 'It strikes me as a bit unusual that a crossbow should be used to kill somebody, Thomas. We've never had it before and I've not heard of anywhere else that has.' He sounded a little put out, shrugging. 'Still, we've got it. Although I've never seen one in the flesh, I'm sure that nobody can carry it around in a pocket. Or handbag,' he qualified, knowing too much to discriminate in the gender of villainy. 'They're only too obviously lethal at short distances and quiet with it. No noise to bring anyone running or looking out of a window to be able to give us a description, though I imagine it must have hurt the poor devil enough to make him scream. If he did, somebody should have heard him.' He tapped thoughtfully at his teeth with the stem of his pipe. 'Ballistics aren't going to help us either. I can't see that there'll be anything on the bolt to identify it coming from a particular crossbow. Even should we find it.'

If Hagbourne thought that his senior was being unduly pessimistic, and he probably did, he kept it unsaid. 'It could have been used from a car,' he pointed out. 'Nobody not an idiot would chance being seen carrying it if he was intending to bang somebody off.'

'My theory entirely,' Rogers agreed. 'And probably from one parked across the street with whoever it was waiting inside. I've checked further along and whatever visibility we've got in this damned mist, it's enough for anybody not myopic to see a man opposite and aim at him. If Stephanakis was facing the door and about to go in, that'd fit the bolt hitting him in the back of the neck.' He was thoughtful again. 'Why in the neck? And particularly when it's dark? Wouldn't it have been more the done thing to shoot him between the shoulderblades or wherever?'

'We've a choice between hitting an intended target by an expert, or a near miss by a novice,' Hagbourne suggested, wishing he could get back to the certainties of his paperwork. 'Or, perhaps, he left his car, crept up behind him wearing trainers and did it at close range.'

'I suppose if it's going to happen it's preferable to have it creep up from behind you than have it look you in the face beforehand,' Rogers said philosophically, moving towards the steps. 'Whichever it was, we won't find out by talking about it. Or why it was done. I'll see your Miss Whicher while you search the body and see if there's a key to the apartment on it. When Dr Twite's finished his eating, if he ever does, and decides to join us, look after him if I'm still inside.'

Rogers, on the move, his nostrils sniffing out the smells of villainy, had a vast impatience for the people he needed doing anything else but what he wanted of them.

3

He hadn't come to strangle her but, cautiously opening the door to Rogers's knocking, she looked at him as though he had. Janet Whicher – that was the name inked on her door card – was, he guessed, in her bespectacled, rather stringy-throat late thirties. Something about her, possibly her wispy brown hair arranged carelessly behind the ears, her shiny skin and thin-lipped prudish mouth, suggested an indifference to a man's interest and a less than outgoing persona. The imitation sheepskin coat she still wore denied him any viewing of her body, thick purple wool stockings hiding her not unshapely legs.

The room in which she sat him after a prolonged inspection of his warrant card was hot and smelling of burned gas, rather heavy on moquette-covered furniture, solemn-looking books and religious pictures. There were no signs of anything like a debauchery-provoking television set or radio. After informing him ungraciously that she had already given details to the other detective, she sat at the side of the gas fire well away from him, telling him of her opening the door at eight-thirty exactly to attend a meeting at which she was due and discovering

Stephanakis bleeding on the doorstep. She had, she said, been badly frightened and shaken, and would he be sure that the blood was washed thoroughly from the step after the body was taken away.

Rogers, agreeing though doubtful that it was possible, said 'You identified the body as that of Mr Stephanakis when you saw it, so you obviously knew him?'

'Only by sight,' she replied, her expression suggesting that he had accused her of an impropriety. 'I don't see him that often and then only when we happen to pass each other. I don't speak to him, if that's what you mean.'

'Do you know what he does for a living?' Her coffee-brown eyes, hugely magnified through the thick spectacle lenses and oddly unsettling, stared at him with what he took to be disfavour.

'It's something to do with gambling.' She had clamped her lips together before saying that. 'I don't know what and I don't want to, but he goes to work just before nine and doesn't come back until two or three in the morning. I know that because he's uncaring enough to wake me up by slamming the door.'

'But here during the day?'

'I imagine so, but as I'm away at work I wouldn't know.' She hesitated a moment, then said, 'He was a blasphemer and he lived in sin.'

'He did?' Rogers put on a disapproving expression though wanting to smile, for he hadn't heard that expression in years. 'You mean he lived with a woman not his lawfully wedded wife?'

'He wouldn't have been killed if he wasn't. That was his punishment.'

He was catching a strong whiff of sexual bigotry from her prudish mouth. 'You mean by a jealous husband or somesuch?'

'No I do not. By Almighty God.' She bobbed her head. 'His divine punishment for the wicked.'

'It comes to all of us, Miss Whicher,' Rogers said solemnly. 'But probably not while we're slogging away down here. You knew the woman, of course?' He was sweating gently under his heavy overcoat, needing to unbutton and open it, but sensed from her peculiar attitude that she would see in it a preliminary to the exposing of the Great Beast itself.

'She's not there. She's been taken away and I saw it happen.'

14

She said it as though it were what the woman had deserved and, when he sat silent and waiting, took it as disbelief. 'I did, I'm quite certain. I was coming back home this evening when I saw her with two men, being pushed into a car. It was further down the street and dark, but I knew it was her. She had on her white coat and she wears her hair down to here.' She touched a finger to the middle of her arm, her expression saying that hair of that length was a sin also.

'Perhaps she was only going out for the evening,' he suggested. 'Why not?'

She bristled at that. 'Because I'm sure not. One man was holding her arm and pushing while the other man opened the door for him to put her in. Then the car drove away towards Haggart Street very fast and with no lights on.'

'Did you see what colour it was, or its number plate?'

'I did not.'

'She wasn't struggling or crying out for help?' He was getting a distinct impression that the room, though brightly lit, had a ceiling of depressingly damp grey cloud.

'She could have before I saw them. Because I didn't doesn't mean it wasn't so. I was some distance away and you must have noticed it's foggy outside.' She was showing more of her disapproval of an obviously thick-witted detective.

'And being foggy, you're quite certain it was her?'

'Of course I am. I wouldn't have said it if I wasn't.'

'Could one of the men have been Stephanakis?'

'No,' she said impatiently. 'He's taller than you are and they were short. I'd have known and told you so.'

'You can describe them?' While she was persisting in getting up his nose, he still had to accept that hers might be helpful evidence.

'No.' A pink flush of warning coloration was rising on her throat. 'Just that they had dark coats on and didn't have hats. Please understand once and for all that I only saw them for a short while when they were getting into the car. And I was looking at her, not them.'

'Of course you were,' Rogers said soothingly. 'I was only wondering why you didn't report it to us at the time if you thought she was being forcibly taken away.' He was now willing, almost willing, to bet a month's salary that she despised not only him, but men in general, was *virgo intacta* and wearing the fact like a police officer's Long Service and Good Conduct medal.

'Because it was none of my business,' she snapped at him. 'You don't seem to believe what I'm telling you now, why should you if I'd told you before? It could have been anything and I wish now that I hadn't mentioned it.'

'I'm not questioning the truth of what you're telling me, Miss Whicher,' he said pacifyingly, his teeth feeling on edge. 'I'm only questioning its interpretation. What time did this happen?'

'At about quarter to seven.' Not visibly pacified, she bit her words off short.

'And you discovered the body at eight-thirty.' He smiled encouragingly at her, but wished he had left her bloody-mindedness to Hagbourne, who would be questioning her later. 'He was killed between your coming home and going out again; outside your door and almost under your window. Will you think back about it and see if you can remember hearing anything? A shout, a car's engine being started, even somebody talking out there; sounds like that.'

'I don't need to think. I heard nothing unusual. I would take no notice of cars in the street. Or of people either.'

Rogers suppressed a rising exasperation. 'Does Stephanakis own a car? Or use one, such as a taxi?'

'If he does, I've never seen it. He walks.'

'Back to the woman then,' he said. 'You know her, naturally. Will you tell me about her?'

'She calls herself Debbie Studley – I think it's Studley – and she lets herself be used by that man. I tried to help her . . .' – the pink flush was rising to her face – ' . . . to save her from the abomination of what she was doing with the body God gave her, but she wouldn't listen. She told me not to bother her, to mind my own business. I told her I was on the Lord's business, and she just laughed and said why didn't I take in a lodger . . . ' Surprisingly, spittle bubbled at the corner of her mouth. 'I can't tell you the other vile things she said to me. They were not womanly and I should have known what she was. When that man wasn't there in the evenings I could hear men going upstairs to her and staying there, and that sort of wickedness gives this house a bad name.'

16

'Tch, tch.' He shook his head as if saddened by the iniquity of it all. 'Apart from the way she lived, what was she like? Her age, appearance, that sort of thing?' He smiled again, although so far she had been wholly unresponsive to his display of white teeth.

'I really couldn't say,' she said unhelpfully, dabbing at her mouth with a rolled-up men's-sized handkerchief. 'She isn't very old and she has yellow hair which makes her look what she is. She paints her face and uses lots of scent.' That, patently, was for her the tie-on label of whoredom and Rogers was thankful that it wasn't the time of the day for him to be smelling of his after-shave lotion.

He said, 'When you say she wasn't very old, could you . . .'

She interrupted him sharply. 'I said I didn't know. There's a photograph of her upstairs and you can find out from that. One of her mother and father, too, that she should be ashamed of keeping.'

He raised his eyebrows. 'You've been to her apartment then?'

'Yes, I told you. When I tried to help her and she wouldn't let me.' Her chin came up. 'But I don't want to talk about her any more.'

Rogers heaved himself from his chair and stood. He thought her a pathetically frustrated bundle of neuroses, probably more cantankerous with herself than with him; wondering what she did for a humanizing vice or two. 'I'm grateful, Miss Whicher,' he lied in the cause of official public relations. 'You've been of great help.'

'Don't forget to get that blood washed off my step,' she reminded him sharply, detaching her attention from him to the glowing bars of the gas fire. 'I won't be able to go out until you do.'

On the seat of a wooden chair near the door he was about to open, he saw a small pile of blue leaflets headed *Church of the New Apocalypse*. He hurried out before she decided in her unfriendly zealotry that policemen were also sinners demanding to be saved. At the moment, other than her, Rogers couldn't think of anybody or anything he wished to be saved from.

4

When Rogers stepped out into the dark and mist-bound street it was to a satisfactory scene of almost completed activity. In it, Dr Twite was talking to Hagbourne while returning a pair of rubber gloves to his briefcase, the Coroner's Officer and a PC were fitting with difficulty a seemingly unco-operative Stephanakis into a green PVC body bag, and Detective Sergeant Magnus, his photographic equipment still assembled, waited on further instructions. Outside the cave of light formed by the flood lamps and held back behind the encircling cars and the major incident coach, a scattering of dimly-seen and spectral-like spectators, unable to view much more than moving heads and a blood-stained door above the enclosing screens, watched patiently for the anticipated gruesome and horrible to appear.

Rogers joined Twite and Hagbourne, the thought occurring to him that the three of them together could reasonably be taken as a gathering of vultures picking at the bones of death. Wilfred Twite, graduate in morbid pathology, slapdash rather than professionally deft in his cutting up of the dead, yet possessed an almost intuitive flair for identifying why and where death had done its embracing. For a man engaged daily in grubbing into its often noisome results, he was an unusually ebullient and cheerful fatness. Managing, as he usually did, to look like the owner of a with-it boutique, he wore a silver-grey suit, a pink shirt and a flaring red tie beneath a kingfisher-blue overcoat. He smoked gold-tipped scented cigarettes held in his mouth, and his incongruous Mexican-style moustache and side-whiskers had saffron tinges to show for it.

Rogers liked him, gave him a friendly smile in greeting and spoke to Hagbourne. 'Use the radio, Thomas,' he said, 'and get a policewoman here. I want her to interrogate Miss Whicher, who seems to believe I'm in league with the forces of Beelzebub and has shut up on me. The missing woman from upstairs is called Debbie Studley and Miss Whicher not only thinks she's been living in sin with Stephanakis, but has also been kidnapped by two men with a car. Also, she suspects her of entertaining men in the apartment in Stephanakis's absence. I want to know more about her. A good description and what else, apart from the

18

dangers of the burning pit, she and Miss Whicher talked about. And while you're about it, have a name check made on the records for her and Stephanakis.'

With Hagbourne gone, he spoke to Twite. 'I see you've decided he's no longer breathing, Wilfred.'

'So I have, old George, and I'm off,' Twite said, affecting displeasure. 'There's nothing here that need have spoiled my dinner.'

'You're a fraud,' Rogers told him amiably, smelling the fumes of brandy and hoping that no zealous policeman he might encounter later would make him blow into a breathalizer. 'You'd bellyache like hell if you didn't see him as found, and I've yet to hear of anything that could stand between you and your eating. How long do you think he's been dead?'

Twite pursed his lips. 'Very roughly, an hour to an hour and a half, and certainly much too early for the onset of rigor. I've taken his temperature, but it's a calculation I'll have to do in the lab. His being out in the cold doesn't help.' He looked at his wristwatch and frowned.

'I thought he'd bled a lot,' Rogers said, prompting a man impatient to be gone into some sort of a diagnosis.

'We usually do when an artery's been severed. I'd say from the position of the bolt in his neck that it chopped through the carotid feeding the brain. Also, smack through his larynx.' He lit a cigarette from the stub of the one he had been smoking. 'If you're going to ask me how long it took him to die, I'm saying it depends. If the artery's completely severed, as I think it has been, probably a minute or two to loss of consciousness. Death intervening ... ' – he shrugged his fat shoulders, cigarette ash sprinkling on to his overcoat – ' ... anything up to four or five minutes. A cut artery'll fairly torrent blood out.'

'Would he be able to move? Walk, I mean, after being hit?' Rogers suspected that Twite, who was articulating his words carefully, had had a brandy too many.

'He might, he mightn't. I'd guess he was shot where he dropped. You haven't found blood anywhere else, have you?'

'No, but come daylight we might.' Rogers blinked several times, feeling mist collecting on his eyelashes and eyebrows. 'Would he be able to yell with that thing sticking in his throat?'

Twite shook his head, scattering more ash. 'It's through his voice-box and I don't think he'd manage more than a whisper, if that.'

They both moved to one side, close against the canvas screens, allowing the two men carrying the bagged-up Stephanakis on a stretcher to pass.

Rogers said, 'I'm surprised a bolt from a crossbow would go in so far as to stick out the other side. Aren't you?'

'If it was shot from across the street or nearer, I'd be surprised if it didn't,' Twite replied. 'Look, I do have somebody waiting for me. Can't we talk about this in the mortuary tomorrow when I examine him properly?'

'A few minutes,' Rogers urged him. 'I'm sure whoever it is won't mind that. Why would you be surprised if it didn't?'

Twite put his briefcase down, a sort of amiable resignation in his expression. 'Damn you, George, make it short. I'm not surprised because it's pointed and at best can travel at up to a couple of hundred miles an hour. I know that because way way back I used to shoot targets with a crossbow.'

'The frustrated warrior in you, Wilfred, and it's going to help. I've only seen photographs of them, so fill me in on the details.'

'And then I'm going,' Twite promised him. He spoke quickly, not giving Rogers any opportunity of interrupting. 'They come in two kinds; one with an enlarged rifle butt, one with a pistol grip. That is not so common, and not used here in any case because the bolt's not so long as this one. They both have gun-type triggers. The prod – the bow part – can be of metal or laminates and built with different tensions; heavy, medium or light and, naturally, it varies their shooting velocities. The light to medium pods, anything up to about an eighty pound pull, can be cocked reasonably easily by hand. Above that you'd need a cocking stirrup or lever, or sheer brute strength. At short ranges, if the bolt and its loading groove are true, the crossbow can approach a rifle's accuracy. The bolts – they're short arrows actually, now called as such, but originally quarrels, so please yourself – are usually made of wood or aluminium, and if I had to choose I think I'd rather be shot with a bullet. Now I'm going to bugger off, so don't try and stop me.' He stooped, snatched at his briefcase and hurried from the enclosure.

20

For a squat fat man with a dinner and brandy inside him he could move with a good turn of speed and Rogers followed him. Catching up with him, short of his white Citroen Safari parked further along the street, he said, 'One more, Wilfred. Can that pistol grip crossbow be folded, sort of, and carried concealed?'

Twite stopped and put a restraining hand on the detective's chest. 'You're a nosy sod, old George, and I've company in the car. The answer's that if there is, it's unknown to me and I can't imagine that it could be.'

Rogers watched him get into the Safari and drive off, a sensible man who seldom allowed work to interfere with his pleasures. He had seen against the light from a street lamp the unmistakable silhouette of a woman in the passenger seat, and he wondered whose wife it was that Twite had kept him from recognizing. While he knew him to be a gourmand with his food, he suspected him – with only a touch of envy – to be equally gluttonous in his appetite for women.

Returning to the enclosure, he found Hagbourne waiting for him, a labelled plastic bag in his hand. 'Anything useful?' Rogers asked him.

'Apart from the wallet and a cheque book, not much.' Hagbourne poked in the bag and took out a cylinder lock key and two small steel keys on a snake-chain. 'The door key was in his coat pocket,' he said. 'These two in his trouser pocket and clipped to a belt loop. Something he was making sure he didn't lose, and they look like desk keys.'

'Just what we wanted. It'll save my ordering you to commit a tort in kicking down his door.' Rogers mounted the steps, avoiding carefully the patches of Stephanakis's blood which he was certain would remain as a stain on the cement in perpetuity, and entered the building. Followed by Hagbourne, he climbed the uncarpeted stairs to a small landing lit dimly by a 25-watt unshaded bulb. There were two doors and a further flight of stairs leading up into shadowed darkness. 'There's nobody up there,' Hagbourne commented. 'I tried it.' One of the landing doors, its handle removed, had a strip of stained wood screwed over the keyhole; the other, a small card pinned to its upper panel with a not very revealing Number 2 typed on it.

Hagbourne fitted the key in its lock, managed a pessimist's

surprise at its actually working, and they walked in to a stifling warmth. Even before switching on a light, the gas fire could be seen to be burning.

The room was cramped and high-ceilinged, and, apart from the ubiquitous smell of burning gas, Rogers's nose detected immediately the fading fragrance of a woman's scent. Reminding him of Nanoushka, it seemed forthrightly aphrodisiacal, though that reaction need only be his admitted susceptibility to a perfume. A couple of shabby mismatched easy chairs and the well-worn patterned carpet were manifestly the legal requirements of an apartment rented as fully furnished. Plushy chairs, a huge sofa, a blondwood sideboard and small single-legged tables, expensive recent additions, had been crowded in with little concern for their different styles and colours or for the space that remained for walking. Beside the old-fashioned tiled mantelpiece containing the gas fire was the largest television set he could remember ever having seen. The room was a cultural desert: there were no books or any reading material but a coloured tabloid newspaper and a telephone directory. While it was generally untidy, Rogers could see no signs of a disturbance.

A door set in the middle of the far wall led into a larger room which had been partitioned into a kiosk-sized lavatory and a shower cubicle, a lilliputian kitchen and a bedroom small enough to be jam-packed with a bed, a wardrobe and a dressing-table loaded with a woman's toilet articles. The bed was colourfully fitted with gold satin pillows and sheets and a continental quilt with a blue cornflower motif. Brushing against it with his leg he felt mild warmth and the surge of contained water. Probably unreasonably, waterbeds were associated in his mind with erotic practices. Behind the quilted bedhead was the sealed door he had seen in the hall. Rogers, subject to claustrophobia, considered that sleeping in there could be better than nothing, but not all that much.

Going back to the sitting-room, he said to Hagbourne, 'You do the bedroom end of it while I sort this out. The woman's handbag could be a useful find.' After turning off the gas fire, his first concern was to find the photographs mentioned by Janet Whicher. He assumed that as she had seen them they would be framed and displayed. They were not and, if concealed in the room, were not readily findable. A drawer in the sideboard contained a dark-blue British passport and an envelope of photo-graphs – of which he took possession – a few bank statements showing an average balance of a thousand or so pounds, a cheque book and some unimportant looking papers he would examine later. All were in Stephanakis's name, nothing of what he had cursorily checked mentioning a Debbie Studley. Apart from one of the sideboard cupboards being stacked with bottles of liquor, the only other article of interest he found was a tiny folder of matches in an ashtray full of lipstick-stained cigarette ends. The folder, in royal-purple, had printed on it in gold a wreathed coronet and the words *Barbizan Club*.

That, Rogers knew, was a gaming club, certainly not one patronized by princes as was implied, owned by the corrupt and tricky Geoffrey Sickert, a former entrepreneur in female flesh under the ambiguous trading name of Sickert Enterprises. Enterprising he had been, for he had made large amounts of money from man's seemingly irrepressible desire to gaze on the exposed breasts of women. A policeman's step or two away from being arrested and charged with running a brothel, upmarket, discreet and highly recommended though it was, he had switched his activities to licensed gaming, making even larger amounts of money from the mistaken convictions of statis-tically heedless men and women that there was profit to be had from it.

Rogers was putting the folder in his wallet when Hagbourne came into the room carrying what was manifestly a heavy green strongbox. He laid it on the carpet and searched his pockets for the keys he had found on Stephanakis's body. 'In the wardrobe,' he said. 'Hidden in a soap powder carton and covered with a bed blanket. The usual row of women's dresses and only a few empty hangers. His gear was with them, including a sharpish dinner suit, a yukky frilled shirt and a made-up bow tie.' Hagbourne appeared not to be thinking much of any of it. 'There's nothing interesting in the drawers but socks and tights and underwear stuff for both of them. Plus about thirty packets of Frenchies. He must have been some goer, mustn't he?'

'They could have been shared around a bit,' Rogers told him. 'I'm sure that Miss Whicher believes she was having it off with ninety per cent of the males in Abbotsburn.'

With Rogers watching, Hagbourne crouched and fitted one of

the keys in the lock of the box, then lifted its lid. 'Bloody hell,' he breathed, his jaw dropping. 'It can't be true.'

Three-quarters full, there was an upper layer of bundles of used £50, £20, £10 and £5 notes, each held together with a rubber band. Getting down beside Hagbourne, Rogers tumbled the bundles with his hands, reaching bottom to discover the box solid with them. In their greed-provoking numbers, in their naked and untraceable availability, he thought them an offence to the spirit.

'Seeing money in used notes like that must be God's ultimate temptation to a needy man,' Rogers muttered, straightening his legs and hoping he hadn't said that only because it wasn't his. It had not been unlike looking into a dazzling light. 'There're several thousands of pounds in there, so shut it up and let somebody else have the chore of counting it.'

Hagbourne, locking the box and standing, handed the keys to Rogers. 'There's one thing we can be sure about, and that is he didn't get it honestly. It'd be in a bank if he had.'

'He does have an account so, tax dodging excluded, I'd agree with you,' Rogers said. 'Your Miss Whicher reckons he's a gambler, and I know somebody here has a connection with the Barbizan.' He frowned, pulling thoughtfully with thumb and finger at his lower lip. 'But dammit, that can't be the answer. Not that much won from a fixer like Sickert. Not unless . . . ah! You said he had a dinner suit. So what if he works for him? Doing something from which he could fiddle the takings?' He shook his head, disagreeing with his own guess. 'No, never with Sickert or I'd lose my certain faith in his essential dishonesty. Having done it himself, he'd know all the answers to thieving, and he'd be on the look-out for it. I don't know why, but villains take a special dislike to being robbed themselves.'

'The Lord forgive me for saying it about a dead man,' Hagbourne said mock piously, 'but what about Stephanakis having done some pimping? He's got all the equipment; a back-street apartment, a waterbed, an adequate supply of Frenchies, an obliging woman who Miss Whicher says entertains ninety per cent of our male citizens, and access to a market where I've heard there's charges of thirty to forty pounds in cash for some inbed humping.' He touched the box with the toe of his shoe. 'Keeping her busy for a year or so could account for that.'

'Good thinking, Thomas,' Rogers smiled, 'although it suggests you've a deplorably squalid mind. I exaggerated the percentage of customers a little, but even that'd still be too much to fit. I'll dig into it back at my office while you're locking up here and then handing that money over to the Admin Chief Superintendent in person. Get him out of bed if you have to. I want that box in his safe and out of our responsibility as soon as possible. Also, I want the place gone over first thing tomorrow by Sergeant Magnus, so make sure everything's secure and a PC's detailed to stand outside the door until he arrives.' He looked at his watch. 'And remember, our missing Debbie Studley may yet return from a quite uneventful evening out with a couple of friends.' He didn't think she would, but was always prepared to be proved wrong.

Passing Janet Whicher's door on the way out nudged his recall of what she had said about Stephanakis having had the equivalent of an Old Testament fire and brimstone death meted out to him. While not believing it for a moment, he considered it not a bad idea at all were Stephanakis found to be the sort of man he and Hagbourne thought him.

5

Rogers's office, on the otherwise deserted second floor of the Headquarters building, was, to him, a late-night bleakness of steel and plastic furniture, of wall displays of crime figures, location flags and statistical columns making anaemic the passions, pain and misery of the offences they represented. On such closed-in occasions he felt surrounded by a universal malevolence which the forces of law and order, and his department in particular, could do little to stem. It supported his long-held opinion that too many of the species *Homo sapiens* carried the black burden of evil beneath the facade of their ordinariness. It had given him a vast cynicism that was the stronger for his concealment of it behind a professional impassivity or a necessary social agreeableness with those whom he considered – with qualifications – as being not too wicked.

Left on his desk blotting pad for his information was a copy of a message sent by Records to Hagbourne. It said that there was no record of a Debbie Studley, but there was a Deborah Mary Stuchley who could possibly be identical. The daughter of a Dr Peter Stuchley of Lilac Cottage, Amford St Michael, she had been reported as a missing person six years previously. Her age was then given as fifteen years, though she appeared older, and her status as 'schoolgirl'. She was described as being five feet two inches tall, of slim build with pale-blonde hair and blue eyes. She had been found three days later at the seaside resort of Thurnholme Bay, refusing to say where she had slept for the two previous nights; or, as it was suspected by the WPC interviewing her, whether she had been associating sexually with a man during the time she had been missing. Supported by her father, she had refused to be medically examined and the case file had been closed. There was no record of a Solon Stephanakis which, for a cynical Rogers, meant no more than that it was a toss-up between his having been a tax-paying citizen of unblemished character or an undetected villain with debts to pay to society.

Appreciating that he was destined to do some possibly embarrassing eggshell questioning, he looked in the directory for Dr Stuchley's telephone number and dialled it, but almost immediately disconnected as he realized that the woman Debbie Studley had by no means been positively identified as Deborah Mary Stuchley and, should he blunder in and find that the doctor's daughter was now living a respectable life, there were likely to be awkward and possibly expensive repercussions.

Checking through what he would call the detritus of death, he examined Stephanakis's passport. Unless it was a clever counterfeit, the apparent Greek was a British citizen, having been born in Birmingham thirty-seven years earlier. His photograph, possibly with all the misrepresentations of passport photographs, showed him as being darkly goodlooking, probably self-admiring with it and a man, Rogers decided, he would have trusted no farther than the other side of his desk. His height was recorded as six feet three inches, his eyes brown and his hair black. There were Rotterdam customs entry and exit stampings in the passport, indicating a number of two-day visits to Holland extending over three years. Rogers said 'Um' about that, though they weren't meaning anything to him other than it was unlikely that they would be holiday visits.

26

There were five photographs in the envelope he had found in the sideboard drawer. Two were of Stephanakis sitting with another man at a bar counter which he could swear did not belong in Abbotsburn or its vicinity, and which had a foreign look about it. Another was of him in a dinner suit looking down his nose at the dealer's end of what Rogers could identify as a baccarat table. The remaining two were of a slightly built girl with long blonde hair and a pouting mouth like a squashed strawberry – he thought looking an unlikely seventeen or so – wearing a white half-length evening dress that showed her thin legs. Holding an empty stemmed glass and standing unsmiling against a background of fleur-de-lis papered wall, hers was a doll-like vapidness of youthful prettiness that would hold no attraction for him. He didn't have to admit to a cerebral brilliance in deciding that she was the missing Deborah Studley or Stuchley, and that her photographs and the one of Stephanakis at a gaming table had been taken at the Barbizan Club. He returned them to his pocket, certain that they would prove useful in nudging reluctant recalls of memory.

Unable to contact Detective Chief Inspector Lingard, his temporarily missing second-in-command, he decided to interview Sickert without a nanny to protect him from whatever scrurrilous allegations he might later choose to make. Using his pending tray to take care of the message form, passport and the other bits and pieces he would look at later, he left the building for his car outside which, he fancifully imagined, seemed to be shivering in a cold mist now thick enough to be designated a fog.

Leaving his car in the almost deserted Lysle Street, he walked through a narrow passage leading from it into an open car park. One of the buildings backing on to it was the rear entrance, marked PRIVATE NO ENTRY, of the Barbizan. Checking that Sickert's white Jaguar was present, he returned to the street. In the darkness, the entrance to the club could misleadingly be taken for the approach to the vault of a bank. Flanked by the shops of a furrier and a dealer in antiques, its set-back heavily studded door would be guarded when closed by a now opened black iron grille. On the inner wall, the club's identity was shown discreetly in gold leaf cursive script as *The Barbizan*, with a deterring *Members Only* below it.

Rogers used a brass bell-push that made a purring sound

inside. He recognized the man who opened the door. For reasons only too visually apparent, he was called Wonk-eye Webber, a thug with convictions for assaults occasioning actual bodily harm and robbery with violence, mostly committed against women. Never a man at best to possess an honest stare, his left eye wobbled in its orbital socket like a faulty compass, never quite certain in which direction it should point. To go with it, he could fairly be described as being unbeautiful, his features seeming to be modelled from grainy putty by inexpert thumbs, a choirboy's pink-lipped mouth stuck on them as an afterthought. Inherited genes had also given him lumpy muscles and an aggressive temperament, though at the expense of an intelligence by which to profit from them. He rarely admitted anything, sometimes not even his name. As a doorkeeper, or whatever he was supposed to be, he made a sham of the enamelled security badge pinned to his straining dinner jacket. There was no sham about his drop-chinned apprehension at seeing Rogers, and it was something that the detective promised himself he would remember.

He stepped past Webber into a carpeted corridor fitted with a small reception desk on which lay a leather book and a telephone, and a visitors' gilt chaise longue. 'I'm here to see Mr Sickert,' he said. 'He's in?'

Webber, closing the door behind him, had shown something that could be read as guilt reprieved. 'You sure tha's all right? I ain't sure he is, and I ain't supposed to let anyone in who ain't a member. Them's my orders.'

'Don't be stupid.' Rogers was cold with him, remembering the women against whom he had used his brutishness. He pointed a finger at the telephone. 'I know he's here, so get on that and tell him. It's what it's there for.'

When he had done so and replaced the receiver, Webber said surlily, 'Mr Sickert says you know the way.'

Rogers climbed stairs that ended at a door with an observation porthole in it. It was opened by another dinner-jacketed man, a whisker more civilized-looking than the doorkeeper and obviously expecting him. Rogers had seen the spacious gaming room before when it had been at rest between sessions. Sparing it a glance as he followed his escort over cinema-style crimson carpeting, he took in the baize-covered tables with their groups of players sitting and standing around them. They were the sort of well-breeched men and women he judged could lose fair amounts of money from their wallets and clutch-bags without worrying too much about a mortgage or having to cash in their unit trust shares. He nonetheless considered them semi-idiots. A large crystal chandelier hung its glittering image of attainable wealth over the roulette table, small gilt side tables and chairs were set against the fleur-de-lis decorated walls for the exhausted and thirsty, and a loaded buffet table screened in a corner of the room was attended by two bare-shouldered, big-breasted and teeth-flashing blondes who would represent Sickert's idea of what were caring hostesses. The room had the murmuring quietness of a prayer meeting, an almost reverential concentration on winning or losing money complemented by the sound of a roulette ball clicking round the rim of the wheel and the quiet slapping of playing cards. The air smelled of cigar and cigarette smoke warring with a heavy blend of women's perfumes. Rogers thought that he might have been mother-naked, his genitals blue with woad, for all that his walking through had been noticed.

The door to Sickert's office was fitted with vertical strips of mirror for one-way viewing and it was knocked on and opened for him by his escort. Sickert, away from his impressively huge desk and smoking a thick green cigar, was warming the seat of his trousers before a marble fireplace. He thrust out a pudgy hand to be shaken and said, 'Nice to see you,' though understandably with no excessive friendliness in his voice. 'You wouldn't be here on business, would you?'

He was a thickset man with the bloat of excessively good living on him. Elizabethan bearded and moustached with a predatory beak of a nose, his gambler's pale-brown eyes were assessing the detective's intent from behind heavy black-framed spectacles. He wore a conventional grey business suit with a white shirt and a muted green tie, wholly dissimilar from the raffishly colourful wide-striped clothing that had offended Rogers's eyes on earlier occasions. Only the gold watch and weighty bracelets on his wrists, illustrating money possessed, were unchanged.

With no acceptable reason for refusing to shake hands, Rogers did so. 'You know I'd come with a warrant and enough men if I were,' he said with a put-on amiability, knowing exactly what Sickert meant. 'One of your dealers has been found dead.'

With his cigar poised in mid-air, Sickert muttered, 'So it *was*

29

him.' Then, to Rogers, louder and unflurried, 'I should have guessed when he didn't turn up.'

'I expect you should,' Rogers said drily. 'Who didn't turn up?' Sickert had remained standing, an indication that the interview was going to be as brief as he could make it.

He gestured impatience. 'Stephanakis. Don't play silly buggers with me. He didn't turn up tonight and I had to cancel his table. I sent one of my staff down to find out and he came back to say the street was full of your lot buzzing round his door, and what looked like somebody who could be him not breathing all that much. I guessed somebody'd be along and as I can't see you wasting your time on a heart attack case I wouldn't be far wrong in thinking he'd met with an accident.' He put his cigar back between his teeth, not noticeably stricken with grief over the death of his employee. 'How?' he demanded around the cigar. 'And you might even tell me why.'

'He was shot with a crossbow bolt and he's dead. No accident and done with intent by somebody who didn't like him.'

'Ah!' Sickert said flippantly, 'that lets me off the hook, doesn't it? I'd have done it with a meat axe.'

'So when did you last see him?' Rogers wasn't prepared to be too informative. To find out what Sickert knew of anything he had to act as a man possessing few hard facts – which wasn't so difficult – and who was fumbling blindly around for them.

'Seeing it's none of my business, I could tell you to go to hell,' the gambler retorted without any particular hostility.

'I know you could, but you won't.' Rogers was unimpressed, that being Sickert's usual attitude with him and not meant to be taken too seriously. 'Especially not when you know I'd find out anyway. When?'

'Half-past two this morning after the punters had cleaned out my bank.' He showed his teeth at his own preposterous statement. 'It's the usual time.'

'And not since? No telephone call? Nothing at all?'

'Nothing at all.' His voice was faintly mocking. 'And I've been here on the premises since six this evening. As I expect you'll also be finding out.'

'What sort of man was he?'

'Stephananakis?' Sickert was rolling a cigar between finger and thumb and Rogers thought he had detected a brief show of anxiety in his eyes. If there had been, it came from his mouth as venom. 'He was a shit,' he spat out. 'An arsehole, if you have to know.' He made an ugly noise in his throat.

'But you were employing him,' Rogers pointed out. He had the impression that Sickert was wanting to distance himself from an inconveniently dead Stephanakis.

'There's no law saying I have to like somebody when I do. He was a good dealer, a professional, and he went down well with the punters. The ladies mostly, and that's as much as I wanted from him.'

'And as honest as the day was long, of course?' Rogers put an edge of derision in his words.

'I doubt it,' Sickert said nastily. 'I've been bounced before by these conniving bastards, as you well know. But I'm not bloody feeble-minded. The feller who showed you in is my nephew. His job is to keep tabs on all the dealers and their play, and he'd know if there was any fiddling. So would the table's profit percentage.' Anxiety shadowed his eyes again. 'Are you trying to tell me different?'

'No, just digging.' Rogers stood waiting for the more that didn't come, then said, 'Why didn't you like him?'

Sickert stared at him, scowling. 'You tell me; I just didn't.'

'Do you know anybody else who disliked him? Enough to kill him?' He knew already the answer to that.

'Don't give me that crap,' Sickert grunted. 'I'm in business here, not paid by you buggers to do your job for you.'

'So you're not,' Rogers agreed patiently. 'He has a woman living with him in his apartment. You know her?'

'I shouldn't think so. What's her name?'

Rogers withdrew the envelope of photographs from inside his overcoat, selected one of the blonde woman and held it out for Sickert to see. 'I'm sure you must,' he said mildly. 'On the evidence of your wallpaper alone she seems to have been here.'

Sickert's expression was one of astonishment and anger. 'So that's where she is, the twisting bitch! With that bastard Stephanakis! Right under my bloody nose!'

'That's the trouble with being so trusting,' Rogers said with unconcealed irony. 'Give me her name so that we know we're talking about the same woman.'

31

'Stuchley,' he snarled angrily. 'Debbie-bloody-Stuchley, so don't come the clever cock with me.' He flung his cigar into the fireplace and stalked across to a Japanese lacquered cabinet, opening it and unscrewing the cap from a brandy bottle. It gave him time to get his blood pressure back under control and, pouring his drink, he said less aggressively, 'It's a good one and it's cold outside. You'll have a drop before you go?

Rogers shook his head. 'Thank you, no. I'm off it. It doesn't do my driving licence any good.' It was a fine hypocrisy, but a civilized excuse for not drinking with a character he expected one day to put handcuffs on, and he had smiled when he said it.

Having muttered a just audible 'Balls to you', Sickert took his brandy to his desk and sat heavily in the huge red leather executive chair he had undoubtedly chosen to reflect his imagined importance. 'Have you finished?' he asked. 'I've got things to do.'

Rogers was genial, deciding to remain standing where he was with no intention of cutting short his interview. 'So have I,' he said, 'but I don't want to have to come back for something you'd forgotten to tell me. She worked for you?'

'She was one of my hostesses; supposed to look after the punters with drinks and snacks, and I paid her over the top for doing it. I didn't know for sure until she'd gone, but she'd been drumming up her own custom on the side.' He drank from his glass, his predatory eyes watching Rogers as if to gauge how he was taking it.

'You mean on her back?' He had wanted to add, 'And you not getting your cut out of the proceeds,' but thought that would be a mite tactless.

'Is there any other way for a tart? And it didn't happen here if that's what you're thinking. I heard that the punters who'd been sold on her went to her flat after she'd finished here.'

'And that was where?'

Sickert, grimacing his irritation and opening a drawer, took out a slim accounts book and flicked through its pages. 'Highfield Crescent,' he said. 'Number eleven, and it must be a right dump.'

'Did you sack her, or what? And when?'

'Six months or so ago, give or take. She just didn't turn up one night and I was told she'd left her flat even before that. I said sod her and got myself another girl. I certainly didn't know she'd moved in with Stephanakis – not for his private screwing.' He scowled, something he seemed fond of doing. 'I'm too soft,' he complained. 'Bloody women run rings round me.'

'We all suffer,' Rogers said, po-faced in agreeing with him. 'She's not there at the moment though. She's missing.'

There was an almost unnoticeable jerk of surprise in Sickert's jowls and his eyes narrowed. 'I shall try very hard not to worry,' he said, despite the fleeting anxiety he had shown from behind his spectacle lenses.

'I'm sure you will.' Rogers knew that the fat man valued women only for the money they could attract in his direction. 'What else do you know about her?'

Sickert drained his glass and heaved his bulk upright from the chair. 'Nothing,' he said flatly. 'She was only working here a year or so ago, and so long as my girls speak good English and have a decent dress or two, look good and smell nice and don't drink on the job, I don't stick my nose into where they come from or what they did when they were there.' He stepped from behind his desk to the door, holding it open. He was now all of a Chamber of Commerce businessman with nothing showing of what had appeared to be an earlier anxiety. 'I've enjoyed talking to you, Mr Rogers,' he said beaming, loud enough to be heard by those at the nearest table, 'I do hope I've been of help.'

Short of hauling him physically back inside – something he would have done had there not been an audience – there was nothing Rogers could do about it. He joined him at the door, smiled a quite false goodwill and said, 'There's always tomorrow, Mr Sickert, and I'll look forward to seeing you again.' He wasn't happy with what he had been told about either Stephanakis or Deborah Stuchley and his had been a coded message he knew the gambler would understand.

Sickert's nephew, no doubt having one sharp eye on the dealers and his other on the office door, was already there to escort him past the gaming tables with the minimum time for allowing a nosy copper to recognize too many of the players. The contemptible Webber at the door also forgot to say 'Goodnight' to him, though he opened the door for him quickly enough.

Outside and in his car, Rogers crawled back to his office in second gear on dipped headlights, worrying now about what limitations he should put on his questions when he interviewed

Dr Stuchley and his wife about their wayward missing daughter. He knew from his previous dealings with Sickert that the gambler was not above using his own version of seignoral rights in obtaining sexual privileges from the women he employed.

6

Well after one o'clock in the morning not being the most accommodating time for interviewing people who had been roused from their beds, and with no further activity possible at the scene of the killing, Rogers decided to relieve of further investigative effort the tired constabulary bodies needing their own beds. And that, with fourteen hours of work behind him and stale blood in his veins, included himself.

On Hagbourne's return from Disraeli Street – to which the missing woman had so far failed to return – he had reported to Rogers that the apartment had been relocked and left with a largish PC stationed outside its door, and that he had handed over the box of money to the Administrative Chief Superintendent. The apocalyptically-minded Janet Whicher had been re-interviewed by Detective Woman Sergeant Millier who had, in Hagbourne's implied opinion, done better at loosening her tongue than had the coarser approaches of her male colleagues. Miss Whicher had, it now appeared, visited Deborah Stuchley in her apartment on three occasions. It had not been until the third and final visit the week previously that she had decided that Deborah was a fallen woman needing to know that, with the world's end fast approaching, she should cleanse herself of the sins into which her submission to the gross appetites of men had led her. Prior to her unwelcomed proselytizing, she had been shown a framed photograph of Deborah's parents. Deborah had said her father was a doctor though had not revealed where he practised. Miss Whicher appeared unable, or unwilling, to give a more detailed description of Deborah than she had already given, or to amplify on the circumstances of her alleged forced departure. In the words of Sergeant Millier, Miss Whicher was still grinding on her back teeth about what had been a hurtful rebuff and it might not be wise to accept as unprejudiced what she had said about Deborah and Stephanakis.

She had been more forthcoming about a visitor she had seen some months earlier when she went upstairs to call on the people living above Deborah's apartment. Passing the door, she had heard angry voices inside. One was a man's, one a woman's. Finding the people she was visiting out she returned downstairs, and was in the hall when the man came running down. He looked angry, ignored her completely and left, not closing the door behind him. Miss Whicher described him as being between 25 and 30 years, quite short with straight yellowish hair – she believed it to have been dyed – and wearing a beige-coloured belted raincoat. She thought his voice had sounded affected and she hadn't seen him before or since. Having decided on Deborah Stuchley's identity – Janet Whicher had patently been mistaken in giving her name as Studley – Rogers put out a *Whereabouts Sought* message for circulation to Divisions. A routine reaction, he guessed it to be unlikely to do much more than insure him against the later possibility of the Chief Constable's, and anybody else's, penetrating hindsight.

With Hagbourne gone to his bed and his fecund wife and Rogers's office so quiet that he would not have been too surprised to have its silence filled with the graveyard sounds of dead voices, he uncharacteristically let the lift carry his 180-odd pounds of bone weariness down to the ground floor and his car.

Bedazzled in the fog by his own headlights and finishing twice with his front wheels straddling footpaths, it was past two o'clock when he parked his car outside his flat. Thankfully he saw no lights in either his or Nanoushka's windows, but was reminded of his abrupt desertion of her, remembering the sight of her sad mouth at the time. He had, he thought, reached the stage of wanting her company when she wasn't with him, being not so sure that he did when she was. Having once held her to be a damned nuisance in her persistent haunting of him, she now occupied as a problem a corner of his off-duty mind.

With only the ghost of her perfume left in his sitting-room and a dried-up piece of steak in the warming drawer of his cooker, he decided on a coffee and a shower instead, falling into bed without the irksome bother of putting on his pyjamas. Despite his body's urging for rest, his brain felt, against his will, a need for a rehashing of the evening's events, and switched when arriving at no useful conclusions, to a squirreling around his being invited into Nanoushka's room for a drink a few evenings before.

It had taken her several dry sherries and some quite conventional talk when, apropos of nothing relevant to it, she had asked him lightly if he liked her.

He had been surprised and said, 'Of course,' with a reassuring and neighbourly bonhomie.

Not so lightly and with her dark-green eyes somehow looking larger and more luminous than they should, she said, 'May I ask something of you that is perhaps not asked by a woman?'

'Of course,' he agreed again.

'You will not be offended?'

'I shouldn't think so, Nanoushka.' He was cautious, wondering what she was getting at, the softly upholstered easy chair enveloping most of him now feeling not so comfortable. 'Policemen are supposed to be thick-skinned, aren't they?'

'I want you to know there is no other . . . not as you might think. I am not, I feel, distasteful to you?'

'Good God, no,' he assured her, hoping it was the only thing she was asking, but fearing it wasn't going to be. Nor could he seem to detach his gaze from the steady regard of her eyes.

'It might be that you would . . . ' she had hesitated, an air of determination about her oddly at variance with her words – ' . . . that you would wish to be my lover.'

He hadn't drunk that much whisky for his brain to be unleashing anything resembling lust, and in his astonished speechlessness it seemed still to be working rationally. Apart from a happy incident in his adolescence – one of the golden apples of his youth – when he had been almost forcibly seduced by his Art School's life-class model, he couldn't recall a woman voicing her desire for him in so unexpected or forthright a manner. She had obviously vetted him in some mysterious female way, then decided that his apparent lukewarmness needed prompting towards the allaying of whatever sexual urgings still remained with her. Hers, he thought, must be the symptoms of a terrible loneliness to have pushed her into doing it. Having held her in a mildly affectionate friendship, never having considered her before in any physical sense, he now suspected that he could be short-sighted in not having been attracted to the niceness of her, to her slim-bodied elegance and grace which had every promise of a continuance in a bed.

'I would – very much,' he said gravely, then lying for the sake of her self-esteem. 'I was about to ask you the same thing, but couldn't bring myself to do it. Do you mean tonight?' You pusillanimous clot, he had sworn at himself; that must have sounded so bloody banal. He felt that he should have made the gesture of scrambling all over her. And that, he had to admit, might be no great shakes. He held no high opinion of himself as a lover, for none of the women who had given generously to him had made the agonized moans and panting sounds apparently considered *de rigueur* for the enjoyed couplings shown on television.

'No,' she said as if he hadn't understood her. 'I would like to feel that we should choose a time that is right for us both.' Then, as if what he had heard had been a casual aside, she reverted to their earlier conversation. 'Your little dog, George. Where is she now?'

He had left her without either of them referring to what she had said; nor, because of an overload of duty commitments, had he spent any time with her until she had, on the previous evening, offered to cook him a meal. He was working out an acceptable way of persuading her to stop wearing bright-red lipstick – it made her look hungrily bloody-mouthed – when his brain decided to close down on its already dwindling consciousness.

He could have been asleep for a week or for only several seconds when the sound of his telephone bell woke him. Fumbling blindly in the darkness for the receiver, far from being fully awake, he grunted into it his irritation at being disturbed. His caller was the duty inspector from the Headquarters Control Room, passing on a request from Detective Chief Inspector Lingard for his attendance at number eighteen Whitehorse Road where a man had been battered to death in the driveway of his house.

Out of bed, his mouth feeling as if full of old doormat, and trying to convince himself that he had not been resuscitated from a premature burial, his watch told him it was four-fifteen and that he had been asleep for all of two hours. Had he given free rein to his feelings and not counted the cost of replacing broken glass, the telephone handset would by now have been hurled savagely through his bedroom window.

7

Rogers felt a perverse satisfaction in driving with bloodshot and straining eyes at a snail's pace through a fog he thought thick enough to be cut into blocks, finding it as bad as he had expected it to be and confirming his right to have been furious. Unable fairly to lay the blame on his second-in-command or the man who had so inopportunely got himself killed, he decided with a lightening of his ill-humour to lay it at the door of the Meteorological Office which had so wrongly forecast a clear night with average temperatures.

Entering Whitehorse Road on the higher outskirts of the town, the short length of which he could only see as a glistening black, he located the house he wanted only by the police patrol car and Lingard's vintage green Bentley standing outside it. The silhouette of a uniformed PC showed in the fuzzy yellow light shining from an open front door. Braking to a halt, he dismounted into a quiet-breathing silence of nothing happening and the dripping of cold water from the few remaining leaves of a pollarded tree under which he had parked.

The short drive he entered ended at an occupied carport attached to the side of the house. Clearly with no dead body awaiting his attention, there was also a complete absence of urgent activity. His first impression that he was at another Stephanakis-like cock-up of delayed attendances he discarded almost immediately, knowing well Lingard's professional adequacy. That and his appearance from the house, his early warning system well in evidence, hurrying out to meet him.

'Morning, George,' he said with more cheerfulness than that time of the morning deserved. 'Sorry to disturb you, but I thought I'd better since he's died on us.'

Detective Chief Inspector David Lingard, one of nature's bachelor exquisites and, paradoxically, a hard case with it, was a man waiting in the wings without visible impatience or unhappiness for the older Rogers to vacate his superintendent's chair of office. Muscularly lean with blond hair – worn a shade too long and shaggy for Rogers's approval – his narrow features thrust out a patrician nose into which he frequently pushed attar of roses-scented snuff. Having an inexplicable admiration for the eighteenth-century dandy Beau Brummell and the society in which he exercised his elegance, Lingard affected a comparable dandyism with impeccably tailored suits, embroidered or extravagantly patterned waistcoats and hand-sewn silk shirts high in the collar and long in the cuffs. These elegances, worn now beneath a sand-coloured camelhair coat, made, not for the first time, the grey-suited and dark-overcoated Rogers feel himself to be a dullish black crow against Lingard's peacockery.

'And I note that you've already buried him.' A tired Rogers felt neither cerebrally brilliant nor particularly far from gritty irritation as he looked pointedly about him as if he had overlooked the obvious.

'Ah, I see,' Lingard said, humouring what he thought his senior's cussedness, he and Rogers being friendly enough to weather professional differences. 'No body left *in situ*. Quite in order, George, as you'll agree. And a pox on what you're thinking. I was called out to what was then an attempted theft and a serious wounding consequent on it, the injured party having been carted off to hospital before I got here. He's an engine driver, one William Kiddle, by the way. Sergeant Tibbet was already here and saw him off and he's now at the hospital keeping me in touch. So far as I can gather from him, Kiddle only just made it to the operating table before dying.'

'Sorry, David.' Rogers cursed his having shown unjustified annoyance. 'Peevishness doesn't become me, does it? How was he killed? Not by a crossbow bolt by any chance?'

Lingard shook his head. 'I was told of that. It made me think twice about dragging you out, but when it became a killing I knew that you'd blow your respected top if I didn't. It was done with a sand wedge that Kiddle brought out with him to bash the ungodly.' He indicated the carport. 'Have a look at the locus before I say my piece.' He called out, 'Switch on the light!' to the PC standing in the doorway.

Close to it with the not too helpful light on, Rogers saw that the carport was an open structure of metal tubes supporting a corrugated PVC roof. The car in it, a bright red Vauxhall saloon, was jacked up at its rear end, its nearside wheel missing from its axle. On the stone-paved flooring a sheet of clear polythene covered a wheel, a cranked socket spanner, wheel nuts and a chromium-plated hub plate. At the rear of the car, sheets of polythene covered a golf club and a saucer-sized bloodstain.

'It's all too damp for dusting for fingerprints,' Lingard answered, anticipating being asked, 'and I've arranged for it to be done after it's been photographed again in daylight. What do you make of it?'

'Only what you're showing me at the moment,' Rogers said drily. 'Which, on the surface, explains damn-all. A minor attempted theft of a car wheel, its owner coming out to see what's going on and being killed for his pains.' He had been watching Lingard's face. 'But I'm sure you're going to tell me there's more.'

'There is,' Lingard conceded. 'What you see doesn't make sense. That wheel doesn't belong to the car. Apart from being more rusty than the others, Mrs Kiddle was certain about it because her husband had all his wheels re-shod with Michelin radials less than a year ago. That wheel on the deck has a different make remould tyre on it. In addition, the jack and spanner are foreigners. His are still in the boot with the spare wheel.'

'Go on,' Rogers told him, knowing his man and refusing to look surprised. 'You've something else up that sleeve of yours.'

Lingard withdrew a tiny ivory box from his coat pocket and pinched snuff up his nose, flapping away unsniffed grains with a green silk handkerchief. 'Not a lot,' he admitted. 'And it was hellishly difficult to get it in any sort of order, mainly because the poor woman was badly shaken and worried about what was happening to her husband. She managed to make me feel all sorts of a callous lout for insisting on digging it out of her. She's at the hospital with Sergeant Jarvis, incidentally, who being a widow herself should be something of a comfort.' His very blue eyes showed his displeasure at what he had had to do. 'Still, I think I got the substance of it. Apparently Mrs Kiddle was disturbed by her husband getting out of bed and putting on his slippers; she thought about quarter past three. He told her that he'd heard somebody messing about with his car, probably about to steal it again. He had a reason for that, George, as you'll hear. Ring for the police, she said. He said something like bugger the police, by the time they got there he'd have lost his car; and he was probably right at that. It seems that Kiddle was a generally aggressive and

40

sturdy cove where his property was concerned and not frightened to mix it when he thought necessary. Once he'd gone downstairs she hopped out of bed and looked out of the window, but could see nothing because it faces the front. Then she heard scraping and what she called hitting noises; and a man's voice, not her husband's, saying something. She says that by this time she was terrified – she'd only just woken up, after all – and in two minds about what to do; whether to dial 999 or to go out and see if her husband was all right. Then she saw two men coming out of the drive, beating a hasty retreat with one of them rolling a car wheel along like a kid's hoop, the other one running with his hand up to his face as if, she says, he didn't want to be recognized. By the time they'd got on to the footpath they were beginning to be lost in the fog, but she seemed certain that they turned into the lane the other side of the next house. She heard an engine being started up, doors banging and so-on, then saw the shape of whatever it was – no lights on it, of course – coming out of the lane and turning towards the town centre. Then she came down and found her husband.'

Lingard paused as Rogers, assuming exaggeratedly that he was likely to drop dead if he didn't, sat himself on the low brick wall that surrounded the drive and garden. Stuffing tobacco into his pipe and lighting it, he said around its stem, 'I'll tell you later, but this is the second time tonight I've heard about two men being involved. You've descriptions?'

'No.' Lingard pulled a disappointed face. 'She didn't see their faces, only thought they wore dark clothing and take your choice about any age, height or build for all she was able to tell me.'

'The same as,' Rogers said, 'and perhaps no more than co-incidence . . . it's this bloody fog. You were saying Mrs Kiddle found her husband.'

'Yes, but I should have mentioned before that he's a golfer and keeps his bag of clubs in the hall. As there's not a sand wedge in the bag now, it's certain the poor chap grabbed it when he charged out. Whether his intent was for self-protection or to commit grievous bodily harm on whoever he found mucking about with his car, I don't suppose we'll ever know. Mrs Kiddle found him knocked cold where that bloodstain is, with the wedge close to him. She really panicked then and ran yelling blue murder to her next door neighbours, which was the first that

41

they'd heard anything of it. They did the emergency ringing for her, covered her husband with a blanket and sensibly left him where he was to wait for the ambulance. Tibbet was the first on the scene and the one who noticed that the wheel was the odd man out.' He grimaced his distaste over what was still bothering him. 'I was the unfeeling bugger who had to hold her back to get any idea of what had happened when all the poor woman wanted was to get to the hospital. Not that she could have seen him before he died, but she'll hate my guts for it.'

He fell silent for a few moments, his hands in his pockets while he gazed sombrely at his shoes. Then he said, 'Too late, but just in case, I put out a circulation for all cars seen out to be checked for occupants or flagged for their registration numbers.'

Rogers also thought it too late. 'We're sure that Kiddle was hit with the wedge?'

'It has blood and hairs on the blade, so it's reasonable to suppose he was. Reconstruction, George. Chummy padding downstairs from bedroom in pyjamas and slippers and going out with wedge in fist. Obviously heard and grabbed by one of the men when he turned corner to carport. Wedge taken from him by second man who bludgeoned him with it to shut him up. Panic stations then and they run for it, job unfinished but taking with them what they'd come for.' His expression reflected a dark promise in his mind. 'I know this. I wouldn't need a sand wedge or anything like it if I ever caught the bastards stealing a wheel from my car.' He meant it, his cherished Bentley being the only feminine thing for which he would admit any affection. 'But murder,' he murmured, shaking his head, 'for a wheel you can buy anywhere.'

'I can't imagine they meant to murder him, and it doesn't explain why they brought a replacement for the wheel they stole,' Rogers pointed out, his voice sounding flat in the blanketing fog. He was now cold as well as dog-tired, his eyes gritty and his numbed brain stumbling in trying the higher slopes of theorizing.

'No, it doesn't,' Lingard agreed. Irritatingly he was looking more bright-eyed, less hagridden, than Rogers felt. 'To round all this off, Mrs Kiddle did tell me that they'd only come back from their holiday yesterday, that it'd rained every day and that their car had been a jinx. She said it'd been stolen while they were there and recovered the same night from where they'd left it. Apparently the police – this was in Holland – sounded as if they thought the Kiddles had imagined the whole thing, and they . . .'

'Holland!' Rogers interrupted him, jerking from his role as a passive listener into standing. 'They'd been to Holland! You're sure?'

Lingard raised his eyebrows, quizzically surprised. 'That's what she told me. What's so important about it?'

'Unacceptable coincidences,' Rogers growled. He did his caged lion act of prowling back and forth in ordering his thinking as he told him about Stephanakis's killing, of his visits to Holland, of the two men abducting Deborah Stuchley, and of the suspiciously close relationship in time between the two murders. 'One coincidence I can stomach,' he finished, 'but two, possibly three, not a chance.'

'Egad, George, I might be a trifle thick, but isn't there a hell of a difference between being knocked over by a crossbow bolt and being bludgeoned with your own golf club you'd thoughtfully brought out with you? You said yourself that they probably hadn't intended killing him. And two men? It isn't unusual for villains to work in pairs. Mutual support and all that.' Lingard, the pragmatist, wasn't going along with Rogers, but needing to be diplomatic in his differing. 'And stealing a car wheel is a common enough pastime of our less worthy citizens.'

'But we don't remember any of them being half-decent enough to replace one, do we.' That niggled Rogers. Thoughtful consideration, even applied to a wheel and tyre inferior to the one stolen, was rarely an attribute of villains. 'It points to somebody not wanting the theft of the original wheel noticed; to somebody who, being surprised doing it, was prepared to attack the owner rather than just run away without it. And when they did run, to make certain that an apparently indispensable wheel went with them.' He snapped a lighter at his gone-out pipe, scowling his perplexity. Unable – for the moment, he qualified to himself – to make illuminating sense of it, he said, 'When we're finished here, I'm afraid that you'll have to see Mrs Kiddle again. I'm sorry to push it on you, David, but disliking you for doing it might at least take her mind off her husband for a few minutes. I want to know where they stayed in Holland and why; the details about the

43

taking of their car and who dealt with it at the Dutch end. Everything you can without having her scream at you.' Too well acquainted with the raw anguish of bereavement, he let his sympathy show, most of it for Mrs Kiddle. 'It's bad luck, but if Mrs Jarvis is still with her, she'll be hating you too.'

He knew, for Woman Sergeant Jarvis whose policeman husband had been blasted to death by the shotgun of a demented pig farmer already had him in her black book for a similar, in her mistaken view, unfeeling callousness in dealing with a bereaved wife.

8

After a stinging hot shower in the Headquarters gymnasium and a mowing of his overnight face stubble with the reserve shaver kept in his office, Rogers felt that, apart from still bleary eyes and having to use again a slightly grubby shirt, he might appear not too wearily impaired. Subabdominal growling from behind his waistband drove him to ordering a breakfast tray from the canteen, eating grilled sausage, bacon and eggs and filling what he thought to be his empty veins with hot coffee as he worked at his desk. Behind him, the windows leaked early morning daylight through the slats of venetian blinds.

Having put in an early bid for a computer crime check on car wheels reported stolen since the year's beginning, he had checked through the print-out flimsy delivered to him. With not so many stolen as he had imagined, for by their very numbers the reports of minor thefts would pass his interest unnoticed, there was only one entry where the theft of a wheel hadn't left its axle vacant. Sending for the crime file, prepared by a PC of the Minor Crimes Unit, he read it while he ate. Fourteen days previously, Martin McNeill, a store manager of St Ogreds Place, Abbotsburn, had reported the theft of a nearside rear wheel and tyre from his Datsun car left at night in the road under a resident's parking permit. He had discovered its loss only when he noticed that the pressure was badly down in the tyre replacing it. The substitution had become apparent because he had recently refurbished his

44

tyres with black paint and a tyre valve cap was missing. The original hub plate had apparently been replaced. McNeill had, among other details, informed the PC that he had only returned from a holiday the evening of the theft.

When coincidences abounded they made Rogers' neck hairs prickle and he wanted to growl, 'I damned well told you so,' to somebody. Instead, he dialled his internal telephone for one of his early turn DCs, instructing him to find out from McNeill without delay where he had been for his holiday, through whom, had his car been taken without consent during it and whatever other information about him and his car's movements he could get.

Checking the time and putting on his coat, which felt heavier than usual, he wrote *8.35 Mortuary* on his booking-out board with a chinagraph pencil and left his office, hoping that nobody else would get himself or herself inconveniently murdered in the meantime.

What had been a cotton wool fog was now thinned to a patchy mist of no consequence, though not helped by the exhaust-smoking traffic filling the streets. Reaching the red-brick hospital—which looked like a former House of Correction and, in Rogers's unshakable belief, was full of understandably terrified patients waiting to have hypodermic needles, glucose drips and enemas pushed into them—he drove into its forecourt, seeing the waiting Lingard seated in his Bentley. Having parked his car in a free space marked *Welfare Visitor* and crossing his fingers in doing so, he approached Lingard who, at close quarters, now showed rough edges and a lessening of his normal panache. 'You've had a hard time, David?' he asked with a post-breakfast amiability.

'Bloody awful,' Lingard replied. 'Jump in and take a seat. The housevet won't be with us until nine.'

Rogers fitted himself in the passenger's bucket seat, careful not to slam the car's ancient door too hard and earn himself a scowl. 'We've another coincidence,' he said, telling Lingard of McNeill's loss. 'If he was just back from a holiday abroad where he'd had his car temporarily stolen, we'd have some idea of what's going on, wouldn't we?'

Lingard scratched at the emerging whiskers on his chin and thought about it. 'Could be,' he agreed, 'if you're talking about drugs. It's probably been done before.'

'Work at how it could be organized and we'll talk about it later.'
Rogers had a theory, but it was a sketchy one with holes in it.
'You've seen Mrs Kiddle?'

Lingard nodded. 'Christ, George, I did feel a shit. Eyes streaming and shaking like nobody's business when I saw her. But she did quieten down and seemed not to mind talking. Jarvis was about to take her home so I kept it short, though as policewomen go she wasn't much help.' He pinched snuff into each of his nostrils in turn, flapping attar of roses-scented air around the interior of the car with his handkerchief. 'God knows why when you consider it must be freezing there, but they'd booked a fortnight in a holiday complex at a place called Konigsfoort through Shad-Awbery Travel; Konigsfoort being about ten kilometres from Utrecht. She thought it was the Wednesday before they came back—anyway, no more than two or three days before—when they found their car had been hijacked. They'd been out for the day, returning in the late evening and leaving it locked in the complex's car park with some of their gear on board. Kiddle—she calls him Bill, by the way—had toothache during the night and went out to it at two-ish to get some pain-killers from the car's medical box and it was gone. Kiddle got the proprietor of the place out of bed to telephone the Utrecht police for him and report the theft. Two mobile bods reached the complex about three-thirty, with both the Kiddles and the proprietor up and waiting. The police did their paperwork with the proprietor interpreting, and that apparently took up a lot of time. Then one of them took Kiddle to the car park to be shown where he'd left it, and there it was; still locked up with nothing missing from it. I suspect that it was all a little embarrassing for poor Kiddle. She said that they found it difficult to understand with the proprietor interpreting, but they did get the idea that the two Dutch coppers were considerably miffed, believing that they were dealing with a couple of English half-wits and not proposing to take any further action.'

'I can imagine it,' Rogers said wryly. 'Us coppers are such an unbelieving lot of sods. But accepting it as so, whoever it was taking it had to have the right ignition key. Or have I been kept in the dark about current developments?'

'I have heard about the use of an all-purpose skeleton key for cars, but I've doubts about it.' Lingard looked at his wristwatch.

'We'll also be an unpopular lot of sods if we don't get ourselves into the mortuary. It's time.'

The mortuary, an essentially discreet basement annexe to the hospital, lay at its rear. A sloping concrete drive for attending hearses led down to a green door which had for Rogers all the attractiveness of the door to a condemned cell. Behind it, where the two detectives waited for the houseman who was himself now late, ran a wide windowless passage, one side of which was banked solid with dark-green refrigerated drawers, each just wide enough and long enough to hold the average dead citizen flat on his or her back. Several of the drawers held name cards on them, two identifying their contents as *Stephanakis, S.* and *Kiddle, W.*, together with the dates of their dying and POLICE endorsed in red. Over the humming of the refrigerated motors there was a sense of brooding there, an imagining of dead eyes looking upwards in the shut-in darkness of their metal coffins.

Rogers was lighting his pipe, considering tobacco smoke an effective prophylactic against any free-ranging bacteria seeking a fresh breeding site, when the door at the far end of the passage opened from the mortuary proper, and the expected houseman entered. A housewoman, actually, as Rogers misnamed her in his mind with pleasure; attractive and amply-bosomed beneath her white coat – so attractive that she made him begin to worry about his grubby shirt.

After they had introduced themselves to her – she was identified as Dr C. Shellabeare by a tag pinned to her coat – she briskly pulled open the drawer containing the sheeted Kiddle. 'Are you making a formal identification of the body?' she asked.

'Neither of us has seen him before,' Roger said, giving her a smile that went unreturned. 'We want to see what the damage is and have a confirmation of the cause of death.'

The exposed features of Kiddle, rough-cast and rugged, had not yet settled into the non-expression of death, but still showed, it seemed, his dying snarl at whoever had done it to him. His sandy hair had been closely shaved in a tonsure down to the greyish skin of his scalp, revealing two pink-lipped mouths of lacerated flesh open to the bone of the skull beneath them.

Dr Shellabeare appeared an extremely serious woman and, standing close to Rogers as he studied what had happened to the unfortunate Kiddle, smelled not so seriously of strongly perfumed soap. She said crisply, 'So far as it is possible to postulate at the moment, it was due to an increase in intracranial pressure. Also, by some subdural haemorrhaging in the parietal lobe, caused obviously by two severe blows with an instrument. I don't believe I should add more because Dr Twite will be operating on him later this morning and will be reporting to you about it.'

Rogers said, 'Thank you.' He thought he had sensed behind her words an undercurrent of hostility. She was unamiable and definitely not in the business of winning constabulary friends.

'Was there a fracturing of the skull, doctor?' Lingard asked, seeming not to have got the message; or, if he had, characteristically disregarding it.

'That, too,' she replied tersely. 'You must wait for Dr Twite's report.' The chromium tube she carried clipped in her breast pocket with an assortment of pens had started to bleep. 'I'm sorry,' she said, not looking it, 'I do have to go. There's nothing more?'

'A formality,' Rogers told her pleasantly. Having changed his mind about her and no longer caring what she might think of his grubby shirt, he had decided against asking how Kiddle had died on his way to the operating table. Doctors were often a little touchy about patients stubborn enough not to respond to what was being done for them. 'We'd like to look at Stephanakis, who's another of our clients, and set for an interview with Dr Twite.' He added uncompromisingly, 'I'm sure we can manage on our own.'

She hesitated, but said nothing and went, leaving them with the impression that they were under deep suspicion of loitering with intent to commit necrophagia. When the door had closed behind her, Rogers said sardonically, 'Forgive her, David. They've probably fumbled things in surgery and she could have been advised to be cagey in case grounds'll be found for a malpractice suit against one of her colleagues.'

'Something I meant to mention earlier,' Lingard said. 'Back at the department, we found spots of blood on the wheel hub taken from Kiddle's car. It could be his splashed around, of course, but it's also possible he managed to get in a swipe at someone before being clobbered himself. Anyway, I've asked the laboratory to do us a really fast grouping on it and on the sand wedge.' For a moment he looked cold-eyed. 'It'd be nice to think we had another fractured skull staggering around waiting to be hand-cuffed, wouldn't it?'

Not answering, though agreeing with him, Rogers pulled open the drawer labelled as holding Stephanakis. 'There you are. As I want you to arrange for Hagbourne to attend the p.m., this is your official viewing of the body and what did it.'

With the bolt still embedded in his neck, Stephanakis looked several degrees more dead than he had when bleeding on Janet Whicher's share of the doorstep, his face a more yellowish colour, his half-open eyes dulled. As a subject not having come under medical treatment, his body, unlike that of Kiddle's, had not yet been stripped of clothing. Despite his contempt for what appeared to have been the dead man's degrading immorality and dishonesty, Rogers could still bring himself to feel a sort of pity for him and for what Twite's scalpels were going to do to his body tissues.

Lingard had been studying the face closely, and he frowned. 'I've seen him before,' he said. 'More than once. A tall cove and quite noticeable. I think usually on his own and walking some-where.' He was plucking pictures from his mind. 'And in a pub, sitting and looking as if he was waiting.' He made a gesture of frustration. 'I can't even remember which pub, but it'll come when I flog it out later.'

Closing the drawer on the dead man, Rogers asked, 'Anything to do with Sickert? The Barbizan?'

'Definitely not.' Lingard was annoyed with himself. 'I'd have remembered and classified him as a suspect by association.'

Outside and walking back up the slope to collect their cars, Rogers said—he thought tactfully—'Those wheels had to come from somewhere, David. If you haven't already done it, put a couple of our chaps on to the breaker's yards. See if we can pick up some information from them.'

'We're already under way so far as the Vauxhall is concerned,' Lingard replied, somewhat put out at his senior assuming a need to remind him. 'Not forgetting the jack and wheel spanner which could be identifiable to the make of car they came from.'

'That too,' Rogers agreed equably. 'And this. I shall be seeing our missing Deborah's father this morning, so I'd like you to visit her old address—that was eleven Highfield Crescent until six months or so ago—and get me some background on her and what she was doing.'

Rogers had all the divisiveness of a man juggling two balls in the air at once, having done damn-all of any consequence about either; though that was mitigated somewhat by the unhelpful habit of the town's citizenry in going to bed for the night. His was, he admitted, a selfish view, having had to be dragged out of his.

9

Possibly because the night fog had been so unhelpfully selective in drifting down from the moor on to Abbotsburn and its deeds of darkness, it and its now tattered mistiness had never reached the surrounding countryside. A pallid sun shone from a pale blue sky empty of cloud as Rogers, heading for Amford St Michael, drove his car along the narrow road that twisted between the massive earthen breasts of the moor, washed now in the purple and brown of dying heather and dead bracken.

Before leaving his office he had telephoned Dr Stuchley. A man with a pleasant and friendly voice, there had been what he thought to be an echo of despair in his 'Oh, my God! Has something happened?' when he told him who he was and that he wished to see him concerning his daughter Deborah. 'She's not . . . she hasn't come to any harm, has she?' Stuchley then asked and Rogers had had to temporize by saying not so far as he knew, but that she was believed to be missing from her apartment and he would explain further when he saw him. He had replaced the telephone with a re-awakened niggle of concern for the disappeared, almost certainly abducted, Deborah. That Janet Whicher hadn't witnessed her being dragged forcibly away meant little; intimidation or deception could have as easily been used to abduct her. That and the later killing of Stephanakis somehow had to be connected.

Lilac Cottage, set back in comparative isolation from the main street of the village, was not strictly a cottage, but an old and sprawling two-storied house with large latticed windows and an ornamental porched door. As a newer extension at the side of the house and approached by a separate path, was a white-painted single-storey structure with a garage. A black notice board on its door displayed the doctor's name and the hours he attended his surgery. Rogers, parking his car outside the house gates and taking his briefcase with him, walked the gravelled drive between hedges of small cypress bushes to the porch, twice lifting and dropping the heavy brass knocker on its door.

The woman opening it was obviously the doctor's wife. Somewhere in her forties and wearing a smooth worsted suit with a paisley foulard scarf knotted around her throat, Rogers classified her as the rangy outdoor type likely to keep a horse and a couple of large dogs. Her good-looking face, on which she wore no make-up, was thin, flat-planed and fresh complexioned, her ash-coloured hair worn straight and short-cropped. There was anxiety in her brown eyes and, cutting short Rogers's introducing himself, she said, 'Please, has something happened to my daughter?'

'So far as I know, nothing serious,' he replied, impassively-faced as he had to be. 'But I think I should explain further to you both together.' He detested this bringer of doom and disaster role he had so often to play, knowing that as the bearer of bad news he would rarely be liked for it.

'I'm sorry,' she said, 'but I am terribly worried. My husband's in his consulting room where he has a surgery in half an hour's time. You don't mind?'

'Of course not,' he answered. It had, anyway, been a no-option asking.

Stepping out into the porch she closed the door behind her, leading him along the lawn at the front of the house to the surgery. Passing through what was manifestly a patients' waiting room with wooden chairs around its perimeter, its walls displaying No Smoking notices in red and a large coloured poster of somebody's diseased lungs, he followed her into what she had called the consulting room.

Stuchley, seated in a leather chair at a desk neatly crowded with books, filing card boxes and unpleasant looking medical equipment which, in Rogers's opinion, should have been kept hidden from his patients, stood when they entered. 'Superintendent,' he said, holding out his hand. 'I can't say this is the

51

happiest of meetings, but I'm grateful you've taken the trouble. Please take a seat.'

While shaking the doctor's hand, Rogers took him in. Fiftyish, he judged. Stockily built and short with a bit of a paunch beneath his elderly herringbone tweed jacket and waistcoat. Greying fair hair, pleasantly honest features with a florid complexion and penetrating blue eyes searching over his gold-wire depressed cleric spectacles. Not, Rogers thought, a man for a horse and large dogs, but one who, under different circumstances, would be naturally affable; the sort of understanding doctor to have sitting at your bedside and taking your pulse if you happened to be dying.

Mrs Stuchley had moved to the window behind her husband, standing against its green curtains while the overcoated Rogers lowered himself into the chair at the side of the desk. 'I'm sorry to be worrying you about your daughter,' he said, opening his briefcase and taking out one of the photographs found in her apartment, 'but would you first confirm that this is of her.' He held it out for both of them to see.

Looking at it from where she stood, Mrs Stuchley nodded without speaking. Her husband leaned forward, peering at it closely. 'Yes,' he said. His face had tightened and he blinked. 'Now tell us, what's happened to her?'

For Rogers, this was the difficult bit. Not having fathered a child himself, he had only a secondhand perception of how deep parental love could run, how much an abuse of it could hurt. And he wasn't in the business of unnecessarily inflicting pain on innocent people, even had he to be sometimes devious and unforthcoming in avoiding it. 'Your daughter Deborah,' he started, keeping his voice expressionless, 'was living in Abbots-burn at a Disraeli Street address. You knew?'

Stuchley shook his head, not looking at the detective and clearly not expecting anything likely to make him happy.

'A man named Stephanakis was murdered outside his apartment there last night and in making our enquiries about possible witnesses we found that your daughter had left her . . . '

'No!' Stuchley had stopped him, his eyebrows down over suddenly angry eyes, his voice choked. 'You're not suggesting she did it!' His wife had put her hand to her mouth, uttering a muffled gasp.

'Let me say what I was about to, doctor,' Rogers hurriedly said. 'I did tell you that she was missing and, from the evidence we have, it seems that she left her apartment at least an hour and a half before he was killed. She was seen by a witness in the street leaving with two men in a car.' When he saw Stuchley about to interject, he held up a dissuading hand. 'Don't jump to a wrong conclusion,' he warned him. 'There's no definite evidence that she left other than by her own wish, though it's certain that she hadn't returned this morning and is now being treated officially as a person missing from her home.'

'But you do think she might have been?' Mrs Stuchley asked him, anxiety in her voice.

'It's a possibility, but no more,' he conceded gently. 'We are looking for her and her description's been circulated throughout the county. There could be a dozen reasons for her going, and I don't think you should fear unduly that she's come to any harm.' The silent anguish straining their expressions was pushing him into expressing unwarranted optimism.

'Please don't take us for fools, superintendent,' Stuchley said, not unpleasantly, 'but you obviously believe there's a connection between that man and Deborah.'

Rogers looked from him to his wife and back again. There was no point in dissembling further, and he had questions to ask. 'They were living together in the apartment,' he told them. 'Does that surprise you?'

Stuchley, looking grim, shook his head. 'Unfortunately not. You think he was killed because they were?'

'That'd be a difficult question to answer, wouldn't it? Considering he's dead and that Deborah's missing?' Rogers needed to avoid suppositions. 'What might help us to find her is for some-body close to her to give me some idea of her recent movements and the names of her friends and associates.'

Stuchley removed his spectacles and began polishing them with his handkerchief, worrying at his thoughts as he did so. Putting them back on, he turned to his wife. 'Mary, my dear,' he said, his eyes giving her a clear message. 'I'd be grateful for my coffee now. And no doubt the superintendent will join me.'

She hesitated for a moment, appearing about to object, then breathed a soft 'Yes, of course' and left the room through a door leading into the house.

53

Stuchley swivelled his chair to face the detective and said, 'You'll excuse my doing that, but my wife doesn't know the whole of what I have to tell you, and I don't wish her to. It'll probably surprise you to know that we are not, unhappily, close to Deborah at all, and we know little of what she does, or with whom.' He sank his chin into his collar and tie, staring at the carpet for several seconds. 'She left home two and a half years ago under circumstances which . . . well, which made it impossible for us to resolve our differences. We didn't know where she went initially, though it must have been away from this area. Much later a friend told me he thought she was working in Abbotsburn.' Sadness came from him in almost perceptible waves. 'I've a country practice here and I rarely go there, but when I did a few months back I saw her passing in a taxi. I think she saw me too, but I couldn't bring myself to acknowledge I'd seen her. Can you imagine what that did to me? It was something I could never tell her mother.' He lifted his head and looked at Rogers as though seeking understanding. 'You know, we do love our children, particularly Deborah, but still found her impossible to live with. Not only because of what she did that we disapproved of, but of the fact that she also did it to us, deceived us . . .' He put a hand to his forehead, rubbing it with his fingertips. 'I'm sorry that I'm unable to be more helpful. I really am. I want to be because we both want to know that she's at least safe and not in any trouble.'

Rogers needed now to tread the exceedingly narrow path between a probing for informative answers and the inadvertent bruising of a father's sensitivities. He said, 'I'm sorry to bring this up, but does any of this stem from Deborah's running off to Thurnholme Bay when she was a schoolgirl? If it does, would you set what you feel you can tell me against my professional need to know.'

Stuchley bit at the bottom lip, frowning. 'You'd know about that, wouldn't you. She'd always denied that anything improper had happened, and while I couldn't believe her, I wanted to. I did what I could to minimise the damage, fooled myself into accepting it to have been one of those growing-up romantic phases an adolescent goes through.' His mouth twitched. 'Painful though, and we all suffered for a while. Then it happened again, though after she'd left school and no more than disappearing all day and then not returning until next morning. And she was taking money . . . not that we begrudged her it although she was given an allowance, but she took it secretly. She lied to us, which was the worst thing, driving her mother to distraction and eventually to a near nervous breakdown. It all came to a head when after one of her absences she said unforgivable things to her mother . . . to me; said that there was a man, that she was going away to live a life of her own. She left when we were both out, taking some of our things with her – family silver, money . . . I just can't . . .' His face suddenly crumpled and he beat on his forehead with the heel of his hand. 'Dear God,' he groaned, squeezing shut his eyes. 'I'm talking about my own daughter.'

A drab yellow and black wasp had been crawling laboriously up the spine of *The British Pharmaceutical Codex* in the row of books on the desk and Stuchley, picking up a record card, slid it shakily though carefully under the insect and removed it. Rising from his chair he turned and moved quickly across to the window overlooking a rear sunlit garden. Holding the card against the window's curtain, he pushed the wasp with his finger into crawling on it. Remaining there, his back to Rogers, his shoulders shook as if he were struggling to control his emotions.

When he spoke, not turning his head, his voice seemed moist with tears. '*Vespa vulgaris*,' he said. 'The common wasp. The poor little thing's a female worker and she's spent . . . she's spent the summer unselfishly feeding a second generation of her kind.' His hand reached to his cheek and brushed at it as he lifted his head to look at the climbing wasp. 'You know, female workers are the only wasps in the brood to have a sting, and that they use only to kill food insects for their younger kin, or against what they may see as an attack on themselves.' He paused clearing his throat. 'A doomed little thing, she's less then six months old and her blood's already running thin. Now that the cold weather's settling in she's ordained by her own life cycle to die. But in her own time if I can help her, not brutally by somebody else who believes her to be a pest of no account.'

Stuchley had said that as though elaborating on a question, clear to the silent Rogers that he had deliberately detached his thinking from his daughter in order to subdue the onset of an embarrassing weeping. The appearance of the wasp on his desk had been too adventitious for him to read into the words anything relevant to what they had been discussing.

When he returned to his chair he was composed, the only sign of his suffering being a moist pinkness to his eyelids. He said, 'Forgive me, superintendent. I allowed myself to exaggerate a little about Deborah, and I don't really know why.'

'You possibly used me as a sort of catharsis,' Rogers suggested. It had been done often enough before and he could understand the doctor's anguish, feel sympathy for him. 'I assure you that I'll confine your confidences to my own office and not broadcast them. However, there is a question or two I have to ask, not too painful to answer I hope. Did Deborah ever identify the man she went with to Thurnholme?'

'No. I tried, but I couldn't get it out of her.'

'She never told you where she had been staying?'

'She never told us about anything that she did.' Stuchley's face lengthened. 'I'm afraid that somewhere I failed her, and I wish I knew where.'

'I now how you feel,' Rogers said, although he actually didn't, 'and it happens to all of us. Where had she been working before leaving home?'

'Until she left, nowhere. She'd enrolled as a student at the College of Art in Abbotsburn, though that didn't last more than a term or two. She tried on a few occasions for situations advertised in the local press, but those she thought suited her needed qualifications she didn't have.' He bit on his lip as if trying to come to a decision. 'I think I should tell you,' he said hesitantly, 'for I'm sure you'll discover it for yourself. I believe Deborah has become addicted to drugs. It could explain her sometimes bizarre behaviour, could it not?'

'Do you know what sort?'

Stuchley shrugged his helplessness. 'One of the amphetamines? Perhaps cocaine, though I hope not.'

'On what basis do you believe she is?'

'I'm her father. Please don't push me about it.'

'I still have to ask,' Rogers persisted. 'Possibly from your own drugs cupboard?'

'No.' Stuchley put sharpness into his voice. 'I don't dispense from my practice.'

Rogers was prepared to drop it, if not to forget. 'This friend of yours who'd heard she was working in Abbotsburn,' he prompted him. 'Did he say where?'

'I don't believe he wished to tell me, but he did say a gaming club.'

'The Barbizan?'

Stuchley looked perplexed. 'The Barbizan?' he echoed. 'He didn't say and I didn't ask, but was that it?'

'Yes, she worked there as a hostess until fairly recently. The man she was living with worked there too.'

'I see.' Stuchley had grimaced at that. 'Was he what you'd call a decent man?'

Rogers swore under his breath. Was he to tell him that his daughter was a whore who had been living with a man who was probably her pimp? Apart from what could only be his criminal handling of too much money to have been obtained honestly. 'Deborah apparently thought so,' he equivocated, 'and I don't know enough about him to give an opinion.'

There were sounds of the scraping of chairs and feet from behind the door of the waiting room and Stuchley frowned, muttering something inaudible. Aloud, he said apologetically, 'If you've nothing further, I'd be grateful if you'd let me deal with my sick and maimed.' He pushed himself up from his chair. 'Could I ask you to let us know immediately if you hear anything of Deborah? My wife . . . she does worry.'

There hadn't been any further questions of importance, and Rogers had risen with him. 'I will, naturally,' he assured him, 'and I'm sorry if I've caused distress to you and Mrs Stuchley.' He meant it; the disintegration of a man into painful weeping, even if only briefly, had been unsettling for him.

Following Stuchley out through the partly-filled waiting room, he remembered that the asked-for coffee had never arrived. If nothing else, it underlined the doctor's sensitivity in sparing his wife any further hurt by the wormwood and gall of their daughter's promiscuity and dishonesty.

10

Rogers, no stranger to occasional exaggeration, had always contended that more routine paperwork passed through his office than through any other Headquarters' department. He was wrong, but that didn't affect his belief in its being a bloody nuisance. When he worked outside, that which he was unable to delegate to a similarly busy Lingard accumulated in his desk trays in depressing quantities. When inside, he had often to overlook it in preference to writing out his notes of interviews conducted, where he had been and why, and to reading through reports from his staff concerning information currently unearthed. Whatever reasons he had for ignoring the routine paper traffic it remained a disciplinary bomb called neglect of duty, a ticking threat to whatever peace of mind he was able to acquire outside a night's sleeping, which, latterly, seemed impossible for him to get.

Among the shoal of papers left on his blotting pad was a sealed envelope from the Administrative Chief Superintendent. Opening it, he found a receipt for one metal security box containing the sum of £53,635 in bank notes of different denominations. He re-worried at its significance, at its possible relationship to the smuggling of drugs, for only a few moments before turning to more graspable matters.

A report from DPC Hopcroft, detailing his interview with Martin McNeill, stated that McNeill had booked his seven-days holiday in Utrecht through the travel agents Shad-Awbery. He had travelled over and returned by ferry, staying alone at the Hotel Terdam, Johannes Vermeerstraat, for the full week. Regularly parking his car overnight in an open courtyard at the rear of the hotel, he was satisfied that it had not been interfered with nor its wheel substituted during the time he was in Holland, insisting that he would have noticed the loss of pressure in it when driving back. Nicholas had checked McNeill's details with RCIO and found nothing recorded against him but a minor traffic offence.

Rogers, already satisfied that the substitution – not the most clever one, he thought, even done in the dark – had been effected outside McNeill's home on his return, was more interested in the Shad-Awbery connection. One booking through them leading to the subsequent theft of a wheel meant nothing; two raised a presumption of something going on a little short of being saintly.

He retrieved Stephanakis's bank statements and cheque book

from his desk drawer and leafed through them. The statements recorded regular cash deposits of £500 and monthly debit payments out of amounts from £40-odd to £300, the cheque numbers only being shown. The few cheque stubs agreed with the most recent large payments out, all being endorsed with the un-illuminating initials of the payees. Rogers was working up an irritation against Stephanakis for being an unhelpfully secretive bugger, against banks in general because he knew it was their policy to refuse even vital information about their dead or alive clients' accounts, when his telephone bell rang.

Calling from the Disraeli Street apartment, it was Detective Sergeant Magnus, his scene of crime specialist who would not think the chore of finding a suspect's cast eyelash in a thickly-piled carpet too difficult or too much of a sweat. 'I've just arrived here, sir,' he said, 'and it looks as if somebody's tried a break-in during the night. Unless,' he added cautiously, 'the kitchen window was already open when you were here.'

'It wasn't, sergeant.' Rogers had gone beyond the point of being surprised at anything now happening. 'Shuffling about on my knees though I was, I'd have noticed it. So would Mr Hagbourne. It's over the sink with white net curtains, yes?'

'That's it.' Magnus sounded relieved. 'The bottom sash is jammed open about nine inches and no further because the window has restraining stubs fitted. There're fresh scratches on the inside of the catch where a blade was used to slip it, and leather glove marks on the outside glass and sill. Access was from a communal yard open to the street behind, then climbing on to an outhouse roof and shinning up a short length of fall pipe. He'd have had to cling on to it while he slipped the catch, and unless he brought a ladder with him he'd need a mate to give him a bunk up on to the outhouse.'

'I presume the PC on the door heard nothing?' Rogers asked. He had scribbled *Sickert?* on his scratch pad.

'No. I did question him. I can't imagine he would have, the kitchen being at the back with two walls intervening. Incidentally, all the windows in the apartment are fitted with restraining stubs. That Stephan-whatsisname must have had something more on his mind than being burgled for his television set.'

'So he must have,' Rogers agreed, deciding not to mention the money found there in case it took the edge from the sergeant's enthusiasm for finding things. 'Bear in mind it could be drugs. I've been told that the woman living with him was on amphetamines or cocaine. Also, there should be a couple of framed photographs belonging to her about the place. If you find them, I want to see them.'

Replacing the receiver, he tried to think out who other than the investigative team and Sickert would know last night of Stephanakis and his death and, possibly, about Deborah being missing from the apartment, coming up only with the man Sickert had said he'd sent to check on his dealer's absence from the club. It was, he decided, flimsy and unverifiable guesswork having regard to the crowd of spectators collected in the street and the compulsive chattiness of some of his colleagues. When his telephone bell rang again, he was looking through the window at a view of sunlit slate roofs and wondering morosely why it wasn't, congruous with his mood, pouring down grey rain.

Recognizably Hagbourne's voice, it sounded as if wary of being overheard. 'I'm at the mortuary, on an open line,' he said. 'Dr Twite's just started on Stephanakis and I think you'll want to come.'

'You think wrong, Thomas. There's a problem?'

'Not exactly, but it's important. We found it when he was undressed and it's not interfering with what Dr Twite's doing.'

'Ten minutes,' Rogers said, closing down on him, consigning all telephones to hell, returning his papers to the pending tray and getting himself into his overcoat.

Even for a man who was certain that he carried the equivalent of a sack of lead on his shoulders, the hospital was an easy enough walk from his office. On the way he hummed repetitively to himself a few bars of *Happy Days are Here Again*, working at convincing his Id or whatever it was that he was in a mood of cheerful optimism, that all was well in a wonderful world, and thinking that it was making no bloody difference at all.

Using the front entrance to the hospital, he walked the highly polished rubber tiling of its corridors, filling his pipe in readiness as he did so and being careful to keep his eyes averted when passing open ward doors. Two yellowed polystyrene air locks, with, between them, a goods lift large enough for a trolley carrying a departed patient, led to the mortuary's door. Rogers, pausing only to light his pipe against the smell of raw flesh and to read the door's *Authorized Entry Only* sign, opened it and entered.

The white-tiled room, familiar to him as an unwelcome reminder of his own mortality, was furnished starkly with two stainless steel necropsy tables, yards of working top benches, a hand wash basin, a wall telephone and a glass cabinet of glittering instruments; the air in it cold and smelling of death, formalin and scented cigarette smoke. Hagbourne was intent on studying with his world-weary pouched eyes a shelf of glass containers of pickled foetuses, organs and fragments of body tissue that the hospital's pathologists had thought worthy of preserving. If he looked a shade paler than his norm, it could have been because he had had as little sleep as Rogers. Twite, bending over one of the tables and illuminated by the shadowless light above him, appeared to be engrossed in bloodily cutting off a naked Stephanakis's head with a scalpel. Making him look even more bulky, he wore an operating theatre khaki gown with a green apron over it, a shapeless cap covering his hair and pale yellow rubber gloves with red-stained fingers. A cigarette jerked in his mouth, dropping ash as he worked.

With Hagbourne moving to one of the working tops, Rogers gave only a hurried glance at what was being done to Stephanakis's throat. He said to Twite in friendly mockery, 'You've a problem, Wilfred? You're going to tell me he wasn't killed by that bolt after all?'

'I'm doing all right, old son,' Twite said, not taking his eyes from his probing around pinkish-white cartilage. 'It's your problem, so have a look at what was in his trousers and do your worrying about that.'

'It's over here, sir,' Hagbourne said. 'We only found it when we took off his trousers.' On Rogers joining him, he indicated folded clothing piled on the bench.

At its side was a contrivance Rogers had not seen before. Attached to a length of brown tape were two foot-long strips of soft transparent plastic, each fitted with small pockets of the same material in columns of three. One pocket contained a folded square of blue tissue paper, the others being empty.

'It was tied round his waist under his trousers with a strip hanging down the outside of each thigh,' Hagbourne explained. 'He's made buttoned slits in the trousers pockets, wide enough when he undid them for his hand to reach in without making too much of a song and dance about it. And there are eighteen pockets altogether.'

'Which explains the money in his wallet, not to mention the loot in his safe box,' Rogers commented, reaching for the blue tissue packet and knowing without surprise what it would contain. It was warming to his spirit that he could occasionally guess at the right answer. 'You've checked this?'

'It's either cocaine or granulated sugar and I can't see any profit for him in selling sugar by the gram.' Hagbourne allowed himself a mild irony now and then.

Carefully unfolding the tissue to reveal the white crystalline powder that resembled frozen snow, Rogers said, 'It's cocaine right enough. I'd like to think this packet was for his own use, but it's a fair bet it was for Deborah's.' He slid the drug back into its pocket, then spoke to Twite. 'Are there any needle marks, Wilfred?'

'No, I've already looked.' Twite had removed the bolt from Stephanakis's neck and was wiping it with his sponge, frowning at it. 'There's nothing to show he sniffed it either; no signs of inflammation in the nasal cavities though that doesn't disprove he could have been an occasional user.' He held out the bolt for Rogers to take. 'I'm no great shakes at metallurgy, but you can see the aluminium's badly oxidized. That means it's a few years old at least, or that it's been left outside exposed to the weather.' He shook his head. 'Whichever it was it's roughed up the surface and wouldn't add to either accuracy or distance.'

Rogers considered that it wouldn't need much of either from across the width of a street, but its possible age could interest him. 'It helps, Wilfred,' he said, handing the bolt – which he thought looked like an oversized ball-point pen with tail feathers – to Hagbourne and wiping his fingertips clean with his spare handkerchief. Not all the blood had been sponged from it. 'You're confirming officially that it killed him?'

Twite was stripping his fat hands of the rubber gloves. 'There's nothing any different from what I said before. It entered the neck close to one of the cervical vertebrae and cut through the internal carotid artery feeding the brain.' He shook his head. 'Bad luck that, it isn't nearly as thick as a cigarette. Penetrating his glottis seems like an afterthought, but it would stop him screaming.

Death was due to a massive haemorrhage, mostly inside him of course, plus whatever consequences shock would have on his nervous system when being humped about by clumsy coppers. Good enough for you?'

'I'm grateful,' Rogers said sardonically. 'I was getting worried. Are you doing Kiddle now?'

'This afternoon, old son, when I've time. I've had a preview of what happened to him and it'll certainly be death from blows inflicted by an instrument. But you know that already, don't you?' He looked Rogers straight in the eyes. 'That's all you need, isn't it?'

'It'll be all the coroner needs,' Rogers answered him. It was enough for him, too. Whatever complications, if any, had occurred en route to the operating table were not going to be exposed by Twite, and would not in any way be relevant to Kiddle's being bludgeoned to death by his own sand wedge. It could, Rogers thought outlandishly, together with the coronary occlusions which dropped elderly bodies on fairways, make golf one of the high risk sporting activities.

Before leaving the mortuary, he instructed Hagbourne to bag up the bits and pieces needed for examination at the Forensic Science Laboratory and brightened his life by telling him that he could return to his normal messing about with criminous documents and figures. And outside, walking back to his office, he thought that the time he had spent humming to his Id must have done something, for he felt reasonably, if not overwhelmingly, optimistic. What about, he wasn't sure; but about something.

11

In his office, his pipe going full blast, Rogers took from the row of books on his desk his Glaister's *Medical Jurisprudence and Toxicology* and the Home Office publication *Drugs: Their Use and Abuse*, refreshing his mind in researching on substances about which he could rarely froth up much interest.

Both authorities referred more to cocaine's harmful effects on the human body and brain than to the euphoric sublimity and heightened physical well-being claimed by its users. Being informed that addicts usually possessed an inborn psychopathic tendency and, later, a psychical degeneration leading frequently to insanity was somethng he had to accept, though from his own experience with addicts he had to question the word 'usually'. Small doses of the powder were alleged to promote happiness, excitement and an excess of mental and physical vigour; and nothing much wrong in that, he thought, were that all. Only it wasn't. Apart from brain damage – he could imagine it resulting in small ulcerated grey holes, each occupied by a purple-blotched worm – and an imaginary sensation of hyperactive insects crawling beneath the surface of the skin, prolonged addiction to it apparently led to terrifying visual hallucinations, paranoid delusions and anorexia.

In women, addiction could cause an increase in eroticism which held in it the threat of nymphomania; in men – unfairly, Rogers considered wryly – it could mean a deadening of physical sexuality which could degenerate into what would normally be uncharacteristic sexual perversions. Acute poisoning by the drug could result in what read as a pretty horrific death from either a painful cardiac failure or suffocating asphyxiation.

Having heard cocaine referred to as 'happy dust', Rogers could only conclude that to be the grimly humorous product of the despairing. He said 'Um' and gazed up at the blue haze of tobacco smoke above his head. Much maligned though it was, and each man to his own poison, his smoking his pipe was very much milk and water stuff by comparison. He was more comfortably considering the question of whether Deborah Stuchley had or had not been addicted to cocaine when his door was tapped on by knuckles and Lingard walked in.

Sitting himself in the visitors' chair at the side of the desk and looking nearly as weary as Rogers felt, he said flippantly, 'I've just learned I'm to live until I reach the age of ninety-five.'

'Bad luck,' Rogers told him feelingly. 'It's probably one of the hazards of being a bachelor. You've been knocking back your Pernods already?'

'Unfortunately not.' Lingard occasionally let rip on what he called his *aperitif anis* in emulation of his admired Beau Brummell. 'If intoxicated I am, it's on two cups of Gaelic tea laced with goat's milk. I was told my fortune by Mrs Ellen MacGluskey, widow and landlady of eleven Highfield Crescent, the onetime lodgings of our missing Deborah. Mrs MacG's apparently a Mark Two type Witch of Endor and a remarkably intelligent one at that. She insisted on reading the creases in my left wrist before she'd tell me anything.' He smiled with mock self-satisfaction. 'Apart from predicting a fascinating and graceful senility for me, she told me that so far as my career is concerned I am destined for the highest of offices; details of which I'm far too modest to repeat.'

'And one or two snippets about Deborah which you can, I hope?' Rogers said drily.

'One or two,' Lingard conceded. 'When I told her that Miss Stuchley had been missing from her apartment since last evening she immediately jumped in and said that she'd known she'd come to a bad end. According to her it'd been written large in the cut of Deborah's jib, plain for anyone with second sight to see. Mrs MacG's in her rawboned fifties, doesn't like us males too much and still a handsome woman for all that. She lets out two of her rooms to lady lodgers only; no feeding, only a little cleaning by a hired help and she doesn't choose to sit out in the hall and act the beady-eyed concierge. So there wasn't going to be much information about Deborah's comings and goings.'

He took out his tiny ivory box, ritualistically tapped a fingernail on its lid, then opened it and inhaled snuff. Doing it was supposed to help him re-arrange scattered thoughts. 'Deborah took a room there about this time last year and stayed for five months,' he said. 'Mrs MacG's not what I'd call the motherly type and wouldn't be excessively interested in her lodgers' private lives and problems. So she says. She liked Deborah, though she found her a wee bittie highly strung and, at times, a wee bittie short-tempered too. She knew she worked at the Barbizan and her coming back to her room at any time after midnight was no problem because both of her lodgers would have a key to the front door. Sometimes Deborah hadn't returned at all, mentioning when she felt the need to that she'd stayed the night with a friend she worked with. She usually slept all morning and ate what main meals she was presumed to have in the town. Restaurant, caff or takeaway joint unknown.'

Lingard paused, giving his senior an opportunity to intervene with his usual awkward question. When none came – Rogers was scratching ash from the bowl of his pipe – he continued. 'There's no suggestion that she was using her room for any fleshly pleasures she needed, and I think Mrs MacG would have choked on her sporran had she thought she was. So far as just who did visit her is concerned, I'm afraid Mrs MacG wasn't much help. Not with names anyway. Fed up to her Gaelic teeth in the past with being dragged all the three or four yards to her front door for her lodgers' convenience, she had bells installed in their rooms. She did occasionally – accidentally, of course – see their visitors on the doorstep, but few for Deborah. One who did call now and then was an extremely tall cove with a black moustache who she said looked like a foreigner.' He cocked a quizzical eyebrow. 'Your client Stephanakis, George?'

'I'd bet on it,' Rogers agreed. 'And on the fact that he was beginning his poaching on Sickert's preserves.' He was thoughtful. 'I wonder if a gambler's blood runs hot enough in his veins for him to be jealous?'

Lingard was dismissive. 'If you're asking me, I'd say as well expect a crocodile's. If we're still of a mind for sticking a label on a suspect, I've a better one. There's another visitor, a young cove about twenty-five and shortish. Mrs MacG runs to about five-feet-seven in her wellies so he'd have to be less than that for her to say it. A blondie with blue eyes like lit-up glowworms she said who she thought was a wee softie, probably because he was polite with her. Clean shaven, smartly dressed and, in her opinion, well-spoken for a Sassenach. He was leaning like mad on Deborah's bell one afternoon when she was out and long enough for Mrs MacG to have to answer the door. When she told him that Miss Stuchley wasn't in – I can imagine she was pretty short with him – he asked where she would be. Bags of frustration in him, brooding eyes and some biting of the lips; a not very composed gent at all. When Mrs MacG told him she hadn't a clue where she was he asked would she pass on a message that Tony had called and would she telephone him during the evening. She said she would and then watched him trot off to where he'd left his car further up the road. There's no joy there either; it was non-descript ordinary in green or blue, or possibly neither. Understandable, considering this happened earlier this year. When she passed on the message to Deborah she got nothing more than a not-too-pleased thank you. She thinks that he came again just before Deborah chucked in her tenancy of her room. She was in this time, being early evening, and she answered the bell herself, but kept him standing on the doormat. Mrs MacG says she couldn't hear what was said from where she was but he sounded as if he were pleading with Deborah to do something, while she was giving him the why don't you ever take no for an answer treatment. He went after a few minutes of that and the sound of the door being slammed. It was then when he passed under a lamp that Mrs MacG thought she recognized him as the wee softie and that he was looking very sorry for himself.'

'Interesting, David,' Rogers said, 'even though a trifle mundane.' The sun coming through the window behind him was nicely warm on his shoulder-blades; soporific almost, and he had had to do his yawning behind closed teeth. 'I haven't got around to telling you in fine detail yet, but the unfriendly female evangelist living below Stephanakis's apartment says she saw what was probably the same man there several months back. He was blond, about the same age and I suppose could become significant by his repeated calls on Deborah. He was in the apartment with her having a shouting match; angry voices and all that, and when he took off it wasn't supposed he left in the happiest of tempers. Your opinion in a few words, David?'

'A discarded lover?' Lingard suggested. 'Though if he was I don't know why he should take on so.'

'My thinking precisely. A persistent one too if he is the same one calling at your Mrs MacGluskey's. He might also be one of those so-called meek little sods like Dr Crippen who'd cut you into small pieces if you impugned his manhood by taking over his girlfriend. Posit Stephanakis pushing his nastiness into a fickle Deborah with that sort breathing down your neck and there are breakers ahead, so to speak.' Rogers in his self-appointed role as a thinker of profound truths was careful in what he now said, for years earlier Lingard had gone crazy over the death in another man's bed of his lover Nancy Frail. 'It's not only elephants who go berserk in musth, David. Men do too, and particularly those who've been left standing on a mat and talking back at a wooden door.' He tapped the stem of his pipe against his teeth, working things out. With Lingard as a possible exception, Rogers was generally mistrustful of men he thought of as Nordic blonds; they were, in his experience, either too pretty for masculine comfort, or too bloody clever for their own good. 'I can't say that I've seen too many of you blue-eyed blond efforts cluttering up Abbotsburn,' he finally said, 'so considering that he seems to be undersized as well, he mightn't be too difficult to put a name to. When you've finished here, do an Identity Sought circulation and hope that we've got one or two uniformed bodies who actually go outside on foot patrol and see people.'

Lingard nodded, nothing in his narrow face expressing that he had already done it. 'While we've quite a few bleached imitators courting our popularity,' he pointed out not too seriously, 'I think we'll sort him out, given time.'

Rogers, his eyelids draggingly heavy, was flogging a brain that would far rather be pulling its own shutters down. It was a weakness for which he had self-contempt and he fought it, for neither he nor Lingard would willingly be the first to concede defeat. 'Right,' he said with an air of brisk alertness, 'let's get back to Stephanakis and McNeill where there've been interesting developments.' After detailing them to Lingard, he continued, 'That could put a different argument to Stephanakis's killing, couldn't it? As a pusher he'd be walking a pretty dangerous path with some excessively nasty characters ready to shut him up should he put a foot wrong. And then there's the addict blowing his shot-up mind because he hasn't enough money to buy his next fix, and it's always cash on delivery or you don't get it. That'd make you love a pusher to distraction, wouldn't it? Too, Stephanakis could be a little something more than that. Because he's visited Holland on several occasions it's possible he's involved in the smuggling end of it.' Straightening himself in his chair, he laid his smoked-out pipe down on his blotting pad and put on a helpful frown of concentration. 'Follow me through while I hypothesize about the system, David, and yell at me if you disagree.'

'All hypotheses accepted as negotiable,' Lingard murmured, recharging his nostrils with his attar of roses snuff. 'I'm agog.'

'First of all,' Rogers started, 'we have to accept that the stuff's coming in from Holland and that's for our drug squad bods to tie up with the Dutch police. Whoever the dealer is this side of the North Sea, he sends the supplier details of any Shad-Awbery client booking a touring holiday in the Utrecht district. They'd need only the dates, the name of the hotel or wherever the client had booked into, the make and registration number of the car, and they're in business. I can't see that it would be too difficult for a couple of villains to locate the car where it was parked for the night, take it away as they did with Kiddle's and unbolt the wheel more or less at their leisure. No spare wheel business for these villains; it's been done too many times and it's far too obvious. We wouldn't know how much of the stuff can be packed into a tyre without making it incapable of sustaining its proper air pressure, but I'd guess kilos enough to satisfy the greediest of the bastards.'

'I doubt it,' Lingard interposed, 'greed being something of a bottomless pit. Don't they push it into Merrie England by the pantechnicon load now?'

'There's always room in a free economy for the smaller entrepreneur,' Rogers said sardonically. 'If I can get on with it, putting the wheel back on and returning the car as found would have passed unnoticed if Kiddle hadn't got toothache and gone out to find it missing. Of course, not necessarily the same for McNeill. The wheel could have been taken off and packed without the car leaving the hotel's park. It'd depend on access and security, which wouldn't be much anyway; even, perhaps, on the physical impossibility of removing it from the park. Whichever, it doesn't matter other than that it resulted in a couple of unaware innocents being used as couriers. It's a sobering thought for somebody, but if the stuff had been sniffed out by Customs on their return they'd have had a hell of a job proving they didn't know anything about it.' He did a brief baring of his teeth. 'How are we doing. David?'

'I'm keeping up with you so far,' Lingard replied. 'Only with the thought that I can't imagine even a sniffer dog's nose being effective through a thickness of airtight rubber.' He was hoping that Rogers would make it short so that he could slip out to the bar of the *Solomon and Sheba* for a revivifying drink.

'No more can I,' Rogers agreed. 'So, back here our dealer has already had the home of the chosen courier cased to see whether it has a lock-up garage, a car port or the use of street parking. He'd also arrange beforehand for the buying of a replacement secondhand wheel and tyre to clap on the courier's car. The rest is a possible following of the car past customs to check that the tyreful of junk gets through safely, a visit the next night to exchange wheels and somebody being more than a few thousand pounds better off for the doing of it.'

'And but for poor old wide-awake Kiddle, no particular problems,' Lingard said. 'Nothing doing at the breakers' yards by the way. Totally and absolutely honest as you well know, and only too anxious to help us.' He roughened his accent, shaking his head in assumed bewilderment. 'There's ain't much call for old wheels, guv, an' nobody says we 'as to keep records if we does manage to sell one or two.'

That didn't surprise Rogers at all. It didn't please him either. He said, 'I don't intend we should get bogged down in narcotics smuggling, so shove the possibility of other wheels being substituted on to the drug squad and Customs and Excise. We know why Kiddle was clobbered, and whoever did it should come out in the wash of what they find. We have to be more concerned about Stephanakis and the why of it. And, naturally, our missing and apparently most unlikeable Deborah, who I hope isn't dead as well.'

'Or, if only kidnapped, not made helpless and subject to the brutish passions of her captor,' Lingard suggested derisively.

'God help her if she is,' Rogers said, straightfaced and solemnly. 'It's a horrible thought, particularly if the man happens to be blond.' He could speak lightly about it because he wasn't yet prepared to be sorry for her; not until he knew. 'However, she could have been removed, or removed herself, to give open house to whoever it was intending to kill Stephanakis. On the other hand, holding her prisoner wouldn't solve anything in the long term, so we can't completely ignore the possibility that she's already buried where we're unlikely to find her, or anchored down in the canal to an old bedstead where we might.'

Rogers stopped and leaned forward, peering as if anxious at Lingard's face. And that had been a bit of an effort with what he thought were creaking noises coming from his own backbone. 'You're overdoing it, David,' he said, officially solicitous, 'and you look done in. Leave me to worry about Deborah and book off. No arguments – put your feet up for two or three hours and, if you feel like it, call in at Shad-Awbery's on the way back and dig out the sneaky mole they seem to have employed there.'

For himself, once a surprised Lingard had left him, Rogers

intended doing his worrying flat on his back and in his own bedroom for at least a couple of hours. Barefaced hypocrisy was a dreadful thing, he admitted comfortingly to himself, but far better than owning to a physical weakness brought on by a mere lack of sleep. Halfway into his overcoat, his telephone bell rang. Poised with one arm sleeved he stared balefully at the handset for a long time, knowing he wasn't being forced to answer the bloody thing, but accepting that he was going to. When he did and Sergeant Magnus told him that he was downstairs with some quite interesting information from his search of the apartment he decided that perhaps he could put off for a few minutes his falling down in what could be first cousin to a coma.

12

Rogers poked a tired finger at the tiny enamelled pillbox and cigarette-sized plastic tube on his blotting pad. The ginger-haired Sergeant Magnus, now standing on the square of carpet on the other side of his desk, had found them concealed in the toe of one of a pair of a woman's mauve shoes in the wardrobe of Stephanakis's bedroom. The pillbox contained a gram or two of white powder that was unmistakably cocaine, the tube the means by which it could be inhaled into the nostrils without wasting grains. Snorting, as Rogers knew its addicts called it, was a method which, when used excessively, caused inflammation of the nasal septum and its later perforation. Magnus's finding it had answered his earlier question as to whether Deborah Stuchley had been a addict. He could now wish her well in not being wherever she was with holes in her nose.

'I know there isn't any more in the apartment or you'd have found it,' Rogers said, 'so it's likely that Stephanakis kept her supplies of it on a fairly short leash. Perhaps only just enough were she paying for it herself, or for her to do what he wanted were she not.' He had already told Magnus of the finding of the cocaine on Stephanakis's body.

'I did get the impression from the stuff I saw there, the dirty laundry and so forth, that she was either flogging herself off with the citizenry, or that he was an indefatigable sexual front runner.' Magnus then added with uncharacteristic primness, 'Either way, they must have been a couple of squalid fornicators.'

'And for his part, an unregretted dead one,' Rogers growled, not believing that anybody in Abbotsburn could be a loser by Stephanakis's sudden going. And, unsettling even to himself, hating to think of the further grief and anguish lying in wait for Dr Stuchley and his wife. 'What's in the case?' he asked.

Magnus had brought in with him a glossy black briefcase and he placed it in front of Rogers. 'It was hidden in the four-inch space under the water-bed,' he said, 'and it's got combination locks. I've already tried a few three-figure strings that don't work.'

Rogers pushed the case back to him. He was having to force his mind to concentrate on Magnus's words, which seemed to float at him as if wrapped in muffling felt. 'Try its back door with your pocket-knife,' he ordered. 'I don't think Stephanakis'll be using it again.'

It was a beautifully crafted piece of leatherwork, but proving poor on security as Magnus attacked its unprotected rear, wrenching apart its riveted hinges and leaving it open for Rogers's inspection.

It contained documents only and those, a disappointed Rogers considered at a cursory viewing, not anything likely to put an identity to Stephanakis's murderer. There was a deed of separation and a matrimonial order relating to an Allegra Stephanakis, interest-numbing letters from a local solicitor referring to their ordering and the matter of a transfer of rental rights of a property called Wattles in Potters Row, Abbotsburn. There was also a trivia of paid telephone bills for Potters Row and Disraeli Street, rental receipts for both properties and more cheque book stubs promising little useful information.

'Not your fault, naturally,' Rogers said, pushing the papers back into the ruptured case for later reading, 'but I don't think it's going to be worth the breaking open. What's so bloody secret about being married and separated that you've got to lock the evidence of it up and keep it under your bed? To hide the fact from Deborah who has since gone missing anyway? Would she give a curse even if she knew?' He brooded on that for a while, watched by Magnus who, knowing the questions were rhetorical and suspecting that his normally stone-cold sober chief had had a drink or two, kept silent. 'Perhaps she would,' he went on, conscious that he may have slurred a word or two. 'There must have been a sliver of lovableness or something about the bastard for some other woman to marry him in the first place. Perhaps he dangled a promise of it in front of Deborah's nose as a bait to get her to earn her share of the housekeeping. How she'd rationalize that, though, with him being a party to her entertaining the hoi polloi in her bed, I can't begin to imagine. Or was she doing it to pay for the cocaine he was supplying her with? It's a possibility she didn't even know he was a pusher, and wet enough to believe he was only getting it for her.' He scowled as if at female stupidity, having to hold his head back to do it from beneath drooping eyelids. 'I imagine she'd be hooked on the stuff and that should tie her to him a damn sight closer than any need for his poncing on her. So would she dodge out and abandon voluntarily her very own pimp? The provider of the means to the euphoria she'd so badly need? Or forget to take her sniffer and her next fix with her? Decide she couldn't be bothered with her make-up equipment and most of her clothes? And that money in the safe box if she knew about it, which I doubt?' He shook his head in frustration, feeling it to be full of hot mattress stuffing. 'Leave it,' he grunted. 'Do you have anything else for me?'

'No framed photographs, quite definitely not, but there was a fingerprint,' Magnus said. 'On the kitchen window. I had a closer look at it and found that a glove had been taken off at some time. I haven't dusted it yet, the glass being still damp, but there's a partial dab up near the catch that was slipped; a twinned loop that's got at least nine characteristics. Bags enough for me to tie it on any suspect coming into the picture.'

'Good fella,' Rogers commended him. 'There could be one now. Try tying it on Albert Raymond Webber, commonly known as Wonk-eye, about whom I've dark suspicions of his having done something unlawful or squalidly nasty from the way the shifty sod looked at me last night.' Pushing himself up from his chair, certain that he weighed a lot more than when he had lowered his body into it, he smiled at Magnus, pleased that he could at least manage that. 'Bugger off now,' he said amiably enough. 'I'm late for an important appointment.'

With the sergeant gone he combed his hair to order in front of the cupboard vanity mirror allowed by the police authority to ranks of superintendent and above, the stark fluorescent lighting reflecting what he hoped was an exaggerated view of deep creases in tired yellow skin and a half-witted glare from blood-shot eyes. Feeling cerebrally diminished and knowing that his capability for driving safely through any kind of traffic would be badly flawed, he rang the Control Room chief inspector and asked him for the use of a patrol car. Driven to the end of the street in which he lived and dropped, being several million light years away from wanting to be at the receiving end of social politenesses or even gentle concern about his condition from a Nanoushka likely to be waiting in ambush, he trod silently with held-back breath past her closed door and up the stairs to his own flat.

Inside, after unhooking the telephone receiver, the umbilical cord tying him to sordid reality, he pushed two of his cushioned chairs together and pulled off shoes that seemed to have become heat-welded to his suffering feet. Slumped in one chair with his legs on the other and his travelling alarm clock wedged only inches from his ear, he was trying to remember whether he had brought his pipe back from the office when he lost his awareness of being anywhere but swaddled comfortably in the depths of his own inner darkness.

13

Before leaving his office, Lingard had spent mole-digging time in acquiring information about the owner of Shad-Awbery Travel. He found him to be James Shadick, somewhere in his fifties, married with three adult children and living in the prestigious Spye Green area where owning a car short of being a Jaguar or a Mercedes was never quite. Being also a former mayor of Abbots-burn, a nonconformist lay preacher and a committee member of the Abbotsburn Businessmen's Fellowship, with no previous convictions recorded against him, Lingard decided with an inner hyperbole that he might risk his professional reputation in giving Shadick the benefit of any doubt that might arise concerning his personal involvement in anything more dishonest than reckless exaggerations about the holiday tours he sold.

Then, possessing his own ideas about restoring animation to a weary body, he had it subjected to a long sweat and a bruising pummelling by an obviously man-hating masseuse at the health sauna he patronized. Following a change of underwear, shirt and socks in his apartment, he revisited the *Solomon and Sheba* to top up his resuscitation with a slice of game pie and a second Pernod, and, finished, to recharge his nervous system with generous pinches of snuff. It was an almost born-again Lingard who left the bar for the High Street in which Shad-Awbery Travel did its business from behind a tasteful facade of green paint and gold-leaf lettering. Inside, there were wall-to-wall racks of holiday brochures and pinned-up posters of African elephants and lions, Egyptian pyramids and camels and, to Lingard's unappreciative eyes, Godforsaken snow-covered mountain slopes littered with chair lifts. There were no customers, but two young women sat behind a counter busy with their desk computers while a tall slender youth with Afro-frizzed hair pinned cards advertizing winter tour bargains to a notice board.

One of the girls, rather formidable-looking in her dark suit, came to the counter and smiled an unlipsticked smile at him. Lingard returned the smile but showed in it, he hoped, the hint of official menace equivalent to the rattling of dangling handcuffs necessary for the smoking out of human moles. 'Good afternoon,' he said, loudly enough for all three to hear. 'I'm Detective Chief Inspector Lingard and I'd like to speak to Mr Shadick on a matter of some importance. Would you tell him that I'm making enquiries concerning the passing from here of information regarding motoring holidays in Holland.'

The girl, faintly puzzled, said, 'Yes, of course. Would you please wait?' then left him. The youth had stiffened, twisting his head briefly to meet the detective's stare in obvious alarm, then breaking away from what must have appeared to him to be accusing blue eyes in a stern face. His stratagem apparently succeeding, Lingard was satisfied and he turned his interest to a scanning of the racked brochures.

Returning, the girl lifted the counter flap and led him through to an inner office where a portly, flannel-suited and spectacled Shadick stood from his desk to shake hands with him. Lingard, giving him an edited version of what had happened to two of his customers and suggesting the possibility of there being others, said finally, 'You'll have gathered by now, Mr Shadick, that I believe you're employing somebody who's selling that information to people capable of committing murder, certainly of smuggling in drugs. I could,' he suggested helpfully to a man whose well-fed features were already reflecting an inner perturbation, 'make a stab at putting a name to him if I knew it.'

'This could prove a very serious matter for my business,' Shadick said. 'You don't think these people could find out for themselves?' He didn't sound as if he himself believed that they could.

Lingard cocked an eyebrow at him. 'Do *you*? For each one, dates of departure and return, destination, accommodation, make and model of car, home address – it'd be a lot for somebody not in the know to ferret out, wouldn't it?'

'Yes, it would,' Shadick agreed with the look of a man having somebody standing painfully on his foot. 'I only employ one man, so why don't you name him if he's the one?'

'Perhaps you'd have him in here and we'll – ', Lingard stopped short as the door opened.

The girl who had shown him in looked around it, her face showing anxious puzzlement. 'Father,' she blurted out, her voice high-pitched with indignation, 'Graham's gone! He never said anything, but I think there's something wrong.'

Shadick's mouth opened and he rose from behind his desk. 'Wrong? What do you mean, Jenny? What's happened?'

Lingard had stood also as she said, 'After the chief inspector came in here he went through to the lavatory. I know he did because I heard it being flushed. Twice, I'm positive. He was in there a long time and when he came out he looked not well – ill, I think. He had his coat on and didn't say anything, but just went out the door making the most peculiar noises.'

Lingard was brisk, inwardly cursing himself for not anticipating flight and wanting now to do several things at once. 'Which way?' he demanded.

She pointed a finger. 'Towards the market place and only just now. I was on the phone and . . .'

He was past her, out of Shadick's office and at the shop door before he shouted back 'He's Graham who?'

'Sleath!' Shadick's daughter called after his departing back. 'His name's Sleath!'

The street, its buildings hard-edged in the pale autumn sunlight that gave out little heat, held no great volume of traffic, and it was too soon after the lunch hour to have more than a sprinkling of shoppers and pedestrians. Lingard, his long legs striding out for the market place, had no difficulty in spotting and identifying the back of the tall Sleath by his excessive narrowness and his round frizzle of hair. About a hundred yards in front of him on the opposite pavement and walking wooden-legged as if in a trance, he appeared not to be looking where he was going and occasionally bumped into people. Certainly he gave no impression of a man anxious to put distance between himself and anticipated disaster. Lingard could have caught him up with ease, but was curious to discover where he intended to go. Not believing that he himself had been seen, he kept his distance to twenty or so yards behind him.

When Sleath turned his dreamlike progress into Canal Street, Lingard knew that there could be only one place for which he was heading and, though under the circumstances it would amount to an over-reaction, his apparent purpose in going there. Were he right, the only thing that would disturb Lingard deeply was the thought of ruining his suit and shirt in having to go in after him.

Reaching the iron bridge crossing the canal, Sleath hesitated only momentarily before climbing down the slope of the grass bank to the towpath and continuing his slow walk to whatever he was seeking. Scrambling down in his wake, Lingard followed into a milieu that seemed to swallow and diminish any sunshine falling on it and which appeared as if in its industrial past it had been tarred over with the essences of coal dust and rust. The blank backs of abandoned buildings abutted the towpath like basalt cliffs and rotting lock gates, long fallen into disuse, rested opened against the canal's flaking stone block walls. Lingard thought that it was colder there than anywhere else and his nostrils, though largely desensitized by snuff, were still perceptive of the stench of rotting vegetation, dead things and chemical effluents rising from the dark and diseased water. Accepting that no person in his or her right mind would choose to walk the canal bank for pleasure, he was unsurprised that he and Sleath were visually the only two persons left in their world. As he reluctantly trod his expensively bespoke shoes in the abrasive ash of the towpath, shortening the distance between them with Sleath apparently oblivious of anybody or anything but his own troubles, he thought he could hear low moaning noises coming from him.

The tall youth halted at the massive timber beam of a lock gate and stood on the edge of the stone wall, gazing down into the canal's sluggishly moving water, his shoulders hunched and his legs shaking. Lingard, now close behind him, heard the dirge-like moaning more clearly and he could have been Sleath's own shadow for all the latter showed any awareness of him, though Lingard could not accept that he was now in ignorance of his presence. Trying not to sound too authoritative, not too obviously a precursor of doom, he said, 'I'd change my mind were I you, laddie. I don't think it's deep enough where you are and you'd die of typhoid fever long before you'd ever drown.'

There was no sign of surprise at his hearing Lingard's voice, but he did stop his lugubrious moaning. When he turned around like an obedient child, Lingard saw what he read as relief in his expression. Gangling and languid in his tallness, pale-skinned and feminine in his features with a soft mouth and wide grey eyes in which apprehension was now superseding the relief, he offended the detective's sensitivity to polychromatic disorder by wearing beneath his chocolate-brown overcoat a light-blue suit with a violently pink shirt and green tie. Unstirred by the cool breeze blowing along the canal, his top-heavy Afro-style hair appeared to have been lacquered in position. Clearly, to Lingard, he could never be a man with bottom enough to place himself too resolutely within reach of the jaws of death.

He said accusingly, 'You weren't actually going to jump in that bilge at all, were you.'

'I'm afraid I was,' Sleath answered in a soft and gentle voice that held the promise of doing remarkable things to the sympathies of elderly women. 'You see, I don't wish to go to prison or anything like that.'

The detective, examining him as if through a quizzing glass and weighing him up as a weak sister, changed course and said, 'You don't look well, you know.' He indicated the lock gate beam. 'You'd better sit before you fall over.'

'I don't feel well,' Sleath whispered, moving to the beam and sitting on it, waiting with his head bowed in dejection and clasping his hands between his thighs.

While Lingard would not classify this less than hairy masculine man as a mole, he was prepared to label him as a contemptible leaker of information. In being so he had, remotely as it might appear, been a party to the death of Kiddle. It was going to be difficult to be civil with him, not to allow his contempt to show. Remaining standing and refilling his nose with his attar of roses against the pervasive smell of polluted water, he said cheerfully, 'You're not supposed to, laddie. It's the day of reckoning, and now's the time to unload yourself of why you did it. Which can't be worse than intending to chuck yourself in the canal. And I think that given some openness about who you passed your information to, you could well be sleeping in your own bed tonight.' He put emphasis in his words. 'You knew, of course, that you were doing it for a drugs dealer?'

Sleath jerked his head up, his mouth open and staring as if at a man who had unexpectedly kicked him. 'No,' he choked out. 'I didn't know. He didn't say.' Then wildly, tears brimming in his eyes, '*Please, sir*, you mustn't believe that. I wouldn't. I just wouldn't. How could I when it was his sister, and he made me –'

'Dammit! Calm down!' Lingard interrupted him, jabbing out an admonitory finger to shut him up. 'And pull yourself together, you're not a bloody girl. How old are you?'

'Nineteen, sir.'

'So don't start calling me sir just because you're in trouble. Are you married?'

He shook his head; no happier, but his hysteria damped down.

'Or living with a woman?'

'No. I live with my parents.'

'Good. So I can take it you aren't going to be altogether pig-headed and deny you've been flogging details of your boss's business to your fellow villain?'

Sleath groaned. 'No, I can't not now. I've been a fool.'

Lingard thought him well-spoken, even a mite prissy, for somebody sporting a freakish hairdo and a gaudy shirt. 'I've no doubt you have,' he said, 'and now you're going to tell me the how of it. I want everything; how it started, what you've done and what you've made out of it. It must be obvious to you that I know more than somewhat, so don't bother to lie to me.' He moved closer to Sleath, imposing his physical presence on him by sitting on the beam at his side. 'Suppose we kick off by you confirming the name of your friendly villain, eh?'

'Mr Stephanakis,' Sleath answered him without hesitation.

'From Disraeli Street, right?' Lingard wasn't surprised, though he had been hoping he would name the very much alive and arrestable Sickert. 'So let's start with Stephanakis, shall we?'

Sleath wasn't looking at him, but engrossed in the backs of his hands, though obviously being unsettlingly conscious of the detective's unblinking regard from so near him. 'I was led into this by Mr Stephanakis,' he started off. 'Back in April or May I had taken a scheduled flight booking to Rotterdam from him. That was the first time I'd set eyes on him and he seemed a very friendly man. When he came in to book again I told him about a cheaper weekend break booking which he accepted and thanked me for being so helpful. The next day I was having my lunch in the pub when he came in and said it was his lucky day because I was just the man he wanted to see. He bought me a drink when he had his and told me he was a partner in a time-share organization dealing in Dutch properties. He did say the name but I've forgotten it – it's somewhere near Utrecht though, I'm certain. He wasn't offering me a full-time job, not yet, but he did say I could earn substantial commissions on the side as I had access to the names of tourists intending to visit that area. He said he could probably persuade his partner to pay up to twenty pounds a time in cash just for information, and a hundred if it resulted in a sale. He had the money, I know, because he showed me it in his wallet and said that some of it could be mine. I said that I didn't think it right, that it . . . well, you know, it wasn't above board. That's the truth, I swear it.' He was uneasy, glancing at Lingard from the corners of his eyes as he fell silent.

Getting nothing from the detective but a slight lifting of his eyebrows, he went on. 'He realized how I felt because he tried to tell me it was all OK, that it was done by everybody in the travel business and then asked me to tell him how my boss could lose anything just because I passed on a few names to somebody who wasn't in competition to him. He had discovered my name from somebody because he said, "Look, Graham, I want to be your friend and to help you. There's no law against it, honestly there isn't, and you won't be brought into any deal whatsoever, I'll swear to that.'' Then he asked me to sleep on it, to say nothing to anybody and see him at his home in Disraeli Street the next evening when he promised to show me publicity brochures. I'd definitely made up my mind not to do it, but made a bit of a fool of myself when I went there and I didn't really have any choice.' A dull red flush came up from behind his shirt collar and he was clenching and unclenching his fists. 'I don't want to go into all that, but I admit that I did give him the names and addresses he wanted over the next few months. I'm sorry about . . .'

'Hold it, laddie!' Lingard said sharply in his ear. He had been about to push snuff into his nose and he held his hand poised. 'I want to know how you made a fool of yourself and had no choice.' He gave Sleath what was meant to be an encouraging smile. 'Don't be bashful. I suspect it was something to do with the woman you mentioned. His sister, did you say?'

'Yes, she said she was. She told me Mr Stephanakis was her brother.'

'I see.' He peered with exaggerated wonderment into Sleath's face, not believing for a second what he was about to say. ''Pon my soul, you didn't finish up raping her, did you? Or committing an indecent assault on her?'

'No, I didn't.' Lingard had managed to strike a small spark of resentment in him. 'If she said so, she's not telling the truth. Neither is he. It was her who started it.'

'Oh, dear,' Lingard frowned. 'All my villains say that to me. You'd better tell me your side of it, hadn't you? And enough this time for me to decide who's telling the truth.'

In between his talking, Sleath had been gnawing at the corner of his mouth, the picture of a man smarting from unjust accusations. He said, 'I called at his house like I told you and his sister answered the door. She said that Mr Stephanakis had been called out on urgent business and would be back later. I was pleased about that, but didn't show it of course. When I said I'd call another evening, she told me her brother would be angry if I wasn't offered a drink. I thought she was his wife until she said that, I really did.'

'Did she happen to say what her name was?'

'Later on. Then she said to call her Debbie.'

'And she was black haired? A big busty woman about thirty?' Lingard was no man to put helpful words in a suspect's mouth.

'No, not at all. She was a small girl, very blonde and I thought about my own age.'

Lingard smiled at him. 'Of course, I remember now. What else did she say or do to drag you inside?'

Sleath looked surprised at that. 'She told me that she was nervous about being on her own because she'd heard some queer noises coming from the back of the house. She thought that there might be burglars trying to get in. I wasn't going anywhere else so like a fool I went in and she sat me on the sofa while she got me the drink. She had one herself and sat next to me. She kept staring at me, asking if I had a girl and what did I do when I finished at work, that sort of thing. She was joshing me, I think, not being serious and giggling a lot. Then she got me another drink.' He swallowed, the red flush re-appearing from behind his shirt collar. 'When she got back on the sofa and lifted her legs onto it I could see she had nothing on under her dress and I . . . well, didn't know what to think. I drank some of the whisky she gave me – I'm used to a few drinks now and again – but straight away I felt funny.' He wagged his head as though bewildered. 'I don't know, I've tried to remember it since. It wasn't that I was drunk or anything like that because then I'm always sick. It was a kind of not caring for anything much, a funny strong feeling with bright lights and happy at being there. Then I think I fell on the carpet because I found I was lying on it with her – with Debbie.'

He had lowered his voice almost to a mumble, then stopped, patently finding the going hard. Lingard, wondering if Deborah had given the daft bugger a cocaine Mickey Finn and finding it difficult to keep a straight face, said, 'Egad, laddie, but you were living dangerously. Do carry on.'

'Yes.' He was looking down at the ground between his feet. 'I don't want to sound indecent but my zip was open – I'm positive she must have done it when I wasn't looking because I never would – and she had her hand inside my trousers stroking . . . stroking my whacker.' His face creased in what seemed to the detective to be an unnecessary show of revulsion. 'Not just that, but her dress was up to her waist and she was holding my hand and pressing it against the top of her legs . . . her thighs, I mean. And that was just when Mr Stephanakis came in – he'd come back

82

early.' He shook his head, his expression woebegone at its recall.

Even for an innocent faced with a straightforward seduction, Lingard was finding his supposed naivety unbelievable, but he went along with it. 'A most disagreeable happening,' he said gravely. 'I imagine he was badly shaken to find you wrestling on the carpet with his sister? And probably believing you were raping her?'

'No,' Sleath protested. 'Because I wasn't, I wasn't near her. He was really very decent about it considering. Not terribly angry and he said that he was sorry it had happened, but that I'd broken the trust between us. I couldn't say what had really happened, could I? Not with her being a lady and saying it was partly her fault for giving me too much to drink.' He swallowed again. 'When she left the room Mr Stephanakis said that although his sister probably looked older she was only fifteen and that anything done with her was a very serious offence in the eyes of the law. Still, he was prepared to overlook it, but only because he still liked me in spite of it and that he'd already told his partner he had contracted to employ me on a proper commission basis. He said that as long as the information kept coming to him his partner would be satisfied, and he could promise that what I had done to his sister could be kept from the police and Mr Shadick. I would have got the sack, wouldn't I? And gone to prison. Like I will now, I suppose. I'm sorry,' he finished lamely, 'I truly am, but I really didn't do anything except what I've told you . . .'

'He paid you as he promised, I suppose?'

'He did give me twenty pounds after the first one,' Sleath admitted unhappily. 'Afterwards he said he was accumulating the rest for me in one big lump. So people wouldn't ever get suspicious.'

'Typical,' Lingard murmured. 'The more they have, the more they want to hang on to it.' Louder, he said, 'I'll have the details later of what clients you shopped to him and how you did it. For the moment, your alleged sexual ravishment demands our attention. It doesn't seem to have lodged under that hair-style of yours that you were set up for it, does it? Would my telling you that your blonde *femme fatale* wasn't his sister make you see what you should've seen before?'

The youth's jaw dropped, opening his mouth to show his stupefaction. 'N-Not?' he stuttered feebly. 'She said she was.'

'She was his freely available live-in doxy and certainly not a day under twenty,' Lingard said flatly, 'so you needn't take her say-so as being anywhere near gospel truth. And if you did go further than you've told me, you might also think about the possibility of your having caught a dose of the clap.' The beam on which he sat, hard on his uncushioned tail-end, now felt painful; at his other end the noxious smell from the canal was becoming an abomination to his nostrils. After the couple of questions to which he wanted Sleath to commit himself and then to brood on, he proposed continuing his interview in the comfort of his office. 'Apart from that, where were you last evening? Say, between seven and nine o'clock?'

Not having recovered from his astonishment and apparent dismay of a few moments earlier, Sleath looked totally bemused. 'Last night?' he faltered. 'Wasn't that when I went out for a drink? Why do you want to know?'

Lingard put surprise in his face, then frowned. 'I'm afraid you're going to have to convince me where you were,' he said, standing up from the beam. 'Somebody killed your friend Stephanakis round about then.' He stared hard at the youth. 'Probably someone with reason to nurse a grudge against him.'

Sleath let loose a despairing groan and, as he lifted his lankiness from his seat, looked as though the detective had just fitted a hangman's noose around his throat. 'He's . . . he's dead?' he stuttered agitatedly. 'Who'd do an awful thing like that?'

Lingard, trying to regard him with complete detachment, found him a difficult subject for appraisement. Overall, he seemed the kind of star-crossed individual on whom heavy trees fell in a gentle breeze, yet, acting as if too wet behind the ears for rational belief, he could be undiluted low cunning in his efforts to get out from under. Flushing a lavatory twice, as he had prior to his half-hearted flight, could suggest either puking, the loosened bowels of frightened guilt, or, as likely, the hurried disposal of incriminating evidence; specifically cocaine. 'Don't ask my opinion about that now,' he told him, his blue eyes giving him no message of comfort. 'There's a possibility that you can fool me and a few old ladies without trying too hard, so we'd better go to my office and sort things out on paper.'

Lingard, walking back with the abject Sleath in tow, searched his mind for the appropriate crime to which he could fit him for the selling of his employers' trading information and found nothing. Should Sleath later find the moral courage to tell him to get lost, he accepted that without evidence of a criminal offence, metaphorically lost he would have to get.

14

Never in any danger of bursting into song or dancing around in carefree abandon, Rogers yet felt that his short period of dreamless unconsciousness had done him good. Taking his second shower of the day, convinced that he could still smell the mortuary's formalin and the dead Stephanakis on his skin, he decided to work off his remaining stiffness by walking back to his office and taking what would be, were he able to cozen the manageress with sweet words, a latish lunch in the Headquarters canteen.

Overlooking the necessity for stealth and making his way down the stairs, he was trapped in ambush by Nanoushka. On the edge of being impatient with her, he felt a shaming guilt that he should be objecting to importunities he could have earlier discouraged. Presented by Nanoushka on a plate, so to speak, that which could seem so sexually desirable in the warm and scented glow of an evening indoors could be significantly less so in the prosaic ordinariness of his daytime thinking. Talking to her now, feeling harassed by the pressures and commitments she was putting on him, he realized that his necessarily short-term physical needs, for weeks itching to be satisfied, were not to be placated by her. In his view an already lonely and unhappy woman, much too serious in her intent that he should make love to her, he feared that what she wanted could only lead to her increased unhappiness when, later, it might be necessary for him to be cruel in the shrugging off of her attachment to him.

Exhibiting as friendly an affection for her as he felt and which he knew would redound to his future discomfiture, he promised in the face of a sad wistfulness that so easily made him feel an ungrateful boor to let her know when he was free from his so far unrewarding investigation. That, he thought as he reached the street and adjusted his mind to the affairs of Stephanakis, should give him the leeway of anything up to a month; by which time she might well have acquired a distaste for him and his sexual diffidence.

At his desk, his brain stimulated to what he hoped was high endeavour by lukewarm coffee and two rounds of hastily put together ham sandwiches, he read through a telephoned report from the police liaison officer attached to the Forensic Science Laboratory. Cautiously endorsed *Subject to written confirmation*, it said that the blood specimens submitted as coming from the scene of the Kiddle murder had been identified to Groups A and O. Group O had been found on the specimens taken from Kiddle's body, from the sole of the sand wedge and that blood scraped and soaked from the surface of a cement flagstone. The specimen recovered from the wheel hub submitted had been identified as Group A. It was possible that Group A blood could also be on the sand wedge but, being contaminated by an overlay of the Group O blood, it needed a more detailed analysis for positive identification. The powder crystals submitted separately had been identified as cocaine with minimal adulteration detected, possibly later to be classified as high grade.

Rogers dismissed the cocaine analysis as peripheral to his immediate needs, being only confirmation of what was already known. But the blood grouping promised to be helpful and, in a sense, satisfying. He could recall Lingard's words in the mortuary, prophetic now: *It'd be nice to think we had another fractured skull staggering around waiting to be handcuffed, wouldn't it?*

Also recalling that one man had been seen by Mrs Kiddle running with his hand to his face, it seemed to him a reasonable assumption that an outraged about-to-be-robbed Kiddle had got in his blow first before having the wedge taken forcibly from him and being felled in his turn. From that there would be a possibility that whoever had been hit by Kiddle and suffered, if not the broken skull one would hope for, at least an injury serious enough to demand medical attention.

Not believing that the man would be fool enough to seek it locally, he nevertheless sent one of his sergeants to check at the hospital, then circulated a request throughout his own force and to neighbouring forces, for enquiries to be made at hospital casualty departments in an effort, medical co-operation permitting, to identify him. He had to ignore doctors in practice completely, for what he had heard derisively miscalled the Hypocritical Oath too often deterred them from helping to bring to justice any person, however criminal, who could claim to be a patient.

He was busy with this, sucking absently on a long gone-out pipe, when the telephone switchboard operator came through to him, asking him if he would accept a call from a Dr Stuchley.

'Superintendent Rogers?' The doctor's pleasant voice sounded high-pitched with emotion. 'I've heard from Deborah! It seems she's all right after all. Will you see me if I come straight away?'

'Of course,' he said, surprised and hard put not to start questioning him over the telephone. 'Or, if you'd prefer, I'll come out to you.'

'No.' Stuchley's refusal was firm. 'You've been put to far too much trouble already, and in any case I can take the opportunity of paying a call or two in town after I've seen you.'

After telling the doctor that he would be met at the reception desk, Rogers disconnected and leaned back in his chair to wait and to think about it. Had it been a sort of diappointment, a twisted sense of frustration, that he felt no relief at this outcome? It seemed such a soft aftermath, an anticlimax, to what he had theorized as being at least a criminal abduction. He was certain that his already considerable dislike for this whore of a girl who had loaded so much unhappiness on to her unfortunate parents would be added to very shortly. Nonetheless, while he hoped that he wasn't doing her an injustice in thinking it, she might now wear more easily the dark cloak of a suspected accessory to whatever arrangements had been made for the murder of Stephanakis. In the meantime, there was the prospect of some heavy going with an anxious father.

When within a shorter time than Rogers would have cared to take to drive the distance from Amford St Michael Stuchley was shown by a PC into his office, the change in his attitude was immediately evident. Shaking hands with the detective, he appeared to be on the verge of a beaming cheerfulness rather than suffering, his floridness heightened and his stockiness made bulkier by his wearing a thick tweed overcoat. Without his spectacles he looked more like an amiable farmer.

'Sit down, doctor,' Rogers said. 'It sounds like good news for you.' Looking at him as he arranged himself in the visitors' chair, it was difficult for Rogers to accept that the genes of either he or his wife could account for the gross immorality and smeary dishonesty possessed by their daughter.

Stuchley put a hand inside his overcoat and withdrew an envelope. 'This,' he said, handing it over the desk to Rogers, 'was put through my surgery door this afternoon.'

Rogers examined the envelope, handing it only by its edges. It was standard correspondence size, white, creased from folding, unaddressed and ripped open, he guessed by impatient fingers. Taking from it the folded sheet of plain paper, he read its pencilled message written in an educated and quite shaky italic: *Daddy. I have not been taken away. I am safe with a friend and where I wish to be. Please don't worry. Love, Debbie.*

Looking up from it, he thought he detected anxiety in Stuchley's eyes watching him. 'I take it you're satisfied that it's in your daughter's handwriting?' he asked.

The doctor looked surprised. 'Absolutely. Quite definitely. As is her mother, and we are only too grateful to know that she's all right. It's such a tremendous weight off our minds.'

'I'm sure it is and I'm pleased for you both.' Rogers was re-reading the note. 'Is this her usual mode of address to you? Does she normally call you Daddy? Would she send her love even after the extremely serious differences you've told me about?'

'Yes, to all that you've asked, Mr Rogers.' He sounded a little flattened. 'I can't think of anything that would come between our love for each other. Or that between her and her mother either.'

'The writing looks shaky,' Rogers pointed out. 'That wouldn't be normal for her, would it?'

'No, it wouldn't, but I'd understand it if she felt herself under stress in writing to me.'

'You don't know the friend she refers to, I assume?'

Etched by pale sunlight coming in bars through the venetian blinds, signs of stress showed in the doctor's own face. He shook his head. 'Of course not. I only wish to God I did.'

Rogers kept the note open in front of him. For several reasons to which he had yet to put names, he didn't like it. It wasn't ringing true and he was faced with a problem. Stuchley, understandably, needed the note to be an assurance of his daughter's safety and there was nothing in Rogers that wanted to destroy that comfort, to return him to the miserable despair he had witnessed earlier that day. His instinct was telling him that the greater probability was that the note had been written under persuasion or threat.

He tapped the envelope with his finger. 'You told me that this was put through your door this afternoon. Did you happen to see who did it?' A stupid question that, he knew, but it had to be asked.

'No. Perhaps it means nothing much because I don't know the time the envelope was put in the door, but my wife remembered seeing a strange lad wearing a motorcycle crash helmet walking past towards our sub-post office. She thought it was about half-past one and I didn't find the envelope until after three o'clock, when I rang you.' His brief smile held in it something of his anxiety and a seeking for confirmation that everything was as he hoped. 'Does he seem likely to you?'

'He could,' Rogers assured him, though not too enthusiastically. 'And why not? It had to be delivered by someone.'

'It's a moot point anyway,' Stuchley said. 'It doesn't matter now that we know she's safe.'

Rogers held the gentle stare from the blue eyes, wondering at the naivety that seemed to co-exist with human decency, and chose his words carefully. 'Well, even though it's now a probability, it's still necessary for me to find out where she is. And I'm sure that you'd want that too. There're matters needing to be cleared and your daughter may have simple answers to them. One is that she appears not to know that Stephanakis, a man she was closely associated with, was killed shortly after she left the apartment. Another is that although she's chosen to tell you that she's safe, she hasn't given you any reason for her going off – which I think under the circumstances she might well have.'

However non-accusative Rogers had tried to make it, it had put the beginnings of doubt in Stuchley's expression. 'What are you trying to say, Mr Rogers?' he asked stiffly. 'That the letter is a forgery, that it doesn't come from my daughter?'

'Not at all. It's one of my more tiresome principles that I don't accept everything wholly as it first appears. And not later either without something to support it.' He smiled sweet reason at the doctor. 'Which doesn't mean that I'm casting doubt on the authenticity of your daughter's note . . .' – *liar*, he told himself – '. . . only that I'm exercising a policeman's prerogative of needing corroborative evidence.' When Stuchley remained silent, he said, 'I don't want you to read into my questions more than what is intended, but I do have several to ask. Knowing you daughter – as I do not – have you any idea of why she should go away like this? And apparently abandoning most of her clothing and make-up in doing so.' He pursed his lips, leaving his own doubt to be read.

Stuchley shook his head helplessly. It could have been Rogers's imagination, but he looked deflated in spirit. 'No. But Deborah is . . . has always been so totally unpredictable that it doesn't surprise me. If she was parting from that man, as I believed she would one day, it would be in her to do it on impulse and concern herself about getting back her clothes later.'

Rogers had noticed that Stephanakis wasn't to be given whatever dignity there was in a name, and that was understandable. 'One thing bothers me a little,' he said. 'I've been wondering how she'd find out so soon about your knowing she was missing, that you'd be worrying about her.'

Stuchley remained silent for long seconds. 'That did cross my mind on the way here,' he admitted. 'You say that she doesn't appear to have heard of that man's death because she hadn't mentioned it in her letter. To me, it's completely explicable that if she had heard of it – and there's no reason why she shouldn't have if she's still somewhere locally – then she would find it difficult to refer to a man she had been living with and about whom she must presume I knew nothing. The other thing is that, being our daughter, she would naturally anticipate that we would be worrying regardless.' He hesitated, then said, 'I would like to ask you a question. Obviously you and your staff have been searching for Deborah, so have you discovered anything about where she might be?'

'No, nothing at all,' Rogers told him bluntly, not wanting to equivocate. 'She could be anywhere and until we get information naming her friends and associates, those close to her now or in the past, there isn't anywhere we can usefully look.'

'Have you tried the gaming club where she worked? The Barbizan, wasn't it? She could be there couldn't she?' If there was such a thing as mild aggression, it was in Stuchley's voice.

'I've tried it, up to a point that is. It's one of the first things I did.' Rogers, suspecting that he was about to be besieged, said patiently, 'When as a police officer I visit a club to which I have no legal right of entry without permission and when I've no grounds at all for obtaining a search warrant, it's highly improbable I'm going to get any co-operation about finding somebody not wishing to be found, or just anyway disinclined for a chat with the police. To assure you, however, I don't believe your daughter and Sickert – he's the club owner – were very friendly on her leaving and I'd certainly be surprised to find her there.'

Stuchley was giving him his blue-eyed stare as if evaluating his sincerity. 'Forgive me, Mr Rogers,' he said with quiet determination, 'but circumstances do change and so do people; my daughter's intentions in particular, as I know well, and she could be there.'

'Yes, she could be,' Rogers agreed. 'While I've no reason to think she is, I'll certainly bear it in mind.'

'I'd be grateful,' Stuchley said. 'And before I forget to mention it, you've raised doubts about the genuineness of my daughter's letter. If only for my wife's peace of mind, I'd prefer you didn't mention them to her, for I naturally wouldn't wish to have her worried unnecessarily. I'd like to make it clear,' he added courteously, 'I neither intend offence nor imply any slur on your handling of what you've so far done.'

'I'm sure you don't,' Rogers said, though uncertain whether he had or had not. 'I do intend holding on to the note. It needs checking for fingerprints, and a laboratory examination might tell us something in addition to what is written on it.'

'One thing,' Stuchley said, standing from his chair. 'Might I ask what the police as a whole have done, or are doing, about dealing with the people degrading and ruining the victims of their greed as appears to have happened to Deborah?'

'Not always enough, I suppose,' Rogers admitted. 'Mainly, of course, because such as your daughter, or their parents, rarely bring themselves to our notice.' He was disapproving. 'Had it occurred to you to tell us of her suspected addiction when you first heard of it we might have been able to do something, even though she may have suffered in the process. Also, hard though it might have been, it would almost certainly have been better for you to have done something positive about her when she first went off the rails as a schoolgirl. While she wasn't guilty of any offence herself, the man who'd had sexual intercourse with her certainly was. So please don't criticize our apparent short-comings when you hadn't even begun to ask for our help.'

Stuchley's eyes had shadowed at Rogers's reproof, though he'd nodded in apparent agreement. He said, 'I do apologize for the form in which I put my question. I should have realized that the enduring protectiveness that parents have for their children isn't necessarily of the best help to the police.' When Rogers made no reply – he couldn't think of one that wouldn't be a banality – Stuchley peered at him as if trying to diagnose an unfamiliar symptom and said, 'Again without offence,' he apologized, 'you could be wrong about the letter, couldn't you?'

'That I could,' Rogers conceded smiling, ever ready to admit that he might be flawed, though not all that badly. 'As easily, if not quite so often fatally, as medical men are about their patients.'

He had managed to wring an answering smile from Stuchley with that and, after seeing him out to his car, returned to his office to smoke his neglected pipe and to do some deep thinking. While he hadn't the slightest reason for suspecting Sickert of being involved in what he had still to consider the abduction of the used and abused Deborah, he felt that in view of Stuchley's own suspicions he should follow them up. Not, he thought, with any hope of getting anywhere for, having seen and questioned Sickert but a few hours earlier, he hadn't yet acquired the necessary fresh ammunition to fire at him and force him into some useful answers.

15

Back behind his desk and switching on his anglepoise lamp against the lemonish-green dusk that crept dying through the windows, Rogers sorted through the papers found in Stephanakis's briefcase, accepting that in his earlier condition of torpor he could have missed an item of immediate interest. It appeared, in fact, that he had not, but seeing again Stephanakis's wife's name, Allegra, reminded him that he had yet to meet anyone who would know more about a man's private and business affairs than his wife. Or, even better, a separated wife as the legal documents showed her to be. Such wives, sympathetically questioned, fostered the promise of a bitter and liberated tongue, an eagerness to unleash informative venom.

It was then – 'Bloody hell' he muttered – that he realized he had forgotten that, separated though she might be, she remained a wife needing to be informed officially and in good time of her husband's death. At the worst, he consoled his sense of a neglected duty, he had only learned of her existence two hours or so ago.

He snatched at his telephone, dialled the number given on one of the Potters Row bills and waited. About to accept that it was not to be answered, it was; a woman's voice, strong and self-confident and with, he thought, a gin-drinker's huskiness. 'Yes? Who is it?' she said. Whoever it was, he seemed to have caught her in a bad moment.

'Good afternoon.' He thought it was still that as he put a suitable gravity in his words for somebody soon to be told she was a widow. 'Mrs Stephanakis?'

'No. Who are you?' She sounded a woman with the potentiality of blasting into his ear.

'My name is Rogers and I'm sorry to bother you,' he said. 'Has Mrs Stephanakis left this address?'

'No, not exactly. It depends on what you want her for. She may not wish to hear whatever it is you are calling about.'

'I don't understand. Is she there or not?'

'She's here when she wishes to be. You need to be more than somebody called Rogers for her to want to be.'

Rogers's exasperation broke loose. 'Madam,' he growled, 'I'm a police officer needing an interview with Mrs Stephanakis, so please don't play games with me. Why I want to speak to her is nobody's business but hers, so will you do me the courtesy of either getting her to the phone or telling me where she is.'

There was a short silence in which, above the faint hissing of static and the scraping of a hand placed over the mouthpiece, he thought he heard muffled laughing. When she answered, her voice had raillery in it. 'My, my,' she said, 'I *am* surprised. Aren't you policemen supposed to be polite to us members of the public?' She was suddenly brusque again. 'My name is Ascroft and if you wish to know anything about the late Mrs Stephanakis you might care to present yourself here in an hour's time.'

Coming in the middle of his saying 'I'm sorry, but . . .', he heard the click of her disconnection like a slammed door. It left him wondering what the hell she had meant by referring to the late Mrs Stephanakis. Not, he was reasonably certain, that she was dead; not in the way she had said it. And then, thinking more about it and being less sure, he could have been speaking to Mrs Stephanakis herself, who might be using the name Ascroft for no doubt adequate reasons of her own. Against that, her voice hadn't been what he had expected from a woman who had chosen to marry somebody like Stephanakis. The call left him vaguely irritated with what had sounded to be a bossy and hard-nosed female – though one with a sense of humour – and, not least, because she must have in her turn thought him a pompous and uptight bugger.

One of the administrative clerks, bringing correspondence and papers for his attention, unwittingly gave him an assurance that the constabulary part of his brain hadn't atrophied completely. From among what was largely routine bumph he fished out two reports. One was another from the liaison officer at the Forensic Science Laboratory who seemed to be having a busy day with Rogers's force; the other, marked URGENT, from Sergeant Magnus. He read that first. It detailed that Magnus had dried off the fingerprint found on the kitchen window of Stephanakis's apartment – Rogers knew that he used a portable hair drier adapted for this – then photographed it and lifted it on tape. Subjected to magnification, the photographed image was identified as a partly smeared twinned loop carrying ten clear characteristics; an insufficient number for proof positive in a court of law, but sufficient for Magnus to be certain that the print had been left on the window glass by the named Albert Raymond Webber. When Magnus claimed certainty, Rogers tended to accept it on the same level of authority as he would the geometric theorem of Pythagoras, had he known exactly what that was. Actually, he was surprised at his own inspired guess that Webber might be involved for, so far as he remembered, he had never been suspected or convicted of breaking offences.

The report from the laboratory's liaison officer, happily not submitted in the sort of scientific terminology that normally made Rogers's back teeth ache, set out the provisional findings derived from a visual examination under magnification of the crossbow bolt removed from Stephanakis's neck. The first was that the bolt was significantly oxidized, suggesting that it had been generally unused for some years, possibly for as many as ten, and, also possibly, exposed to some weathering. The second finding was that there had been a recent displacement of surface oxides on the bolt in the form of a number of microscopic striae, these caused by friction between the bolt and the groove in the crossbow from which it had been fired. This striation suggested that the bolt had been used once, at the most twice, after a long period of disuse during which the oxidization had occurred.

Having already been told most of that by Twite, it didn't sound as if it was going to help him all that much, but he supposed it could mean something, assuming that he might find the time to think about it for more than a minute or so. He lifted his internal telephone and dialled Lingard's office number. 'Ah, you're back,' he said unnecessarily when Lingard answered it. 'Order up some tea and I'll be along in a few minutes.'

Further along the corridor and with only a view of a grossly untidy metal scrap dealer's yard from its windows, Lingard's office was fitted with the same soulless metal and plastic furniture as Rogers's, bureaucratically adjusted to his lower rank by, among other things, a two drawers less commodious desk, a non-rotating chair for sitting at it and a smaller rectangle of carpet. Unlike Rogers, who suffered the starkness of his own office without complaint, Lingard had hung on the birch-grey emulsioned wall area around him framed reproduction prints of Gillray and Cruikshank caricatures, a steel engraving of Bath's Royal Crescent and a black and white drawing of his admired and emulated George Bryan Brummell. On his desk were two silver-framed photographs. One was of his cherished green veteran Bentley with an elegant blond Afghan hound at the driving wheel looking uncannily like the detective himself; the other, of the long dead, once beautiful courtesan Nancy Frail whose ghost was destined to haunt him to his grave and, he was certain, well beyond it.

Rogers sat on the visitors' chair and, in between drinking unenthusiastically at a cup of canteen tea, brought Lingard up to date on the laboratory's blood grouping report and the enquiries he had initiated, the identification of Webber's fingerprint and, finally, the delivery of the Deborah Stuchley note. 'Last things first, David,' he said. 'What do you think of it?'

Lingard was definite. 'It pongs to the high heavens,' he drawled. 'I'd say she's either heavily tied up in the knocking off of Stephanakis, or she knew enough about it not to have waited to be around when the balloon went up.'

'Not under compulsion?' Rogers suggested, airing his own tentative theory. 'And if not, why should she bother to send it? By her father's own account they hadn't been on speaking terms for God knows how long. And if you think about it, what was the message meant to achieve? She doesn't say where she is or why she's there. She doesn't even say why she's assuming her father would have doubts about her safety. Why should he when he didn't even know she was missing from anywhere until I told him, let alone ever knowing that she'd been living in Disraeli Street with a toad like Stephanakis.' He was frowning his dissatisfaction with what he was saying. 'Why should she leave her clothing behind? Well, most of it anyway. And her cocaine and the nose tube she used to sniff it? Why would she need a couple of men for escorts if she was going of her own volition? And, more significant, it's hard to believe it could be coincidental, what was the reason for her being taken away so shortly before Stephanakis was shot down on his way to join her?'

'You could have a point,' Lingard accepted. 'Possibly several. But whatever, don't be thinking she wasn't involved in chummy's drug trafficking. She was, and I'll tell you all when you've finished. But whichever way we look at it, it doesn't wholly invalidate my suggestions. The note could have been written in an attempt to pull the plug on the nasty suspicions of the police; to perhaps suggest *sotto voce* that we might chuck in our hand at trying to find her.'

'Yes, it could,' Rogers conceded. 'In fact it had that effect on her father until I rather put the damper on it. Poor devil! His wife, too. What else has she done to crucify them?'

'I found the mole for you.' His contempt showed plainly in Lingard's narrow face. 'As we'd reckoned, one of Shad-Awbery's employees, a weak sister of a chap called Sleath. Stephanakis and Deborah set him up with the you've-been-screwing-my-under-aged-sister routine, then threatened him with the chop if he didn't cough up the information wanted.' He gave Rogers the gist of Sleath's confession made on the canal towpath, pushing snuff into his nostrils as he did so and scenting the air with attar of roses until it gave ground to the more robust smell of Rogers's tobacco smoke.

'You've dreamed him up,' Rogers said, smiling broadly. 'I can't believe they're made like that any more.'

'That's what I thought, but when I tried to sort him out here I wasn't so sure. I'm still not. Now and again I thought I smelt he could've been hating Stephanakis's guts in a pretty feeble sort of way, though that might have developed after our towpath chat when he realized he'd been conned. For all that, I've a feeling he's a liar and probably coming this wet and innocent business with me as a cover-up for something. While he led me to believe that his romantic interlude with Deborah included nothing worse than her paying her respects to his exotica, there's a likelihood the stupid drip went the whole hog. He was certainly fretting about something because he asked if I thought he should drop in at the hospital's postules and pox department just in case. Aids seemed to be on his mind after what I'd told him and he was doing a gentle sort of sweat about that too.' Lingard showed his teeth as if to excuse an uncharacteristic credulity. 'Mind, it is possible that Deborah laced his drinks with a pinch or two of cocaine and I've heard that it's a great loosener of trouser zips; so possibly I've been a little hard on him.'

'The mere suspicion that he might have Aids seems punishment enough, and I thank God I'm of a saintly and celibate persuasion,' Rogers said with mock piety, conscious now that he was sitting on the chair certainly occupied by Sleath during his interrogation and hoping rather wildly that viruses on the loose couldn't burrow like worms through thicknesses of fabric. 'Do you think he's now on cocaine, as well as everything else? That he swilled it away when you walked into Shad-Awberys and flashed your warrant card?'

'That's anybody's guess. He didn't have any on him and he's

not throwing a fit about the prospect of having his home searched. Whatever, I tossed him over to the Drug Squad and as they haven't put him down I imagine they've given him a reasonably clean bill and taken him home to his mummy.'

'You're a hard sod, David. Where did he do his passing of information? At the apartment?'

'He says at the Black Dog pub where he has his lunch. And I believe him because that's where I now remember seeing Stephanakis waiting on an occasion or two. It's also where he says he spent a couple of relevant hours last evening – which I've yet to check.'

'Did Stephanakis ever mention Sickert's name to Sleath?'

Lingard shook his head. 'I shouldn't think so. It'd be a damfool thing to do, wouldn't it? I asked him, of course, and he certainly looked dim enough to be telling the truth about that.'

Rogers brooded on the fact of Sleath, searching for anything perverse enough for him to poke his finger at and not finding it. 'He's your baby, David, so keep him in your sights,' he said, not committing himself to absolving Sleath merely because of his wetness. 'About Webber. Send a couple of our heftier DCs out to pick him up for questioning. We've got him for attempted housebreaking if nothing else, but he's certainly tied in with Stephanakis's drug pushing. It might be he was trying to clear tracks after the killing, or grabbing the loot before we found it. And that,' he added, 'could have been on the orders of Sickert whose wrists were surely designed by God to fit my handcuffs exactly.'

Lingard was wagging his head again. 'I'll give you most of that, George, but a favour. Not the two bods from the department. I'd like Webber just for myself.' There was a fleeting hardness in his expression, his eyes darkening.

'If you want him, of course,' Rogers agreed, slightly puzzled. 'But why? He's a brutal bastard and you won't get the Queen's Police Medal just because he's a handful for one man to bring in. He might even rough up that suit of yours,' he observed humorously, believing it might make Lingard have second thoughts.

'He did that years back.' Lingard's expression had returned to being elegantly casual. 'And if you think I've a personal animus against him, you're so damned right. You mayn't remember, but I went to his lodgings on the Wilcot Estate – a bloody jungle it was then – to rope him in on an attempted robbery charge. He fooled me by doing the civilized villain act and coming without causing any undue bother. Outside in the front garden he suddenly landed one under my ear, though not enough to floor me. We finished up with him banging the juice out of me in a stinking mess of mud, paper rubbish and dog crap, and me like a bloody idiot trying to quieten him down with a proper regard for using only sufficient force to effect an arrest.' Lingard's face reflected an inner fury at his recollection of it. 'All the time he was yelling that this something or other of a bastard – that was me – was trying to kill him and we soon had spectators looking at us from over the hedge. What irked me most was that they were not only enjoying it, but were potential witnesses preventing me from taking him apart by just being there. I nailed him in the end, though not until he'd ripped my shirt, ruined my suit and shoes, and half strangled me with my own tie. Since when, apart from getting away with the charge and the assault on me, he gives me the old two-fingered 'up yours' when we see each other. It's always one too many for me, George, and all I can hope for now is that he'll resist being arrested. He really does owe me that.'

'You think you owe it to your *amour propre*, David,' Rogers corrected him. Lingard was a hard case when upset and, thuggish as he might be, Webber would suffer if it came to violence. 'I'm not likely to lose any sleep over Webber, but I wouldn't want you charged with GBH or whatever and suspended.'

'Worry not,' Lingard said flippantly, not having been refused a request with which he knew he would have gone his own way irrespective. 'To him that meteth it out, so shall it be meteth back to him in full measure.'

'As for me,' Rogers said standing, 'I've to pass on the news to Stephanakis's wife that she's now a widow. And if I'm right in believing I've already spoken to her, she sounds to be as tough and unfeeling as an old boot.' He was straight-faced in his exaggeration. 'I'm sure you'll agree that we leaders of men have to choose, as I have, the most dangerous and trying of jobs.'

In a way, he hoped that she was as tough and unfeeling as he had exaggerated, for he knew that he would never lose the phobia he had of breaking the black news of a death to a woman and having to deal with her grief, a task for which he knew he was ill-suited.

16

With an infuriating perversity, one of Rogers's telephones rang at the moment when, virtually straitjacketed, he was putting on his overcoat to leave the office. That his caller proved unexpectedly to be Sickert went some way to mitigate the perverseness.

Sickert's voice sounded uncomfortable, his usually controlled insolence and dislike of authority missing. He said that he was at the club with a problem or two, that he couldn't leave it to visit Rogers's office because he had an unmissable appointment later, so would Rogers care to look in before seven-thirty for whatever it was that worried him.

Rogers, unwilling as a matter of tactics to show anything but a lukewarm interest, told him that he was busy but would try and squeeze him in between what would patently be more important enquiries tending to lead to an imminent arrest. He left his office with an unwarranted optimism that Sickert might possibly have the chill water of fear running through his veins and a conscience-stricken need in him to confess to something or other. Dreaming of the unlikely was, Rogers admitted to himself, the mind's compensation for being convinced otherwise.

The entrance to Potters Row, situated in the old centre of the ancient town, was to be negotiated down steps dropping steeply through a narrow entrance between a derelict Anglo-Saxon church and the King Aethelred's Kitchen restaurant. When Rogers parked his car alongside the church the evening was dark with a cold polished half-moon hanging between trailing wisps of high cirrus in an indigo sky. It was chilly, but with no promise of the previous night's mist. Potters Row, with its houses on one side and a high lichen-blotched embrasured wall on the other, was more prosaically a dead-end street, and not a particularly well-lit one. It still retained its centuries-old stone setts, irregularly proud and ankle-spraining to unwary feet, down which the detective made his way. The slate-tiled houses in greenstone or plaster were stepped down to accommodate the ground's steep slope, most of them having tubs or containers of shrubs and flowers at their gardenless fronts. Apart from the chimneys sprouting television aerials and the doors a rash of electric bell pushes, the street had probably looked much the same for the past two or three hundred years. It wasn't the sort of milieu in which Rogers could picture Stephanakis.

The house he looked for was at the lower end of the slope, a small nameplate on it just readable in the light of his pencil torch as *Wattles*. Of pale-blue painted plaster, it had small curtained windows with opened deep-blue shutters. Its matching blue door with a pebble-glass porthole was flanked by two stone urns in which white chrysanthemums glimmered palely in the moonlight. Pressing the brass bell-bush he found on the door stile and hearing its remote response, he waited. She wasn't long in answering it; not, he saw through the irregularities of the porthole, putting on an inner light, but switching on the lamp in the door's architrave immediately above him. Apparently satisfied with whatever distorted image she could see of him and obviously not overly nervous of being confronted by a visiting thug or intending rapist on her step, she opened the door. Unable to see her shadowed face clearly and maintaining his gravity, he said, 'Detective Superintendent Rogers, and I spoke to you earlier. You're Miss Ascroft?'

'I knew what you'd look like,' she replied. 'Come in.' Heard in the flesh and not over a telephone cable, her voice was educated and, though slightly husky, nicely modulated.

Following her in to warm air, he thought it an odd start by what seemed an odd woman. He should, his instinct was telling him, have brought a policewoman with him. The room into which she led him, shadowed and smelling of smouldering incense sticks, looked comfortable in the greens and golds of its fabrics, in its glossy mahogany furniture and open wood-burning fire. There were books in plenty, a small bar in a corner and, apparently less necessary to civilized living, a very small television set and a portable radio. A cream-coloured chihuahua the size of one of his shoes, curled shivering on a sofa, watched him from bulging black eyes.

'Don't panic,' she said, giving him a brief smile. 'She only savages people who're near enough her own weight. Somewhat like her owner.'

He saw a tallish woman of about thirty years, not beautiful, but attractive with thick red-gold hair that looked shiny with wet varnish, a pale tea-coloured skin stretched taut over the bone structure of her face, deep-green eyes under dark eyebrows and a generous mouth set in a pleasant curve. Her nose was almost as prominent as his own, though femininely shapely and less thrusting. Her unremarkable body with its small breasts was dressed in a loose moss-green turtleneck sweater and woollen skirt, around her neck a string of golf-ball sized yellow beads. Despite what might be seen as a few visual imperfections, she had presence and impact, adding up to some sort of a response in him that brought absurdly to his mind words like lapis-lazuli, porphyry, jade and samphire, though there was little about her to suggest any of them. It could have been his imagination, but he thought he read in the eyes studying him an almost predatory interest not usually extended to him by women; certainly never within the first few minutes of their meeting.

Not reacting to her humour about the dog and herself, he cleared his throat and said, 'I do have some bad news to pass on about Mr Stephanakis.' He saw what he sought in her face. 'You *are* Mrs Stephanakis, aren't you?'

'I was,' she said calmly, 'and trying to get his name out of my life. For your information I'm now known by my family name of Allegra Ascroft. And in case it bothers you, I've already been told that he was killed last night. So has my solicitor and I'd have thought he would have contacted you by now.'

'I see.' Rogers wasn't particularly surprised at her attitude. Few wives legally separated from their husbands necessarily went hysterical over their loss unless they had somehow managed to take everything they owned with them. 'May I ask who told you?'

'By all means,' she said agreeably enough, 'though I don't propose telling you. If that's all you've come for, I'm sorry you've wasted your time.' She gave him another smile. 'I understand that the sun's probably over the yardarm by now and I'm going to have a drink. Will you join me?'

'The sun's been over it for the past hour,' he told her, 'and thank you, no. But I'm afraid I do have necessary questions to ask you about your husband.'

She walked over to the bar and stood behind it. 'That's fine,' she said, creasing her eyes in good humour, 'but no drink, no answering necessary questions. I don't care to drink on my own.'

Rogers moved to join her, conceding a sort of defeat, though not feeling unduly cast down about it. It was certainly preferable to having her weep tears on him. 'An extremely weak whisky, please,' he said, having seen a black-labelled bottle of the stuff waiting in a cluster of others behind the bar. 'May I sit?' On her nod he sat himself on one of the tall leather-padded bar stools at the counter.

He watched in silence as she poured herself a vodka with a pink mixer and then his whisky, pushing a small bottle of soda water across for his own diluting of it. Having now accepted that she was in no way an archetypal widow, that she was manifestly miles from being an ignorant and drug-addicted trollop, he had now to rationalize how she, like Deborah after her, could stomach being associated in any way with human rubbish such as Stephanakis. Never having understood women, it wasn't going to be easy.

She walked out from behind the bar and sat on the stool near the detective, her knees almost touching his. It had, he thought, been a studied move. 'Don't take me too seriously,' she said lightly, stretching behind him and retrieving her vodka from the counter, 'but isn't it usual for a widow to get herself sloshed in a celebration of grief?' She drank deeply from her glass, watching him with what he took to be teasing amusement.

'It's been done,' he said neutrally, lifting his own glass and letting the diluted whisky just touch his mouth. He could be mistaken, but he was thinking that she was halfway to being sloshed already, notwithstanding what she had said about not drinking on her own. 'I'm in a difficult position, Miss Ascroft, and . . .'

She cut him short. '*Mrs* Ascroft,' she corrected him sharply. 'It's obvious I'd never pass as a Miss, and nor would I wish to. And I imagine you are now wondering if I'm as dead rotten as he was. I don't suppose it would satisfy you my saying I'm not, so that'll be something you'll have to judge for yourself.'

She could have been reading his mind. 'Not for one moment,' he assured her, wishing she would let him get on with it in his own way. 'Did your nameless friend who told you of your husband's death mention the circumstances of his dying?'

'First of all, would you mind not calling him my husband. He isn't. He hasn't been for a long time and he can't be now, can he?' She bobbed her head as if in acknowledgment of his agreement. 'That he was killed with a crossbow arrow, yes I was told.' She sounded wholly indifferent. 'Why are you bothering? It won't help him, and whoever did it was doing lots of people a good turn.'

'I wouldn't argue you out of that. In that way was he rotten?'

'Oh, do come off it. If you're investigating why he was killed you won't need me to tell you that.'

'You'd obviously know his friends and associates, Mrs Ascroft. You could help me there.'

'I've been separated, living apart from him for over a year. Even before that we weren't exactly on speaking terms. When we were, he'd never tell me anything of what he did. Apart from his dealing work at the club, of course. The only person I knew he was at all close to – apart from several women, naturally – was a rather nasty man who worked at the club with him. He's the doorman there; at least he was then. He used to come here occasionally and don't ask me why because I don't know. I'd be told to lose myself, or they'd go into the kitchen and talk.' She looked at his untouched whisky on the counter and frowned. 'You're not drinking. I meant what I said, you know.'

'I'm sorry,' he said, reaching for the glass and this time swallowing a small mouthful. 'I'd forgotten I had it. Had the man a dodgy eye?'

'Yes, an ugly brute. His name's Webber.' She said it as if referring to a nauseous stench.

'He did things for your husb . . . for Stephanakis?'

'He must have done, but he worked for Geoffrey Sickert. They both did.'

Rogers stared at her. There seemed to have been an emphasis in what she had just said. 'Stephanakis was into drugs. Into cocaine and selling it. You knew that?' He saw in her eyes that she had, and also that she wasn't giving much of a damn about it anyway.

She twirled the stem of her glass between finger and thumb, her expression momentarily serious. 'An odd question this, but you are sure he's dead, are you? It's not somebody else?'

'He was when I saw him outside his apartment in Disraeli Street, and even more so in the mortuary.' Because she had shown nothing at his mention of Disraeli Street, he was satisfied that she knew of it. 'I can't think there could be any doubt about his identity when he was found dead by a neighbour who knew him by sight. And I did think that he still resembled something like his passport photograph. Why is there that doubt in your mind?'

She shrugged. 'I do take it that you wouldn't wish me to end up in your mortuary and give you something else to think about.'

'An unpleasing thought,' he murmured. 'You really think they would?'

'Somebody did, didn't they? Why wouldn't they believe I was involved as well? My telling you what I know about the drug dealings wouldn't give you much more than I imagine you already know, but it would certainly get back to . . . ' She grimaced and shrugged again. 'Well, you'd know that too, wouldn't you?'

'As Stephanakis hasn't a long enough arm to be able to reach you from the mortuary, you must mean Sickert, yes?'

'I used to work for him at the Barbizan,'she said obliquely. 'It's where I met Stephanakis. As you'd have eventually got round to asking me I'm telling you now. It's no business of yours and it's nothing I'm proud of either. We all make our mistakes, don't we, and I was fool enough to be misled into marrying a five-star pig. You understand?' There was amused mockery in her words, but her mouth showed bitterness behind it. 'You'd better because you won't get any more. Other than, perhaps, that I've been decontaminated by time and a long absence from the pig's quite abominable presence, ending up as I am now with a dislike for all you untrustworthy bastards. I've rarely met one anyway who wasn't a sex-mad pig at heart.'

She had warned him not to take her words too seriously, though he thought that they had to have some truth in them. 'It's appallingly true,' he exaggerated amiably, 'and you can't be too careful with any of us.'

'I should have made an exception of policemen,' she smiled back as if joshing him. 'Possibly a policeman one could count on not being a five-star pig.'

Odd that, he thought. Unless he was mistaken her eyes were showing a warmness, and what she had said could perhaps reasonably be interpreted as an invitation. Because she hadn't known him for much more than twenty minutes and three or four swallows at her vodka, he could safely put paid to any illusions he might have – and he didn't believe he'd ever had any – that he possessed what could be called an instant appeal to women. He

105

had little hesitation in putting what she had said down to her seeking some sort of an advantage from him, and it wasn't an unusual enough feminine ploy for him to get a high blood pressure over it.

'Regretfully, I'm out of the running,' he said, assuming a smiling ruefulness. 'I've a short-tempered seventeen-stone wife, eight children and crumbling discs in my backbone. And, anyway, I certainly could never be trusted.'

'Liar,' she said, laughing white teeth and pink tongue. 'You're just running scared.'

Rogers liked her despite his suspicions, and they were easy with each other, but knowing that he had gone too far with his humour he cut it short by saying, 'I take it you knew Deborah Stuchley?'

She had shrugged almost imperceptibly at that and said, 'She was one of the reasons I left him and I suppose I should be grateful for that.'

'She's missing from the apartment she shared with him. You knew that, did you?'

'Of course I did and I heard that she'd had enough sense to leave him before he was killed. So am I supposed to know where she is?' She answered her own question. 'I don't. Nor do I wish to.'

'You could tell me what you know about her.' Her slim legs, carelessly crossed, had been too near his own for him to be indifferent to them. Snail-slowly, he had moved his own away from them. She would, he guessed, if with a serious intent, be a woman far more determined and clutching than the mild Nanoushka could ever be. It made him very cautious.

She turned down her mouth. 'You want me to be bitchy? Right, and so I will for I never liked Stuchley and she never liked me. She's a cow. A not very nice type who isn't so particular who she sleeps with and with a very unladylike temper when she's upset. Not that she's a spoiled only child like me – she isn't. Just spoiled, I imagine, by a sloppy family who didn't know how to cope with her sort of selfishness, though they sounded respectable enough. I heard her say once that her father – I think she said her father – was a doctor living somewhere around here.'

'Her father is,' Rogers said.

'So it was her father; I wasn't sure.' It was obvious that she didn't care a damn either. 'You know she used to live with Geoffrey Sickert? I was still tied up with my – with the pig then and working there. It wasn't too many days after she started there as a hostess that Sickert was entertaining her after hours in the room over his office.' She held his gaze as though needing to convince him of something. 'Which, I may add, I couldn't describe and would be unforgivingly insulted should you ask me to. Going to bed with him was an understood arrangement with the hostesses, though I'll say this for him; when he invited me up there and I told him I wasn't interested in being entertained by him in particular, he took it like a lamb and never bothered me again. Of course, that could have been because the pig had got me the job and he and Sickert were as thick as thieves anyway. And getting me the job was no more than he owed me considering that I'd lost more money than I'd actually had at the time on his table and so badly needed one. But doing it the hard way wasn't Stuchley's idea at all and she was soon being bedded and boarded at the suite Sickert has at the Kinnisdale Grange Hotel.'

'When she left him for Stephanakis,' Rogers said, 'were he and Sickert quite so friendly after what'd happened?'

'I don't know, I'd left by then, though it doesn't surprise me that she'd gone stale on him.' She looked at his glass. 'You're empty and I want another,' she said peremptorily.

'You're pushing me.' Rogers looked down his nose at her. 'Is this your threat of no whisky, no words, again?'

'That's it precisely,' she said, already risen from her stool and moving around the bar counter.

While she poured his whisky, too lavishly for him to ever drink the whole of it, he tried unsuccessfully to beat down the tiny chihuahua's black-eyed staring at him, then tried to fathom what was going on behind the intelligent forehead of the woman who owned her. Specifically, he wondered again at the excess of friendliness where there might have been wariness and even dislike. It didn't get him very far, but he did promise himself that he would keep to a polite remoteness.

When, having placed the drinks at his side, she resumed her seat, he drowned his whisky in soda water and said a trite 'Cheers', tipping the glass to take in a cautious driblet. When she answered him with what he took to be 'Salud, dinero y amor' and put back a man-sized swallow of her vodka, he said, 'Did your . . . sorry, did Stephanakis have any nonfriends, anybody disliking him sufficiently to shoot a crossbow bolt into him?'

She was serious and used her words carefully. 'You said to me that he was into drugs, and who am I to say that you are wrong? Wouldn't you think that if he was he wouldn't win any friends, only have rather desperately sick addicts hanging on to his goodwill and the availability of what he sold for when the insects started to bite? As I've heard it, drug peddlers don't hand out credit and if availability in particular was held back from any one of those who couldn't pay for a fix, wouldn't you think that there might be some dislike, some need to get his own back?'

'Or *her* own back,' he postulated. 'Women do take the stuff as well.' He smiled at her encouragingly. 'You wouldn't put names to any you know, I suppose? Male or female?'

She was back to her cool affability. 'You suppose right, and I'm not even sorry. They're sick people, sick enough to be forgiven should they make the extermination of drug dealers a habit.'

'Given somewhere other than my bailiwick, not too bad a suggestion,' he agreed, 'though never say that I said so.' Whatever else she was doing, she was not yet prepared to put her nicely manicured finger on her late husband or, indeed, on any of his customers. And that, he considered, could be due more to fear from whatever organization was manipulating the local drug racket than to any affection or respect for Stephanakis or the others she could improbably have. He dropped the subject, needing to keep on her friendly side. 'There's been a blond man chasing around after Miss Stuchley,' he said. 'Calling on her at her lodgings and her apartment, and making himself a nuisance it seems. He could be a reject lover, she could be owing him money – anything. He's youngish, clean-shaven and has blue eyes; is well-spoken and well-dressed. You know?'

She wrinkled her nose. He could, apparently, read into that what he wished. 'I saw her once with a man I thought was fair-haired and might fit. That was a long time ago though. As far as I could see, she'd been given a lift to the club and was out of the car and giving him what I'd call an earful of trouble over something or other she hadn't liked.' She cocked her head at him. 'Would he be the man you mean?'

108

'He could be. Would you detail what you saw, when it was and where?'

'I'm trying to remember it properly,' she said, drinking from her glass and looking beyond him as if bringing back a visual recall of it. 'It was about this time last year, just before I left the Barbizan and about nine in the evening. I'm sure of the time because I was going in through the car park entrance to start getting ready for the evening. Stuchley was in the car park and standing at the open door – the passenger's door – of the car and talking into it. I remember the engine was running because I saw lots of exhaust smoke, so she'd probably been brought in it. It was dark at the time, but the interior light was on and I could see the back of his head. I wouldn't swear to it, but my memory tells me he had very fair hair. Whatever the colour, it wasn't doing him any good with her and she was laying into him, that being something she was awfully good at. I must admit I was taking my time at opening the door to go in, but I needn't have bothered because I don't believe either of them noticed me anyway. In between Stuchley's choking him off for something I couldn't catch on to, he, stupid man, was pleading with her – well, grovelling almost. Then I went in and didn't hear any more. When I saw her later she, of course, was back to her normal self – that is, bitchy and self-opinionated – and never a whisper to me or anyone else so far as I know about what had been going on.' She creased her eyes at him. 'Would I make a good detective?' she asked.

'You might,' he assured her, straight-faced, unwilling to even imagine the clashing of antlers she would cause in his department's offices. 'Particularly if you can also give me a better description of the man and one of the car. And you'd be decidedly useful if you had heard his name mentioned, if you'd seen him before or since.'

'You must be an ungrateful beast to work for,' she said caustically, though her eyes still showed warmness, 'and I don't think I'd like to. Because I wasn't all that interested at the time, I don't know for sure whether the name Tony was said by Stuchley then, or by somebody else on a different occasion altogether. While I didn't see his face – you don't when you're looking at the back of a head in semidarkness – he seemed quite young. As much as I heard of him – which wasn't much – he was well-spoken, a milk-and-water sort of a man. The car – well, it had four wheels and was fitted with an interior light, which is about all I can remember after a year and not being terribly interested in cars anyway. So far as I know, I'd never seen him before, I've certainly not seen him since and with Stuchley having been in some way tied to him, I wouldn't wish to.'

She drank from her glass again and he looked at his wrist-watch. It was near to the time when he was seeing Sickert and he thought it could be profitable to leave a question or two for another interview if for no other reason than that she might recall more after a period of thinking about what he had asked, or unconsciously contradict herself in something she had said. And, he hoped, he might then find her several degrees cooler than she now appeared to be under the green wool of her sweater and skirt.

'I'm sorry,' he said, rising from his stool, 'but I've another appointment. There are more questions, so perhaps I may see you again?'

She stood with him, near enough for him to smell the scent she wore. 'You and me,' she said astonishingly, her deep-green eyes showing clearly her meaning and intent. 'I have a strange feeling that we already know each other intimately. Do you think we might have been lovers in a different life?' She was quite serious.

Rogers, blank-faced, stared at her while he tried to think of something sensible that wouldn't be wounding to her. If she really believed that, if that were a true inner conviction, who was he in his ignorance of the metaphysical, or whatever it was, to dispute it? He had to admit that, without visibly trying, she was temptation writ large enough to fire any man in breeding condition to want to feed on her flesh. He could suppose dispassionately that a different Rogers, not a police officer and not on duty, who was not still in need of enough sleep and had no strong aversion to following on after a toad like Stephanakis, could – just could – take a woman like her up on it. As it was, though feeling as weak a sister as Lingard had held Sleath to be, he made his effort of disentanglement by saying, 'You flatter me, Mrs Ascroft; but I think if I were somebody else in a previous life – which I don't altogether accept I was – you would be flattering him also.' That didn't sound right and wasn't quite what he meant, but it would have to do.

110

She smiled at him and reached, touching the side of his face with the backs of her fingers. 'Don't think you're getting away with that,' she warned him. 'I shall probably think of something.'

That had been done and said in a joking mood and he felt that he might be clear of her dangled hook. 'I must go,' he said, moving towards the door. Then he stopped, turning back to her. 'I'm sorry, I'd overlooked it,' he apologized. 'Stephanakis had all the documents relating to your separation, the renting of this property and the payment of your bills locked away. Is there a reason why he should want to keep you and your marriage under cover?'

With an abrupt change of mood she looked at him as if he had made a remark in bad taste. 'I'll think about it,' she said, 'and possibly let you know. Or possibly not. It all depends.' She gave him a brief smile, walked to the door and opened it. 'And now you'd better go, hadn't you?'

Outside in the moon-shadowed darkness he made his way up the slope of uneven setts towards his car. At one stage in his mulling over his interview with her he shook his head despondently. He was growing old and stuff-shirted. He must be. In retrospect, he thought that any man with hair on his chest and a proper regard for the consoling of newly widowed wives, though one who hadn't been forced to ask an apparently awkward final question, would by now have been in bed with the undeniably delectable, undoubtedly hungry Allegra Ascroft. When he tripped on a protruding sett and hurt his toe, he couldn't even be bothered to put any feeling into the obscenity he swore.

17

Because Lingard had a fastidious distaste for those not of his ilk sitting in the passenger seat of his cherished Bentley – and Webber was definitely not of it – he took over one of the CID vans in anticipation of an arrest. This, ironically called the Q car, was a shabby and apparently uncared for nondescript with a standard engine that had no difficulty in keeping down to any built-up area's speed limits, being kept unwashed to the extent that it would always be difficult to recollect its colour or, with its radiator and boot badges missing, to put a name to its make or model. Driving it now through dark streets towards the East Thorpe Estate in his continuing search for Webber, he was committing to his memory the interview leading to it.

His knocking on Webber's door in Nobbers Street had been answered by his wife, a hugely fat woman who, in the darkness, had appeared to fill most of the doorway. Switching on the inside light showed a face that had been attractive and was still pleasant; a woman appearing to be far too good for Webber. But then, in Lingard's opinion, so would any woman be. Her expression, set by maturity, told him that she was probably losing out to life through no fault of her own. Lingard accepted that she need not necessarily be blamed for having committed an act of grossness in marrying Webber and he had been gentle with her, calling her 'madam', which seemed to do her suppressed femininity a lot of good. Later, he had even offered her a pinch of his snuff, a rare consideration on his part, and she had been gracious in her acceptance of it.

She had said 'What's he done now? You can't see him because he's packed his bags and hopped it,' when Lingard produced his warrant card and enquired whether her husband was in. Inviting him inside because of whom she called the bloody people next door, she proved to be surprisingly voluble in answering his questions, her eagerness unconcealed that the detective should find her husband and lock him up. He had warmed to her, taking unconcealed advantage of the fact that she was a woman whose ill-treatment and neglect by her husband was about to be rewarded by her discarding the loyalty he had abused. She told him that his job kept him at the club late and as a result he normally came home halfway through the night. Because of this he slept in the spare bedroom; something, Lingard read in her expression, that caused her no heartache at all. That past night, or rather early morning because it was about five o'clock and late for him – though it wasn't the first time by any means – she had been awakened by him crashing about and swearing in a loud voice downstairs as he often did in argument, though she found later that he had been on his own. Then he staggered upstairs into his bedroom where he did more crashing about, enough to wake the dead, God help them, she had said. Though she feared him

112

physically, it decided her into getting up. When she looked
through the door of the spare room, she said she had found him
boozed to his stinking eyebrows and moaning about wanting to
smash some bugger's face in. He was throwing his clothes in a
couple of suitcases he'd brought upstairs – she reckoned he had
pinched them from someone because they were nearly new and
she hadn't seen them before, and she noticed – couldn't help but
notice in fact – what she took to be a folded handkerchief taped to
the side of his face with streaks of blood running from beneath it.
She had placed a sausage-like finger on her left cheekbone to
indicate just where it had been. She asked her husband what was
going on and after telling her to mind her own effing business, he
said that he was going to Scotland on business and he'd let her
know where when he got there. When she asked him what he
had done to his face he got mad and slammed the door on her and
she went back to her bed, not getting up again until she heard
him leave the house and drive away in his car.

Asked by Lingard its description, she said that it was a Morris
something or other, coloured red and, never having been taken
out in it, all she could remember of the number plates was that
they had the letters YUM on them. But no doubt, she had added
with the only touch of malice he had heard, his bloody skinny
whoring tart had, her and her God knows whose poor little
bastard of a baby it was. She was called Maureen, at least that was
the name he had once chucked at her during a row, and lived at 59
Keighley Road on the East Thorpe Estate, according to a letter
asking for money she had happened to see by accident. And, she
told Lingard angrily, as if the mention of the woman Maureen
had lit a fire in her, if the bleeder had done somebody up he
deserved to be sent down and she didn't ever want him back in
her house because she'd had enough of him to last her the rest of
her life. She had looked blankly at Lingard when he asked if she
knew whether her husband had been trafficking in drugs, in
cocaine in particular, and he was inclined to believe her when she
said that she didn't know but wouldn't be at all surprised that he
had. Nor, she had admitted equally uncomprehendingly, had
she ever heard of him owning or using a crossbow or even
mentioning one.

But, she had added, as if unwilling to let it go at that, if he was
mixed up in anything really nasty it would be with his mate called

113

Dog or something like it who he was always hanging around with and who she knew he'd been with several times on all-night jobs for his boss at the club. Then, as if she were intent on unloading enough on her husband to ensure that he didn't come back, she told him that a man she didn't know who said he was from the club had called during the afternoon to see him. He hadn't, the man said, turned up for work and Mr Sickert – he was the boss man she'd mentioned before – wanted to know where he was. For reasons she didn't explain, she merely said that he had gone out that morning, she didn't know where to, and hadn't seen him since.

Then she had gone to her kitchen and produced for Lingard a blood-soaked towel which she had found pushed behind the bath after her husband had gone. Wrapping it in the sheets of a newspaper she had given him, he retained it for a blood-grouping examination at the laboratory. His searching of Webber's room, which she had readily allowed, was a wasted effort because manifestly he had been careful to take everything of a personal nature with him. With an injured Webber now being well into the frame as a suspect for the killing of Kiddle, the room would be worth a search by Magnus for any material evidence likely to connect him with it, and for traces of cocaine.

Leaving Mrs Webber, he told her that he would be sending round a policewoman to see her, to give her whatever help and advice was possible. Apart from her misfortune in possessing a cumbersome jumbo-sized body, she struck him as a woman lamentably short on whatever benefits there were to be had in a marriage.

Keighley Road was one of fifty or so roads set in a grid pattern on the estate, each with its rows of depressingly ordinary semi-detached houses identical in design, garageless and befoggingly difficult for Lingard to find in the darkness. He had hesitated in parking the van at the road's entrance, sensing that somebody was watching him, that another intelligence had latched itself onto his awareness strongly enough for him to feel it. It could be Webber, though he didn't think so. Seeing nobody and feeling an imaginative idiot, he moved away to check the cars standing along its length for Webber's Morris. It wasn't in the road, but in the process of looking for it he had located number 59 and he returned to it when he had finished.

Standing on the pavement outside the house and studying it, he pinched snuff into his nostrils as a defence against the greasy smell of food being cooked somewhere in the vicinity. When the road seemed clear of its occasional pedestrian, he walked over the unkempt grass of the small lawn and placed his ear close to the glass of a window showing curtained light. Rendered largely inaudible by thumping music from a television set or a radio, he heard snatches of a conversation; a woman's voice whining in complaint, a man answering her in monosyllables, too brief for his identification as Webber.

Lingard knew now that with Webber as a suspect for murder he should send for a cover in arresting him. There were factors discouraging him from doing so. In the absence of the Morris car and from what he had heard of the woman Maureen, there was no guarantee that the man she seemed to be complaining at was Webber. Further, he was definitely in no mood to again be made a fool of by his *bête noire* were it found that the latter's stated intent of going to Scotland was a fact and that he had gone. Too, it left him saddled with the possibility that Mrs Webber could have been mistaken about the address, leaving him to blunder into a civil damages suit; or otherwise being unknowing that the woman had a husband living with her who might be justifiably resentful about his home being invaded by a posse of police bent on arresting a man believed to be his wife's lover. He thought it a problem in something or other that the Lord Chief Justice could have toyed with for hours; hours which he himself didn't have.

Convinced that carefree insouciance suited his thinking better, he crept soundlessly along the narrow passage ending at a solid wooden gate leading to a rear garden. After doing a visual reconnaissance of the garden by dim moonlight, he found a small stone and jammed it in the latch to prevent its being opened from the inside. Then, having removed a metal lid from a dustbin kept inside the garden, he balanced it precariously on the top of the gate. Returning to the front he knocked loudly on the door, immediately moving to the window and listening. Apart from the music there was a quietness in the room in which, he convinced himself, he could sense a sudden cessation of breathing, its being held in apprehensive suspension. Then the music snapped off and he heard the man whispering, footfalls crossing the room and a door opening. He was back at the front door as a crack of light showed at its bottom and a woman's voice called out, 'Who's there? What do you want?'

It was no civilized way of answering a knock on the door and Lingard felt a lot happier. 'I'm a police officer,' he said, not too loudly. 'Please open the door.'

The woman who opened it was manifestly the bloody skinny whoring tart Maureen so graphically described by Mrs Webber. What she hadn't fleshed out for Lingard was the waist-length yellow hair, her blued-up eyes and the sullen red mouth. His identification was hardly flawed by her wearing a quite respectable black dress and being without the evidence of a baby. Producing his warrant card – which she only glanced at – he stepped into the hall and said, 'May I speak with Mr Webber, please.'

She scowled at him. 'Who said he was here, because he ain't. And who said you could come pushing in as if you owned the sodding place?'

Lingard smiled disarmingly. 'I'm terribly sorry, I thought I heard you asking me in. Fetch him, there's a good girl,' he urged her. 'You'll probably find him hiding in the kitchen.' Her eyes, shifty between the black-lined lids, had told him that his guess could be a good one.

She actually started as if to do what he had asked, then hesitated. As she did so, Lingard heard the ringing clatter of the dustbin lid falling on to concrete. 'Excuse me,' he said, pushing past her and a child's pushchair as he headed at speed for where he expected to find the back door, her screaming following him out through it. Leaving the lighting in the house for the comparative darkness of the garden gave him a few moments of a blindness he hadn't counted on, and during it he could hear scrambling noises from the end of the garden. With what vision was returning to him in the half-darkness, he saw the shadowed figure of his quarry pulling himself over a high panel fencing that was silhouetted in light shining from behind, and then dropping down its other side in a loud crunching and cracking of breaking glass.

Lingard was already running across soft and lumpy soil when over the confused sound of more breaking glass he heard a hoarse shout of anger, a scraping noise and then a thwacking sound as if an oversized open hand had been slapped against a side of beef. There was a groan, a short silence and then a woman calling in the darkness for somebody named Bob.

Pulling himself to the top of the fence and straddling it painfully, Lingard looked down into a back garden illuminated dimly by light coming from the open door and a window of the house to which it was attached. Immediately below him were the remains of a large cold frame, its interior a welter of smashed glass and broken woodwork. Webber, apparently unconscious, lay unmoving on his back alongside it, his legs in its ruins. A slim and youngish man with a heavy moustache stood looking up at Lingard, holding a gardening spade as if to use it as a weapon. The woman he had heard calling out, now silent, stood outlined in the illuminated doorway. The body of a small white cat lay near a partially-dug hole at the foot of the fence and three or four feet from the cold frame.

Lingard, irritatingly aware that his overcoat and suit were now fouled with the slimy moulds his hands could feel on the fence, was still able to say nonchalantly, 'Good evening. I'm a police officer and I'm coming down.' He then swung himself over and dropped to a piece of the ground not occupied by bodies or shattered glass.

The man from whom menace had fled pushed his spade into the earth. 'Bloody hell,' he said apprehensively, 'I haven't clobbered your mate, have I? I thought he was going to bash me.'

'He was running from justice, so don't worry,' Lingard assured him, adding a silent 'At least for the moment' as he took in what had been done to Webber. Most definitely unconscious from the blow he had received, he was snorting stertorously and bubbling blood from between broken teeth, his breath exhaling a pungency of beer. The blade of the spade had also struck him over the cheekbone on which his wife had said he had worn a taped handkerchief. Were that so, it had been driven into his cheek together with a mess of bloody flesh. One of the legs of his trousers was black with blood from the thigh downwards. Apart from all that, Lingard considered, not being wholly unsympathetic, he seemed not too bad.

He turned to the man at his side. 'What's your name, old son?'

'Mr Cull,' he answered him. 'He's not going to die, is he?'

'He mightn't if you do what I tell you and do it fast. You've a phone?' Receiving a nod, he said, 'Get on it and dial nine-nine-

nine for an ambulance. Tell them he's been in an accident and there's the possibility of a severed artery.'

With Cull back in his house, Lingard put his hands under Webber's armpits and hoisted him into a sitting position against the fence, believing in a recall of first aid instructions from way back that it would clear his breathing. It seemed to, allowing Webber to suffer silently his discomfort instead of snorting it. Opening his pocket-knife, he sawed a long slit in the bloody trouser leg, finding the blood pulsing from a deep cut on the inner side of the thigh. It needed to be stopped and the only clean handkerchief he had was the green silk one from the breast pocket of his jacket. Cursing at its imminent loss, he knotted it tightly around the thigh above the cut, inserting his closed knife beneath it and twisting to tighten it, holding it there to stem the bleeding. With the thumb of his other hand he searched for a pressure point on the artery he believed to be draining Webber's life away.

As he waited for the bleeding to diminish, he noticed that his own trousers and the skirt of his overcoat were smeared with blood. Webber's blood which, he was certain, would later be classified as Group A; the same blood that had been shed during the killing of Kiddle. He couldn't bear to think what else from the fence he had climbed would show on his clothing in the light. It was all Webber's fault and only mitigated by the fact that by no stretch of the imagination could the doing of it be described as one of the slippery bastard's better efforts. If he survived, which Lingard thought was possible if he could stop the bleeding, it appeared unlikely that he would be in a condition to answer pointed questions for several days. He wasn't looking too healthy now, his face having what seemed to be a livid tinge to it, the injured cheekbone caved in as if it had been broken. Lingard released his hold on the tourniquet for a moment or two to put the pad of his forefinger against the side of Webber's throat, feeling the throbbing pulse thin and reedy. 'Don't you die on me, you selfish sod,' he whispered to him. 'Not now, anyway.' It was one of the detective's beliefs that every man should know someone on whom he could expend whatever hate was in his system, and Webber suited his own particular book admirably.

Cull, appearing suddenly at his side, said, 'It's on its way. Is he all right?'

'Not being a veterinary, all I can say is that he isn't going to get up on his feet and wallop you back,' Lingard told him, not too amiably. Crouching over Webber to hold the tourniquet tight was a torture to his calf muscles and there was nothing he could do about it. 'While we're waiting, tell me what happened and how you came to do it with a spade.' Cull didn't strike the detective as a man quick on the trigger in using violence, though he knew that invading another's garden at night on the estate was, not illogically, interpreted as a declaration of intended violence; or, when not that, as an intent to break into the house and steal something.

'I was burying our cat,' he said. 'My wife told me when I got home from work just now that he was knocked down and killed in the road outside. She found him lying in the gutter and didn't see who done it. She's fond of him and wanted me to bury him straight away and not have him put in the dustbin, which we never would. I was doing it, digging the hole over there, when I heard some woman screaming blue murder and then this bloke was climbing over my fence and smashing into my cold frame. Course, I didn't know you was chasing him, I thought he attacked that woman I heard. I could see the way he looked at me and yelled that he was going to have a go at me and I was frightened for my wife. So I landed him one with the spade which I had in my hand anyway. It was instinctive, like.'

Lingard could hear from several roads away the raucous siren of the approaching ambulance, grateful that Webber would soon be taken off his hands. The woman Maureen had apparently tired of screaming some time ago. He needed to see her in a hurry before she did anything obstructive about the suitcases Webber was supposed to have brought with him. He said to Cull, 'I'll get an officer to come and take a statement from you. Don't worry yourself too much, old son, it isn't going to be the end of the world.'

Which was, perhaps, a trifle too comforting. He hadn't liked to tell him that there was a possibility that some legal pedant on the staff of the Crown Prosecution Service (who had never been startled in his garden at night by a drunken and violent intruder and reacted from fear), taking due notice of what seemed to be the judiciary's dicta that little more than polite words or the equivalent of a light slap on the wrist should be used by members of the public in the face of violence, would order his prosecution for whatever offence Webber's injuries would sustain in a court.

And further, if Webber did die, he could take his culpability for Kiddle's murder with him. That he would presumably then come under the jurisdiction of what Lingard thought of as the Higher Authority was of no comfort to him at all.

18

Rogers, having parked his car in a street of closed and shuttered shops, rang the door bell of a darkened Barbizan Club and waited. Unless Sickert was intending to be uncharacteristically forthcoming about whatever was bothering him, Rogers felt that this interview, not of his own seeking, was premature, too unlikely, with the little evidence he had, to result in any bruising, let alone bleeding. He had never underrated Sickert's intelligence, his bloody-mindedness or his ruthless and sharp-witted cunning. It meant that it was essential he was given no reason to believe that Rogers was doing anything but sounding off with the generalized suspicions of a rather thick but well-meaning detective baffled by the lack of progress in his investigation.

Sickert answered the bell's ringing himself, a certain indication that he was alone on the premises. If he was worried – as Rogers hoped he was – his eyes behind the black-framed spectacles were concealing it. Inconsistently, his small beard was untidy as if he had been scratching at it, and he smelled ripely of brandy. Not offering to do his usual handshaking, which had to mean something, he said perfunctorily, 'I'm glad you could get here,' standing aside for the detective to enter.

Following Sickert along the passage, up the stairs and through the gaming room, its tables shrouded in green fabric sheets, Rogers noticed how the minimal illumination and the absence of players gave it a tawdriness. His nostrils breathed in an enclosed air depleted of its oxygen by having passed through too many lungs and containing the residual smells of food, the flat fragrances of women's scents and stale cigarette and cigar smoke.

In his office, Sickert fell back heavily in his big red chair as if exhausted, picked up a still smouldering cigar from an ashtray on his desk and began drawing on it.

Rogers pulled up a black lacquered chair to face the fat gambler from the side of his leather-topped and brass-handled desk. He smiled amiable encouragement at him. 'I never thought you'd have the sort of problems you'd want me to sort out,' he said. 'So what can I do to help?'

'It's something that's been giving me aggro, and it's a question of protecting my good name.' Sickert, rolling the cigar between his finger and thumb, frowned at it. 'It's about my dealer being clobbered and him being tied up with this club. It means I don't want to have my licence objected to just because of him.'

That a man like Sickert didn't choke to a purple-faced death on this outrageous claim to a good name was, Rogers considered, something God had carelessly overlooked in organizing the inner mechanisms of Homo sapiens. He said, 'You mean Stephanakis, of course? The one you said was an arsehole but still kept him working for you?'

'I didn't mean bloody Julius Caesar!' Sickert showed sudden irritation over the detective's tactless reminder, but swallowed it as quickly as it had arisen. 'I was going to tell you what I should've told you when you were here before. Did you find anything bent at his place?'

'If you mean evidence of a serious criminal nature involving him, and possibly others, yes we did.' Rogers was being deliberately unforthcoming.

Sickert grunted, obviously having expected something more specific. 'Would that be the powder?' he asked guardedly then, seeing Roger's shut expression, added, 'I thought it might be cocaine.'

'What was it you were going to tell me, and didn't?' Rogers knew that would be accepted as a coded message saying yes to his question.

'I bloody well knew it,' Sickert muttered, back to frowning at his cigar. 'I suspected the bastard was pushing it behind my back, probably in the club as well. I meant to tell you last night, but you were practically accusing me of knowing where the Stuchley bint was and Christ knows what else you were thinking.'

'True, I wouldn't have expected you to do anything like report-

121

ing any suspicions about your Stephanakis to us, but believing he was a pusher – which he was – couldn't you have got rid of him?' Rogers hoped that he wasn't sounding too naive to be true.

'I only suspected. I didn't think I could throw the bastard out legally without proof. He could have sued me for everything I've got.'

Rogers nodded his understanding. 'And now that he's dead it naturally worries you.'

'Well, Christ!' he burst out, his jowls reddening. 'Of course it bloody well worries me! Aren't you saying he was clobbered because he was into pushing coke? And me, just because I'm the stupid bugger who happened to be employing him, probably believed to be in with him. For all I know that's what you think too.'

Rogers stared at him, inwardly surprised at his associating himself, though only as an imputed theory, with Stephanakis's activities. It was, he decided, a clever, if risky, bluff designed to protect him from the accusations of informers. Whatever Sickert meant, Rogers had to disclaim and to equivocate. He wagged his head dismissively. 'I don't get you. Is that the problem you wanted to unload on me? If I thought you had had even half a sniff of anything you'd got from Stephanakis, you'd be in a cell by now.'

Sickert pushed back a sleeve of his jacket and looked pointedly at his wristwatch, then rose from his chair and went to the lacquered drinks cabinet that should have belonged to a more civilized somebody. 'You've taken a weight off my mind,' he said, almost showing his relief as he poured what looked to be a prodigality of brandy into a glass. 'You know I've always been on the side of the law and I wish I'd told you about Stephanakis before. I'm sorry I had to bother you.' His apology was a form of dismissal and he pointedly expected the detective to go.

Choosing not to take in what was obvious from Sickert's words, Rogers remained seated. 'It's been no bother,' he assured him: 'In fact, what you've told me could be very useful indeed. There's one thing though. You obviously believe Stephanakis was murdered as the result of his pushing drugs. Is that a guess? Or do you know something that I don't?'

Sickert scowled, the brandy glass halted on its way to his mouth. 'I'm sure I didn't say that. It was you who said it or you didn't hear me right. How would I know why the dumb bastard was clobbered?'

'If you say not,' Rogers murmured. 'But while we're on about his being murdered, I was intending asking you if your door-keeper Webber was available; if he's the chap you sent to Stephanakis's apartment to find out why he hadn't reported for work.' He smiled companionably at a man who, though his partly used cigar was still smoking on its ashtray, was paying a concentrated attention to the piercing of a fresh one and beginning to show signs of unease. 'For the records, you appreciate,' he reassured him.

'You mentioning it like that, I think he was.' His unease was changing to what was his normal hostility to Rogers, and that under restraint. 'Now that you know, so what?'

'It was just for that? For no other reason?'

'I'm trying bloody hard to understand you, but don't know what you're getting at.'

Rogers pulled a face as though irritated with himself. 'Of course, I hadn't told you, had I? Webber tried to break into the rear of the apartment during the night and obligingly left his fingerprints for us to find.' He flapped a hand at Sickert's chair. 'Why don't you sit down. I'm sure you'll find this interesting, what with you seeming to have been employing a flock of villains here and no doubt wanting to put things right about it. The good name of the club, I mean,' he said helpfully.

Try as he might to conceal it, Sickert was – as Allegra Ascroft had taunted the detective himself earlier – running scared. He returned to his seat, puffing jerkily at the cigar between his teeth. 'Get it over with, Rogers,' he said grittily, his eyes behind the spectacle lenses not wholly reflecting the confidence in his words. 'I haven't got all bloody night to sit here and explain that I don't have to know what my staff get up to after they've left here and when I'm not breathing down their necks. So Webber breaks into Stephanakis's place: what's it to me?' Seeing no likelihood of an answer in Roger's face, he asked, 'Have you knocked him off?'

'We're looking for him. You'd obviously know where we can pick him up.'

Sickert shook his head vigorously. Had he shown a flicker of relief? It was hard to tell. 'Like hell I do,' he said forcefully. 'He was supposed to be working here this afternoon, but didn't turn up. I sent round to his home to find out why and his wife said he'd shoved off somewhere she didn't know where. That's all, and I don't care whether I see the useless bastard again or not.'

'He'll come,' Rogers said, as if matters were already wrapped up and settled. 'I'll say this in his favour; when he does he'll be talkative, he always has been. You know, trying to get out from under by informing on all and sundry who had anything to do with whatever villainy he was up to.' He shook his head as if what he had said had saddened him, but never taking his policeman's unblinking stare from Sickert's eyes. 'It's a terrible world when you can't even trust a fellow villain, isn't it?'

It was doubtful that Sickert had understood the implication in Rogers's words for he rasped, 'While it's no skin off my nose, you must know as well as I do that Webber's a bloody romancer and a liar when he's in trouble.' He drained his glass of its remaining brandy. For all the effect it had had on him it could have been mineral water.

'A not unusual response from villains when they're only a couple of steps away from chokey,' Rogers agreed mildly, 'but not being a window cleaner he won't be able to dispute the significance of leaving his fingerprint on some upstairs window glass, will he?' He scratched thoughtfully at his chin with a thumbnail, keeping his unrelenting regard on Sickert who, in what seemed to be a ragged irritation with the detective, appeared to have forgotten about his appointment. 'What do you think of this as a theory?' he asked, as if he were wanting the gambler's help. He hadn't much belief in it himself, but it could, if it came to it, be a useful starter for putting the pressure on. 'Our so far unknown drug dealer, using your Stephanakis with his no doubt very useful connections at the club as a pusher, has reason to believe he's being robbed of large amounts of loot that should be forthcoming from the drugs being peddled. It's a little awkward for him because he can't very well complain about it to the fraud squad, can he? Still, he does have options. One, and I'm trying to put myself into his mind, is the unthinkable one of cutting his losses by forgetting it, though this would mean a loss of face among his fellow villains and the certainty of being considered an easy mark for future rip-offs. Another that would come naturally to a thuggish mind is the more profitable and satisfying one of giving Stephanakis the old heave-ho by putting him down personally. Or, more likely, if he's of a nervous disposition . . . ' – he aimed a brief grimace at Sickert which could mean anything the gambler might fear it to mean – ' . . . to have it done for him by an equally thuggish accomplice. He could then have steps taken to recover the loot from over his dead body, together with any evidence there might be in the apartment connecting the dealer with anything in such bad taste as having an interest in drugs. In fact,' he said as if it had just occurred to him, 'that could be why Webber was so set on breaking into the apartment. A little late with us having already been there but better, I imagine, than not at all.' He cocked an interrogative eyebrow at Sickert. 'They're your two chaps and you obviously know them better than I do, so how does all this strike you as a possibility?'

He imagined that he could hear the whirring and clicking of Sickert's brain in the silence that followed, though there was no imagination about the grating noise that came from the back of his throat. 'A load of bloody tit,' he finally growled around the cigar he had been maltreating between his teeth. It need only have been the light from his desk lamp, but there appeared to be a shine of sweat on his forehead. 'While I wouldn't trust the prat not to cut his grandma's throat, Webber's too bloody pig-stupid for the stuff you're dreaming up. He couldn't open a door unless some bugger showed him how to do it. But whatever it is, it's nothing to do with me and I'm not interested.' He stood, resting his fat spread-eagled fingers on the leather surface of his desk, very obviously having no affection for the detective. 'My appointment,' he said, scowling. 'You've made me late.'

'I haven't finished,' Rogers said, about to change his approach and put an interrogator's bite into his words. 'No more than I'd finished last night. I'm surprised you thought fit not to tell me that Miss Stuchley used to live with you, that she'd once moved into your place at the Kinnisdale Grange. Considering that I told you she'd been living with Stephanakis and was now missing, it would have been relevant, wouldn't it?' He was about to test the gambler's reactions to an accusation he guessed wouldn't hold water, but which could be reckoned as a middling possibility.

Sickert's eyes showed his amazement, then annoyance. 'For Christ's sake! What in the hell are you on about now?'

'When a woman's been living with a man and leaves him for another, it could be considered by some police officer less understanding than myself to provide a reason for the man to feel sexually aggrieved. And my experience is that sexually aggrieved men can be resentful, jealous and even homicidal; men who understandably have a motive for doing something about it. It seems to me you could have been any of those things?' There was nothing in Rogers's face suggesting a man prepared to be understanding.

Sickert showed his teeth in a smile of derision and sank back into his chair, holding his cigar and stabbing it at Rogers. 'Me, jealous over that tart?' he jeered. 'Me knocking off Stephanakis because of her? You must be bloody mad. I gave her a whirl for a month or two if it's any business of yours, but that's all it was. Easy come, easy go, and her lot don't need any encouraging when there's a job as a hostess at the end of it. And Stephanakis? If the bastard had upset me over anything I'd have certainly done him over good and proper, but that wouldn't be killing him and having you give me unnecessary aggro.'

'Do you also suppose that Miss Stuchley could have been encouraged by somebody with a snort of cocaine? You knew, of course, she was an addict?'

Sickert had. It was in his eyes before he denied it by saying, 'Like hell I did. But if she was, she was getting it from Stephanakis. And she wasn't likely to be telling me, was she?'

'I understand that before she moved into your bed at the hotel, you used to entertain her in a room upstairs. Was that so?'

'That's right; her and a few others. I don't make any secret of the fact that women go for me and I do something about it.' His mouth was ugly, his expression showing the contempt of a man who had seen expected danger recede. It hadn't taken long for him to revert to his open hostility to the detective. 'You're welcome to use it for yourself, if that's what you're getting at. There'd be no charge, naturally, and I've no doubt I could organize a scrubber for you.'

'I'd certainly like to check it out,' Rogers said, unruffled by the pettiness of the insult. 'Miss Stuchley's still missing and I'd hate to think I'd overlooked the possibility that you're in the habit of providing a bolt-hole for any woman tasteless enough to have been to bed with you.'

An angry Sickert stood from his chair and crushed his cigar to extinction in the ashtray. 'You'd better watch your mouth,

126

Rogers, or you can get stuffed so far as the room is concerned. I've got nothing to hide so you can have your look and then bugger off.' Small bubbles of saliva had appeared at a corner of his mouth. 'I don't want the bad publicity I'd get by you trying to fit me for whatever it is you've dreamed up in your tiny mind.'

'It's unusually accommodating of you,' Rogers said with irritating politeness. 'I'd finished talking with you anyway.' Deborah Stuchley's whereabouts had weighed lightly on his mind when he had asked to see the room, for had Sickert abducted her he would have been uncharacteristically cretinous to keep her on the club premises. Cocaine and the topography of the upper rooms for his future reference had weighed the heavier.

Sickert, leaving the office with Rogers following at his heels, unlocked a door situated in an alcove and concealed by a high wooden screen. Steep carpeted stairs rose to finish at a small landing giving access to two doors and an overhead trapdoor, almost certainly leading to the roof space. That, he noted, was partly covered by a spider's dusty web, denoting no recent access to it. Sickert opened one of the doors, switched on a light and said, 'Don't be all bloody evening, I've still got my appointment to keep.' Climbing the stairs had neither improved his breathing nor tempered his glowering anger.

With him, Rogers stepped into a room larger than he had expected, a room, but for its bed, functionally furnished as a self-contained suite. The bed, not by any means to be accepted as one meant primarily for sleeping in, was a commodious double fitted with a mauve patterned duvet and black satin bed linen, femininely flounced and fitted with an enclosing white netting canopy over its head. A basically masculine touch was shown by a virtual picture gallery on the walls of framed poster-sized sepia prints of horned and hooved priapic satyrs working their different ways through a progression of seemingly double-jointed and overripe women. So far as he could see there were no signs of a recent occupancy, though his nose was detecting the ghost of a woman's scent that might suggest it. It looked the kind of room which a former flesh peddler such as Sickert might, when not using it himself, rent out after the gaming had ended to a discreet enough member of the club and an accommodating hostess.

'A civilizing exhibition of classical art,' Rogers commented with heavy sarcasm, leaving the room for the second door on the landing. 'Another one? Another bed?'

Not answering him, Sickert opened the door and switched on a light. Dusty as if unused for months, the room was stacked to confusion with furniture and furnishings undoubtedly stored from his closed-down skin show enterprise and, from his willingness in opening it to the detective, probably innocent as a store for cocaine. But only probably, for any refusal or reluctance on Sickert's part to show either room would certainly have roused a deeper suspicion than existed already.

'Satisfied?' Sickert snarled at him. 'Because if you bloody well are, shove off and . . . ' In pulling the door towards him and forcibly slamming it, its knob had come off in his hand, surprising him into cutting short his own words.

From the gambler's vicious expression it could be read that in his anger he had tried to tear the door from its hinges, the door standing in proxy for the detective on whom he would have preferred to expend his violence. For all that, even because of it, Rogers knew him then as a man who was going to come, to be as edible to the law's appetite as the cheapest of cheap thieves who stole milk from doorsteps. He showed his teeth at him with the certainty that it would never be taken as a friendly smile and said, 'I'll let you know later if I'm satisfied,' and started down the stairs with Sickert following, though making no effort to catch up with him.

Walking along the street to his car, Rogers accepted that he had gained little from his interrogation of a man he could now be satisfied was concerned in some way with the handling of cocaine. Being a little less satisfied that he was involved in Stephanakis's murder and Deborah Stuchley's abduction meant no more than a slight hiccup in the certainty of his logic. He couldn't believe that he was doing Sickert an injustice for, owning to a talent for dishonesty and violence, he was capable of committing most crimes in which there would be an element of profit at little risk to himself.

Being the owner of a prickly conscience and often subjecting himself to self-censure, Rogers was conscious that he hadn't asked Sickert – as he had intended – about any sexual relationship which might have existed between him and Allegra Ascroft; admitting to himself that he hadn't – a weakness, he conceded –

because he feared the answer. Bringing her into his thinking brought back her remark about the feeling of insects starting to bite in drug deprivation. As far as he was aware it was a symptom not generally known, and her knowing it could indicate either that she had experienced it herself or had been closer to the drug's use than she had admitted. He loudly grunted his exasperation about it, startling an elderly woman passing him in the dark street into quickening her pace to get away from him.

Why in the hell, he niggled at himself as he climbed into his car, should he be so concerned about whether she had been Sickert's casual lover or not; or whether she had been blowing her brains ceiling high on her toad of a husband's cocaine. And, for all that he might know, still was. Not conscious that he was doing it, he slammed the door of the car almost as violently as had Sickert the door of his storeroom.

19

Lingard, his loyalty to Rogers unquestioned, considered him a friend as well as a colleague. Rogers had, at some risk to his own career, once curbed his junior's loss of personal control over the death of Nancy Frail by knocking him senseless with the solid root ball of a potted shrub when he ran amok and tried to kill the man he suspected of murdering her. With no ill feelings by either, he had worked his way back to professional respectability and to being Rogers's second-in-command. It being in the nature of any second-in-command to lust after his senior's chair, Lingard did so, confident with no false modesty that he could hold the post as successfully, if not more so. While he respected Rogers's dedication and professionalism, it would never mean that he regarded him as the better man. What he didn't appreciate was that Rogers, having been a second-in-command himself, was well aware of how he felt, the situation occasionally affording him some quiet amusement.

It was logical that, consciously or subconsciously, the golf club killing of Kiddle was of more importance to Lingard than the murder of Stephanakis, his concentration on it the greater. That the two appeared somehow to be interlinked was a bonus, for he might then clear up both killings at the same time. It was, he admitted freely to himself, one of the principal reasons for his not wanting Webber to die just yet, or to suffer an incapacitating loss of recent memory from the blow he had received. In support of this he had made an emotional effort to feel sorry for him, though not quite making it. There was, however, a mad irony about it all that amused the now far from elegant detective. He had set out with an intent to enforce some justifiable mayhem on the unspeakable Webber, then found himself straining a gut and a thumb in trying to stop him dying. In addition, being almost a repetition of his previous encounter with him, his trousers, shoes, overcoat and silk handkerchief were stained with garden soil or blood or the green slime of algae. The only comfort he could dredge from his defeat by ill circumstance was the remote possibility that if it was examined in better visibility than livid moonlight it might not be so bad as it now appeared.

He had searched Webber's clothing, necessarily one-handed and with difficulty, and taken from the pockets a wallet, a ring of several keys and a large folding knife in which Webber would have difficulty in justifying a legal possession, releasing the pressure of his tiring thumb on the artery only when the attendants on the ambulance took over the deeply unconscious man. He was, they agreed as they rolled him deftly on to a stretcher and loaded him aboard, not too far from promising to be a case of Dead on Arrival.

Using the unfortunate Robert Cull's telephone, Lingard called for a detective from the department to attend and to take a statement concerning what was, in his opinion, the justified wounding of a violently rampaging Webber by an unaggressive citizen engaged in the non-aggressive act of burying his dead cat. Then, with the assistance of Cull and a kitchen chair, he climbed over the fence and dropped back into the garden of 59 Keighley Road.

The back door from which Webber had fled was still open and he knocked on it, walking into the kitchen and through to the hall. The woman Maureen was in what appeared to be the sitting-room, seated in an easy chair in a hunched crouch and staring blank-eyed at something he could not see. She appeared neither surprised nor anything else, showing only a slight movement of her eyes in recognition of his entering the room.

Younger than he had thought her on his earlier entry, she was pallid, thin, small-breasted and narrow-hipped in her black dress, a long strand of her yellow hair showing a pinky dampness at its end as if she had been sucking at it. Her overlipsticked mouth proclaimed a hardness not reflected in the little girl immaturity of her face, leaving the question of which was the dominant factor to guesswork. She looked, he thought, ruinously used. The room, its furniture of dark-stained wood and mud-coloured upholstery, was overhot from a burning electric fire. At one side of it stood a wooden frame holding steaming infant's clothing; at its other, a television set showing a black and white picture she was watching with the sound turned down. Around the room was an untidy scattering of plastic toys and women's shoes. Opened beer cans and two food-stained plates, each with a fork on it, lay on the square of florid carpet near the easy chairs. With a strong smell of vinegar and fried fish in the air, it was close to being squalid.

He stood waiting, smelling somewhat foul himself he thought, and wondering how a woman who had been screaming to the high heavens only a short while ago could now detach herself from the apparent trauma of Webber's flight so soon after it. When she had apparently decided that he wasn't going away, she gave him her attention, for what it was. 'You woke him up,' she accused him without spirit. 'He won't go back to sleep again.'

'I'm profoundly sorry.' Though Lingard considered that it could have been caused by her own screaming, apologizing promised an easier passage than denying it. 'I'll try not to do it again.' He looked down at his besmirched overcoat and trousers, at his soil-smeared shoes, and saw them to be as bad as he had feared. 'I hope you'll excuse my dirtiness,' he said, 'but I fell down in your garden. And forgive me, I imagine that you're more concerned about what happened to your friend?'

'You did it, didn' you?' She sounded mildly resentful. 'Albert said you would, an' I heard the ambulance. I didn' think you was a copper anyway because when you knocked the door he said "That's them" and tol' me to tell you he wasn' in.'

131

'I'm afraid that he was sadly mistaken.' Lingard fetched out his warrant card, holding it outstretched so that she could read it, then returning it to his pocket after he had seen her mouth moving soundlessly at his name and rank. 'Now you tell me what your name is, please,' he said.

'Miss Titmuss.' Her black-rimmed eyes were wary.

'Maureen Titmuss?'

'Yes.' She bristled, he obviously having committed some kind of a solecism in disclosing that he knew her forename.

'And being a Miss, I take it you're living here on your own with Albert doing his best to help by visiting now and again. Is that the situation?' It pained Lingard to refer to the contemptible Webber as Albert – he would have felt easier with the derisory Wonk-eye – but he knew it had to be for the promotion of informative harmony.

'He's just a friend, yes,' she said with what seemed an incredible belief in the detective's naïveté.

Lingard gave her a smile. 'It's nice to have a friend when you've a problem or when you're in trouble, isn't it? Is he also your baby's father?'

'Yes.' She apparently disassociated that from being just friends. 'He's goin' to marry me when he can.'

'I'm sure he will,' Lingard said, mainly because saying that he was sure he wouldn't wasn't going to help anyone and would only spread grief. 'Now, who did your Albert think I was when I knocked on the door?'

She shrugged and looked up at his face, something in her own changing to what could be taken for a softening of her attitude towards him. 'I don't know, he didn' say. Just that his job was dangerous an' they was after him. So he had to go to somewhere else an' we was goin' to go with him tomorrow.'

'To Scotland?'

She looked surprised. 'Is that where? He never tol' me. All I know is he said he was goin' to be done over, an' he was, wasn' he?'

'Not by me,' Lingard assured her, keeping the regret for not having been responsible from his voice. 'I'm afraid he fell into your neighbour's cold frame and is now in hospital.'

'He's bad?' She certainly now gave Webber a fair measure of visible concern.

'He's cut about a bit,' he equivocated. 'They'll probably let you in to see him tomorrow if all's well, but definitely not before.'

'I can't with Kevin upstairs, can I?' A thought manifestly occurred to her. 'If it wasn' you after Albert like he said, what was you here for?'

He pursed his lips. 'Well, there's quite a minor kerfuffle going on about a couple of newish suitcases for a start.' He saw her eyes flick towards and then away from the sofa lodged against the wall on her left. 'I'm told he brought them here this morning.'

'If he did, I ain't seen them,' she disclaimed, looking everywhere but at the sofa.

Lingard felt as sorry for her as he had for Webber's wife. Stripped of the thin veneer of her hardness, temporary though it might be, he could see that she wasn't all that far off in years from when she could have been regarded as somebody's innocent little schoolgirl as yet unaffected by the curse of pubescent sexuality. Patently dim-witted and dangerously naive, she could, without doubt, be manipulated by any man taking the trouble to be pleasant to her and to confound her with whatever words she wanted to hear from him.

'I'm sure you've not,' he told her, gazing casually around the room. 'For reasons of his own, Albert might have hidden them behind the furniture without your knowing. Behind the sofa would be somewhere I'd choose.' He strode across to it, seeing from the corner of his eye the confirmation of it in her expression.

Two new navy-blue cases, one larger than the other, had been wedged against the wall by the back of the sofa and he had to move it to get them out. 'You've not seen them before?' he asked her.

'I don't think so,' she said hesitantly, not remotely in the manner of a hardened liar and allowing Lingard to deal with her gently.

'You'd have remembered, wouldn't you?' he smiled, switching off the soundless television set and lifting the larger of the cases on to it. Taking from his pocket the ring of keys found on Webber, he used one to unlock it. 'If you really are detachable from that chair, Maureen,' he said, drawing her into co-operating with him by the familiarity of an encouraging grin, 'please come and stand by the side of me. I'm going to search the suitcases in your

133

presence, and I want you to try and remember what I do and what I find.'

When she was at his side, giving out heat like a black stove and apparently too apprehensive to be other than docile, he lifted the lid. Were simulated leather bomber jackets, faded jeans, and underpants overprinted with the rear view of a breeding bull and an allusive pink snake motif the material of back streets *haute couture*, then, Lingard thought fastidiously, Webber must have been somewhere in the top twenty well-dressed men. A search of the pockets revealed nothing of immediate interest to him. The smaller case, lifted on to the television set and opened, proved to be the more profitable, containing a small collection of hard porn magazines, bank and credit card agency documents and four packets, each declared by the issuing bank's label to contain twenty-five £10 notes. Riffling through them with his thumb and checking the run of serial numbers told him that they were an as yet uncirculated issue.

'There's a thousand pounds here,' he said to her. 'You've seen them before?'

She shook her head, swirling the long yellow hair. 'No, I never did.'

'Albert mentioned them to you, of course?'

'No, he didn'. He was prob'ly looking after them for some-one.'

Lingard pinched attar of roses snuff from his tiny ivory box and inhaled it, as much to anaesthetize his nose against the distressingly sour smell coming from the girl as to feed his addiction. He thought it might be her body's reaction to an understandable fear of what sorrow there might be in store for her. So far, he was prepared to believe her – up to a point. And that point was where she would feel bound to defend her thuggish lover against the bogey of the law. 'Sit down, Maureen,' he said, relocking the cases as she did so. 'I want to ask you a few questions. Believe me, I'm not trying to get you into trouble . . . ' – he looked around the untidy and depressing room, sniffing the air as if tasting its unpleasantness with his nose – ' . . . because I think you've enough of it already with all this. And you do have to think of Kevin, haven't you? So I know you won't hold anything back from me and you'll be on a cross-my-heart-and-hope-to-die promise to be truthful.'

She looked worried, almost fearful. 'I don' want to get Albert in trouble.'

'Good Lord, no,' he protested. 'It's just that if he hadn't been carted off to hospital in a hurry he'd have certainly told me about Dog . . . ' – he frowned his frustration, snapping finger and thumb together as if prompting recall – ' . . . you know, Dog who was his friend and who used to come here with him.'

'Oh, *him*. That's Dog Gogarty, but he didn' really like it. He said call him Danny, an' I did.'

Lingard's features tried not to have the look of a man who had hit a dimly seen target first time. 'I knew it was something like that. He's the youngish blond chap, isn't he? And short with it?'

'No, he ain't,' she said with a shade of scorn in her voice. 'You're mixin' him up with somebody else. Danny's got brown hair and he's not all that young. An' he's nearly as big as Albert.'

A miss that time, Lingard conceded, and he had better be more careful or chuck in his guessing. 'But if I remember rightly, he does have a brogue?'

Her forehead creased in perplexity. 'Do you mean the way he stammers? He said it was done by him bein' bitten by a man-eatin' sheep when he was a little boy.' Even she almost smiled at its preposterousness.

'A man with a sense of humour,' he told her, giving up his pretence of knowing the Gogarty character. 'What does he do for a living?'

'He said he was a mechanic. Anyway, somethin' like it an' he used to mend Albert's car. He was kind like that.'

For Lingard, it was like hitting the nerve that caused the reflex kick of a leg. 'Ah!' he exclaimed as if satisfied. 'That could account for him bringing those spare car wheels here, couldn't it?'

She looked troubled, twisting her fingers together. 'It was Albert's, his wheel. He used to leave it here when him an' Danny had to go on a special job because he wanted the space.' It must have been something in the detective's expression as he was working that out that prompted her to add, 'Straight, I've seen him take it out of his car, so I know it is. He puts it under the stairs an' takes it away when he comes back.'

'I expect he had a good reason for doing it,' he said agreeably. 'How many times has it happened?'

She screwed her face in thought. 'Three ... four times: I dunno, I can't really remember.'

'And would he have left it here, say, yesterday? He'd need it wouldn't he if he was going to Scotland?' He thought he could see the picture clearly now. It would have been difficult, if not impossible, for Webber, being checked by the police at any time during his driving to retrieve the cocaine-filled wheel and replace it with another, to explain the reason for his carrying two disparate spares.

'You aren' goin' to take it?' She was alarmed, her eyes large with it. 'He said I wasn' to tell about it, an' he'll be angry if it's gone.'

'Show me it, Maureen,' he said with a little more authority in his voice, deciding that he might now relinquish his distasteful pretence of fighting Webber's corner for him. 'We'll decide what to do when I've seen it. In any event, I don't think your Albert will be in a position to be angry with anybody for a long time yet.'

Not appearing to appreciate the implications in what he had said, she rose from her chair and went out into the hall. The wheel, stored in a cupboard beneath the stairs, was dusty, its tyre manifestly not having been in contact with a road, wet or dry, for a long time and flabby from underinflation. Though there was nothing on it to indicate its having come from a Morris car, Lingard was prepared to accept that it had. Not overly important in itself, it confirmed to his immense satisfaction that Webber – should he not bleed to death in hospital – and Gogarty – should it be decided that he had a criminal togetherness with Webber – were each in their separate ways a probable few steps from a long prison sentence for the manslaughter of William Kiddle and for their part in the trafficking in dangerous drugs.

He closed the door on the wheel that would have to wait for its later collection. 'Do you know where your friend Danny lives?' he asked. 'The garage or whatever where he works?'

She wrinkled her forehead. 'He never said. Not Albert either.'

'Where's Albert's car now? It isn't in the road.' He was prepared to feel sorry for her in her approaching descent to the problems inevitably arising from her having allowed Webber into her bed. He suspected also from her odd behaviour that she might be on the tail end of a cocaine jag, a part of the wreckage such a man as Webber always left in the wake of his downfall. If

136

she was an addict, it would have to keep for another time, and perhaps for somebody else to deal with.

'In the next road,' she said, pointing a finger in its direction. 'He tol' me it was safer there because his wife had a private detective on to him an' she'd stop us goin' away.' Tears suddenly welled in her eyes and ran black streaks down her pallid cheeks. 'You said he wouldn' be back for a long time,' she whimpered. 'What's me and my baby goin' to do if he don'?'

It wasn't a question the detective could answer and, keeping his distance, he reached and patted her shoulder consolingly. 'We'll think of something while you show me around the house,' he said, giving her some hope though not himself believing there was much of it going for her. 'Just in case your Albert's left any more bits and pieces for you and me to worry about.'

It was a cursory and visual search, an unsuccessful one in which, unconvinced that he would find any more wheels or cocaine that hadn't been carefully hidden, he had touched nothing and found nothing. The latter would be the drug squad's concern in organized and meticulous searches of whatever buildings he had favoured as his habitat. He hoped that the baby he saw asleep in his cot with a rubber teat in his mouth would somehow, against all the odds, avoid taking after his execrable progenitor – he couldn't think of him as a father – either in appearance or persona.

Having already realized that she possessed no telephone, he told her that he would be leaving her for a minute or two to summon a policewoman to help with whatever needed to be done. Taking the small suitcase and what he guessed was a £1000 redundancy payment inside it, he left her sitting obediently in her chair with the television picture and sound switched on.

Reaching the end of the road, he had confirmation that it had not been his imagination when parking the van in sensing that he was being watched. It now stood bare-axled on stacks of old bricks, its four wheels and the spare having been stolen in what he could only see as a truly appropriate irony of fate. While it would inevitably suggest a downright carelessness that a police vehicle in the charge of a detective chief inspector should be looted, Lingard felt it a small comfort that whoever had been responsible for it had been good enough not to have set fire to it, and to have left its radio intact. Non-residential drivers of ve-

hicles choosing to visit the East Thorpe Estate during the hours of
darkness clearly did so at their own peril.

20

Entering the office to hear the telephone ringing before he could
get his overcoat off and his breath back after climbing two flights
of stairs with an effort he would not have noticed at any other
time, he lifted the receiver. 'Rogers here,' he said, concealing his
irritation at not being given time to get himself organized.

It was Allegra Ascroft, her husky voice tight with a hardly
held-back anger. 'I didn't think you'd do that,' she flung at him
without preamble. 'Damn you! Why did you?'

Driven by his irritability and wondering what the devil, he
growled, 'I expect I'm damned already without you adding
your weight to it, Mrs Ascroft; so what are you yelling at me
about?'

'You should know. The man we were talking about has just
rung me and you can guess what he said.' She was clearly
spoiling for a fight. 'Why did you have to tell him you'd been to
see me?'

'He told you that did he?' Sickert had been more clever than he
had thought. Because Stephanakis's wife hadn't been mentioned
in his interview, the gambler would have guessed that he had
seen her and was also holding back on whatever she had said.

'He said you'd just left him, that you'd questioned him about
me and . . . you know, the pig, the one who was killed, and
whether I'd had something to do with it and what he was dealing
in. For God's sake! How could you think that of me?'

'Calm down,' he said sharply, though his irritability had
largely gone. 'Stop yelling and listen to me. I think none of those
things and if you've let him trick you into admitting I'd been to
see you, bigger fool you. True, I've only just left him but you'll
have to take my word for it that I neither mentioned your name
nor referred to you in any context whatever. But I do now want to
know exactly what he said and why.'

But for a tiny scraping noise there was silence on the line and when he was beginning to think that she might have left him hanging on, she spoke, her voice low with a gentleness he took to indicate a submission he didn't want. 'I'm sorry, I truly am. I should have known you wouldn't.'

'It's all right,' he soothed her, though it wasn't quite. 'It's not your fault. I'd have probably thought the same. Tell me what he was calling you about.'

'No, I can't. I mean, not on the phone. He threatened me in his slimy way about what I'd already made up my mind to tell you. Not in his actual words, but he meant some rough handling.' There was a further silent waiting until she added pleadingly, 'Will you come tonight? It might be that I shall have to go away tomorrow. He told me I should and I'm not sure what will happen if I don't.'

Damn it! he swore silently. He didn't know how much of her story to believe. The ambiguous threats that could always be defended as meaning something else probably, for that was typically Sickert in his dealings with women. For the other part – he shrugged imaginary shoulders in his mind – he didn't know her well enough to decide. But with her promising him information about a man she must have known better than somewhat, he had to see her.

'If there's substance in your personal safety being threatened,' he told her, 'I don't think it wise that I should be seen coming to your place. Certainly your coming here isn't an alternative.' He looked at his wristwatch. 'Shortly before nine-thirty, go to the restaurant end of your street. Don't worry if you feel you're being followed. Don't look round in any event and turn right past the old church. There's an unlit lane about a hundred yards along on your left and my car will be in it. It's a blue Escort and there are three sevens on the number plate. If I'm not there you'll find the passenger door unlocked. Climb in, lock it and wait.'

Her voice was wrapping itself around him like warm honey. 'It's so nice of you to be concerned about me. I do really feel safe now and I can't tell you how grateful I am.'

She seemed bent on making this a personal matter and it was 'Oh, bloody hell!' in his mind, already feeling the gossamer strands of a woman's intent falling softly on him. 'You're now a potential witness,' he told her, realizing his ungraciousness but needing to damp her down, 'and I have to be concerned. Please

139

don't be thinking that there's anything particularly dangerous or exciting in this; there isn't. It'll be all too boringly routine. You understand what I've told you?'

'Yes,' she said, her voice remaining warm. 'To the letter, and *I* think it's exciting.'

'Have it your way,' he said, 'but in the meantime, please don't go out until the time I asked you to.' He closed down, wondering why she made him feel so bloody ordinary, his words banal. He needed to convince himself that she was definitely somebody with whom he would be happier were they several miles apart.

At his desk, and in pen-scratching time, he made his notes of the Sickert interview, reflecting on the perversity of the order of things which far too often brought fresh information to light at the wrong time. Then, on the basis of knowing himself to be as capable as the next in missing the significance of a shred of information too casually accepted, he retrieved the documents in the investigation from his desk drawer, together with those exhibits he had managed to retain, and re-examined them. It was when he was looking at the photograph taken of Deborah Stuchley in the club and wondering at her lack of taste and squeamishness in making so free the wormwood and gall of her body to the exploitation of men debased enough to pay for it, that the thought occurred to him. Unwilling to disturb further what peace of mind the Stuchleys had left to them, he used his telephone to call the sergeant at Lizard Common, the section covering the unpoliced village of Amford St Michael. Putting questions to him, he received the answers he had anticipated without any feeling that they had advanced his investigation.

He was reflecting on them when his door was knocked on and Lingard entered, Rogers having left a note on his desk to see him on his return. He stared at him as if at an apparition; stared at his fouled trousers, overcoat and shoes, and at his overall dishevelment. 'Sit down, David,' he said with an amused concern which, while no remedy for bruised feelings, he thought less hurtful than the laughter he felt rising in him. 'Do I take it you've been pigging it again, trying to arrest your friend Wonk-eye?'

Lingard, probably battling against letting out words incompatible with good order and discipline, sat himself in the visitors' chair and summoned up a semblance of amiability. 'Gad,

George,' he said. 'Never from Webber. It was perverse fate and the flat end of a garden spade that did him. I haven't had time to put anything on paper yet, even to get out of these stinking togs, but you'd better hear me now.'

It took him fifteen minutes to give what he considered a necessarily detailed account of how he had never got around to thumping Webber while Rogers listened carefully, looking mostly thoughtful and letting his pipe go out. Lingard, in his tying up of loose ends, said, 'The veterinaries are operating on Webber now; they can have finished for all I know and so far as anybody's told me. You ask me and I'd say he has a fifty-fifty chance, what with losing the blood he did and that dreadful smash on the side of his head. If we look at what happened to him in terms of proving he's the chap poor old Kiddle walloped with his sand wedge, then I think that having been walloped again by Cull the People's Friend in the same place with a spade could effectively negative whatever evidence there was of it.' He had been about to push snuff into his nose and he held his hand poised. 'Take it from me, it's a load of rubbish about lightning not striking some unfortunate character twice in the same place; deserved or undeserved.'

Rogers looked almost beatific. 'I'm trying to think of Sickert hearing about Webber being in hospital, wondering why he isn't on his way to Scotland and not knowing whether he's been baring his soul to us or not.'

'He'll hear soon enough. I know the hospital bods will have told his wife because I gave them his home address. And I suspect that Sickert won't be leaving her alone until he knows for sure that Webber left for Scotland.'

'Mental torment,' Rogers said musingly, 'otherwise known as worry, is a fine thing to make somebody do something damned stupid. I think we might leave him for the moment to his own disasters. That chap Gogarty, you've identified him?'

'Ah, yes.' Lingard was liking that. 'He's one Daniel Oswald Gogarty, hence the name Dog. He has a conviction recorded against him for the theft of a car by fraud, his punishment amounting to a terrible twenty-four hours community service. Don't have a cardiac arrest, George, but he's employed as a fitter at Garnsey's Tyre and Exhaust Services and lives locally with an aunt and uncle. Calling there hot on the trail, I was told by his

141

aunt that he wasn't at home, having been sent to Scotland this morning to collect a car for his employer.'

'I rather think I've heard that particular story twice this evening,' Rogers commented drily.

'You're so right. I chatted on the phone to well-known honest citizen Adam Garnsey who's been able to do helpful things in the past to my Bentley, and he, of course, knows nothing about a car to be collected. Or about visits to Scotland if it comes to that. In fact, he was considerably peeved at the prospect of Gogarty – who he seems to regard rather highly – not going to be doing his stuff with tyres and exhaust pipes tomorrow morning.'

'I imagine he'd have his share of disappearance money; smelling strongly of Sickert's safe, no doubt?'

'Strongly. A stench of panic stations. Redundancy money for men who could be gabby liabilities if they're caught up by us. The notes we have from Webber's case are new and sequentially numbered, so we might be able to prove their local issue.' Lingard wasn't looking too hopeful. 'Might,' he repeated for emphasis. 'Incidentally, before I nod off and forget, I found Webber's car in Bishopgarth Road, which is where he was making for in hopping over the Culls' fence, and where their cat was found dead. It'd be a pleasing poetic justice if he was the one whose car had run over it. Naturally, there was no spare wheel on board and unfortunately nothing else either.' He rubbed his finger along the ridge of his nose, a man putting forward a winning suggestion. 'He and Gogarty, George. I think we can be satisfied that they're going to come for Kiddle's death. So what do you feel about them being the two coves wheeling away the Stuchley female?'

'They could be,' Rogers agreed, though patently not over-excited at the suggestion. 'And, as far as any evidence we don't have goes, so also could any two others. It'd mean Webber in particular would have had an extremely busy night, if we assume that it'd be about a quarter to seven when he and Gogarty would be abducting or collecting her and taking her off to some unknown accommodation. It's more likely to have been a forcible abduction because so far as we can see she probably left without any of her clothing and cosmetics; certainly without the boxful of money she must have known about, and leaving behind some, if not all, her cocaine and the tube she used in snorting it.' He

142

wagged his head, suggesting an inability to rationalize it. 'With Stephanakis's body being tripped over by Miss Whicher at eight-thirty and with Hagbourne and his troops at work by nine at least, we have Sickert worrying enough about the unexpected absence of his card dealer to send Webber round to Disraeli Street to find out what's going on. Webber, if we can believe Sickert, reports back that what with the police buzzing around Stephanakis's front door and him lying there unbreathing, he takes it that somebody's put him down. That, so far as Sickert is concerned, is that. Stephanakis won't be turning up for work and he might as well wipe away his tears and go on with the pain and anguish of running his club.' Rogers was taking the opportunity of expending some of his stored-up cynicism.

'At about eleven-thirty when I should by any account have been in bed,' he continued, 'I saw Webber doing his doorman-cum-bouncer stint at the Barbizan. I could have been mistaken in believing that he thought I'd come to jump on him for something he'd done and was uneasy about, but on reflection I'm sure not. It was all there in his eyes and a good enough pointer, even if a non-evidential one that wouldn't be worth a pinch of your snuff in a court.' He brooded on that for a few moments, wondering why he couldn't feel more enthusiasm for what he was working out. 'Some time after I'd left the club – I'd imagine very loosely between one and, say, two o'clock – Webber, possibly with Gogarty but certainly according to Magnus with another man, was attempting to break into Stephanakis's apartment. We know this because he was stupid enough to leave us his fingerprint. Also, typically Webber I'm sure, he was either too thick to know that we'd put a PC at the front or, if he knew – which I think he must have – too thuggish to give a damn that we had.'

'Or being under serious pressure from Sickert,' Lingard suggested. He had been gazing gloomily at the secondary problem of his soiled trouser legs. 'I shouldn't think he'd have much of a choice.'

Rogers stared into the ashy bowl of his gone-out pipe and thought about it. 'No, I don't believe he would,' he said. 'I'm sure you're right. As sure as I am that he isn't the type to allow his fingernails to be pulled out by Sickert in preference to taking the chance of being disturbed by a PC who he'd be prepared to bash anyway. So, after trying it and having been rather put off by

Stephanakis's anti-crime fittings, he's detailed for a wheel-changing job at Whitehorse Road. He goes there at three o'clock or thereabouts and, from what you've told me, has Gogarty again as his back-up man. Having done what he's there for and killing Kiddle sort of *en passant* – I think with you that we shall end up accepting that there was no intent to murder – he finishes up doing some bleeding himself. We can only guess that between then and five o'clock when he returned home in a bit of a paddy, he and Gogarty delivered the wheelful of cocaine to somebody and had a no doubt fraught meeting with Sickert who was probably, anyway, the somebody receiving the cocaine.'

Lingard said, 'I've already pinned my best shirt on Gogarty not being a party to the walloping and that, when he's thought about it, being sweatily desperate to say so to Webber's disadvantage. He's got a sense of humour with his stammer, so he can't be all bad.'

'He'll need not to be from where I'm looking at him. If his name's anything to go by, he's probably in Ireland by now. The Scotland bit must have been a blind, handed out by Sickert with the redundancy money. I hope you can find him because, apart from Webber's fingerprint, which if he's capable he'll deny is his anyway, we've no real evidence to connect either with anything I've been laying out as a sort of scenario.' Rogers could sense that Lingard was wholly confident of finding and exploiting a supposedly garrulous Gogarty, and that was good. But having a confidence based solely on what it was hoped somebody would say, or was going to do, was not a lot better than having none at all.

'Absolutely no sweat,' Lingard assured him, more cheerfully than he actually looked. 'Even if I have to verbally kneecap him into coughing up.'

'About Webber,' Rogers said. 'One thing I'm reasonably sure about – and it's my instinct that's talking – is that he didn't shoot Stephanakis. He's certainly manipulated by Sickert, but if he has more than the brain of a palaeolithic primitive I'd be surprised. I somehow can't see him having the intelligence to load and use a crossbow without shooting the bolt through one of his own feet. If he had orders to clobber Stephanakis he'd have used brute force on him with an iron bar. Such as, for example, that he used on the unfortunate Kiddle.'

'I'm not with you all the way on that,' Lingard objected. 'I'd say there's a fair bit of cunning in him and that's intelligence of a sort. I'll stick with him as a bod doing it for Sickert for the time being.'

'I couldn't argue that Sickert isn't behind his killing,' Rogers said reasonably, 'or, indeed, that he'd been pushed into doing the job himself. In fact, I've just come hot from being questioned by him about the possibility of Webber being arrested and making all sorts of nasty and unjustified accusations against him. He was, I'm sure, referring to his drug dealing activities, though naturally he wasn't fool enough to want to take me into his confidence. To warm his blood up a bit, I did get around to hinting that he might have killed Stephanakis from jealousy and what have you about Deborah, whom he used to bed down with off and on. That was a pretty damp squib and it didn't produce any reaction I could quarrel with.' He told Lingard the substance of his second visit to the Barbizan and, arising from it, of the threats he had apparently levelled at Stephanakis's widow.

'Under that blubber and bluster of his,' he said, 'he's a badly frightened man who's scratching around to cover up his involvement in something very nasty. Drugs for money, of course. He's still the same clever bugger and I just hope that Mrs Ascroft tells me enough so that I'm not forced to bring him inside on hope alone.' Rogers didn't look too worried about that possibility.

'Do I detect in your thinking that the Stuchley female had been stored in the room with the smutty pictures?' Lingard used his patrician nose to express his distaste.

'She could have been. Certainly some woman had been within a few hours of my being there. If she'd put the Judas kiss on Stephanakis for Sickert, he'd want to hide her in one way or another, wouldn't he? But not, I fancy, anywhere in the club when he'd invited me there to find out about Webber. A pity I hadn't known then that you'd already arrested him,' he mused. 'I could have made him sweat a very satisfactory amount of blood. Still, that's by the way. Weren't you more or less leaning towards her having been dealt with more permanently by having her tied to a bedstead at the bottom of the canal?'

'You suggested that, not me,' Lingard reminded him. 'And you certainly said you were fairly happy she'd written the note, although probably under compulsion.'

'Her father identified it, not me. He could have allowed himself to accept a forgery; wishful thinking, needing to console a grieving wife and so-on. Or, deliberately deceiving himself because the alternative was unthinkable to him. It's happened before.' He looked savage for a moment. 'In a different way we're the same. We have to accept she's still alive and under restraint because without any evidence the alternative's so far out of our ability to decide.' He turned the pages on which he had earlier written his notes. 'You know we've both been hazarding guesses about your blond character Tony having been one of her customers or lovers and now finding himself a dissatisfied reject, wanting to strangle her or somesuch?'

'We haven't found him yet,' Lingard said on the defensive. 'We haven't had all that much time, and nothing much to go on anyway.'

'I'm not being critical, David,' Rogers pointed out mildly. 'I wanted you to remind me of his description.'

Lingard raised his eyebrows. 'You've something up your sleeve and I can smell cheese in a mousetrap. You know as well as I do what he's like; about twenty-five, short with blue eyes, blond hair, clean shaven, well-spoken and according to Mrs MacGlusky a wee softie. You've found him?'

'I don't know for certain, but what's the description we've circulated of Deborah?'

Lingard cast a searching glance at Rogers, then frowned as he brought her out from his memory. 'Twenty-one years ... between five feet two and four inches ... slim build ... pale blonde hair ... blue eyes ...' He stopped, banging the heel of his hand against his temple. 'You're only thinking so?' he said.

Seeing the exasperation in Lingard's face, Rogers wasn't about to rub it in, he himself having been given a gentle nudge in that direction by Allegra Ascroft's then unregarded remark that Deborah wasn't a spoiled only child. 'So far, yes,' he agreed. 'Having constabulary oriented minds, I suppose that we've accepted without too much thought that our blond character was, or had been, sexually involved with her; that he'd been tossed out on his ear and was now frustrated to the point of haunting her and being nasty about Stephanakis for presumably taking his place. All surmise, of course, so what if he wasn't any of those things? Think on it, David, now that you've obviously compared their descriptions.'

'I have and I should've seen it before. You're going to tell me she has a brother?'

'She has. Two, in fact, and both unmarried. One we can forget because he's currently doing relief work in the middle of the Sahara or somewhere adjacent; the other's a junior doctor or houseman at the Thurnholme Bay Cottage Hospital, and his name's Anthony. Without our getting overheated about it, our sexually frustrated troublemaker might actually be a loving and well-disposed brother trying to help a younger sister needing to be dragged from a pit she's dug for herself, but who doesn't believe she should be and why won't he mind his own bloody business.'

'You've checked with her father?'

'Definitely not. I don't want to stir things up with a couple who I think have problems enough. Somehow, I've the feeling that Stuchley wouldn't have approved – at least he wouldn't prior to her being abducted – of his sons getting themselves tainted by association with their sister's whorishness.'

'I'm sure you're right, George,' Lingard said. 'You want me to check him out, of course?'

'Of course. When you've changed out of those offensive clothes of yours that are smelling up my office. I don't know where he lives, but try not to see him at the hospital if he happens to be working this late. I don't think that having Deborah for a sister would be regarded as a career asset for a junior doctor.' Rogers smiled broadly at a recollection he had not yet passed on to Lingard. 'I don't think he's likely to do all that well anyway, because he's been described to me on very good authority as being a grovelling milk-and-water sort of chap who drives a nondescript car fitted with four wheels, an interior light that works and a smoking exhaust. Lovely useful stuff that might help you to identify him,' he added drily.

'I don't know how I'd manage without it,' Lingard told him, standing to leave without being visibly moved by his senior's humour. His murmured 'Wherever did I get the impression that slavery had been abolished?' was only just audible as he closed the door behind him.

In the absence of the Assistant Chief Constable, who was able to leave his office with a clear conscience at six o'clock daily, Rogers assumed a ready consent from him had he been able to ask and took his spare shaver to his private washroom. There, looking in the mirror with pouched eyes scribbled with the pink capillaries of fatigue, disgruntled by a stubbled gauntness of features made more pronounced by the unshaded light bulb, he saw a confirmation of his need for renovation. Using his shaver and the lotions and deodorizer he found there, he made himself reasonably presentable for his interview with Allegra Ascroft. He would, he tried to convince his reflection that didn't now look too bad, almost certainly have done the same were his interview with a guaranteed non-starter such as Janet Whicher.

21

Before occupying one of the wall embrasures in Potters Row, Rogers checked out the others for anyone he might identify as having been sent there by Sickert, ignoring as an irrelevance the two manifestly over-affectionate juveniles who had fled with an untypical fear of exposure at his approach. Standing motionless and pipeless midway between two street lamps, his dark clothing made him one with the deep shadow cast into the embrasure by the moon. He was passed a few times by pedestrians, none of whom noticed him or seemed to have the interest in the house he himself was watching. For autumn, it wasn't a bad late evening. Unsurrounded by his usual tobacco smoke, the air in his immediate vicinity smelled sweetly of wood smoke and chrysanthemums, and the half-moon was now hanging in a sky clear of cloud.

Exactly a minute before nine-thirty the door of *Wattles* opened on an inside darkness and Allegra Ascroft stepped out, turning to her right and walking lithely up the slope towards the street's exit. Clearly visible in the moonlight, she was wearing a white belted raincoat – it prompted Rogers to recollect the description he had been given of Deborah Stuchley's coat on the evening of her abduction – with a handbag slung over one shoulder.

Prompting the detective to recollection wasn't the only thing the sight of her did. Keeping to the shadows where he could, and following behind her at a distance calculated to keep her covered without any possibility of an observer thinking them associated, he knew that the basic lower half of his mind was already seeking an ascendancy over what he considered to be his staid and cautious upper half. He accounted it a minor virtue that he could still keep most of his mind on what he was there for, deciding to dwell rather on the occasional solitary male who could be considered a threat and his aching thigh and calf muscles as he trod the steepness of the slope after her.

Though she was the subject of predatory, sometimes drunken, masculine scrutiny as she passed along the upper street, she reached the lane where he had left his car and turned into it without arousing in him any suspicion that she might be being watched. She was sitting in the car's passenger seat, a shadowed figure in the darkness, when he reached it. 'Good evening again,' he said pleasantly, climbing in. 'I shouldn't think you were followed, but it'd be as well if I moved from here.' The scent she wore, which he wished she had not, replaced the more usual, less dangerous, blue fug of tobacco smoke that haunted the interior of his car.

'I didn't know.' She sounded amused. 'I didn't worry either, knowing you'd be somewhere near.' It must have been his one-off use of the ACC's exotic lotions that made her add inconsequentially, 'You smell nice. I like it.'

He had no ready answer to that and, after too long a pause, said almost jocularly, 'Madam, just so long as you don't go on thinking I've been taking your name in vain,' starting the engine to conceal his sudden awkwardness.

Leaving the lane, he did a mental run down on where he could park and talk without exposing them both to being seen, and the reason for their being there misinterpreted by any patrolling and inquisitive PC; a place also to discourage any eroticism likely to be floating around in the confines of a perfumed and warmed-up car. He was a clot, he concluded gloomily; a clot running scared, as she had earlier accused him. One of his sociological criteria – he tried to convince himself it was rooted in reality – was that any woman would be a threat to his peace of mind could he not imagine himself holding back from her under a shared shower. Allegra Ascroft was definitely one to avoid happening on in that situation.

The sight of the graceless multi-storied car stack, silhouetted against the moonlit sky like an enormous gasholder, decided him. Driving in silence the steep spiral route to the top level open to the sky, he parked the car with its nose against the concrete parapet overlooking the lacklustre saffron street lights of the town. Now beyond being rectified without embarrassment, he saw there were no other cars there; and, he half-heartedly cursed himself, anybody not cretinous should have anticipated that on a late evening.

Allegra Ascroft had been silent since leaving the lane and he had the uncomfortable suspicion that she had been laughing at him. It didn't quite fit in with what she had told him over the telephone and he started a little more brusquely than was deserved. 'Mrs Ascroft,' he said, almost interrogatively, 'I'd be grateful if you'd be explicit about the complaint you made to me this evening. If Sickert has threatened you in the terms you suggest, I'm sure we need to take it seriously.'

She was fairly brusque herself then. 'I take it seriously enough to have decided to follow his advice and go away from here for two or three weeks. I probably know Geoffrey Sickert better than you; know just what he's capable of.'

'Tell me how he threatened you.' He considered that scent such as she wore so provocatively should be made an illegal substance.

'He telephoned this evening, as I told you, and first of all said that you'd been questioning him about the pig being killed.' She was looking sideways at him while he, appearing to be studying the strings of street lights spread out below them, was thinking she would find it easier to start without having his eyes boring holes into hers. 'I realize now that he lied about you believing I'd had a hand in killing him because he was holding back my supposed share of drugs money. I should have known then, but I didn't stop to think because he's so oily and convincing when he wishes to be and made it sound so completely possible. Then he said, did I understand how dangerous it was to talk to the police or anyone else about what Stef – that's what he always called him – had done on the side without his knowledge. He said he was seriously worried about my safety and suggested I should go somewhere abroad on holiday and stay there until things blew over.'

Rogers turned to her, staring at a face that looked less self-assured in the half-light, her eyes large and softly gleaming. 'And naturally Sickert wouldn't threaten you unless he himself had something to hide,' he pointed out. 'Something you obviously know about.'

She sighed. 'I almost told you before, but put it off. Anyway, I only know what the pig told me when we were together. He had once hinted that Sickert was his supplier, though he never said it in so many words. Nor did I realize then that he was supplying it to more than a few people he met at the club; as a sort of favour he'd told me. I honestly didn't know then how much he was involved in it. What later worried me about him was his explaining to me how large amounts of money could be passed through a business like the club, and he did say that he believed Sickert might be doing it.'

'While you were together, did Stephanakis keep large amounts of money in the house?'

'He did have a small strong box, but he never said, and I never knew, what was in it. I don't know whether it means anything to you, but he used to go to Holland – I think to Utrecht – several times a year. He said it was connected with his work at the club, though how that could be he didn't explain. Now I'm certain it was about drugs and that he was doing it for Sickert.'

'Aren't you rather guessing about Sickert?'

'I'm sure not. Once when I was working at the club I overheard him and the pig in his office talking about a flight to Rotterdam, so I did have an inkling they were both up to something that I couldn't see had anything to do with the club. Certainly while I was there I never saw any Dutch at the tables or anywhere else.'

Rogers wasn't wholly happy with what she was telling him. He said, 'Rotterdam's probably the nearest airport to Utrecht, so did Stephanakis tell you that's where he went?'

'No, he never told me. He used to say "All over" if I ever bothered to ask him.' She opened her shoulder bag and took a white envelope from it, handing it to him. 'I thought you'd be interested in this. I copied it from a letter he accidentally left in the bureau once. I don't know why, but I thought it could be an insurance for me one day.'

Rogers switched on the light and took a slip of paper from the envelope. Written on it in large italic – obviously hers – was *Christof Pronck, Keizergracht 18–7, Utrecht*. While it wasn't exactly white-hot as evidence, he thought it might put a Rijkspolitie finger on the Dutch connection. Returning the slip to the envelope, he put it in his jacket pocket and switched back into darkness. 'I imagine you read what was in the letter?' he said.

'Yes. It was some nonsense about organizing a package holiday flight for gamblers. Knowing him, it couldn't have meant that at all.'

'Do you have anything else connecting Sickert with drugs?' He was about to put her credibility to the test.

'No, only what I've told you.' She must have read the dissatisfaction he had put in his voice. 'Isn't it any good?'

Good in the legal sense it was not, being almost entirely non-admissible hearsay evidence from a dead man, but being neither much better nor worse than similar information with which he normally had to work. Perhaps – only perhaps – an item or two of it might trip Sickert into a hasty lie to his eventual downfall. 'It's useful, and I'm grateful,' he equivocated. 'But it's nothing on which I could arrest him. I'd need evidence of his possession of cocaine to remove him as a threat to you.' He left that hanging in the air.

'I see,' she said, biting at her lower lip. 'Then you can't do anything about him?'

She hadn't succumbed to embroidering what she knew and he was now prepared, more or less, to trust her. 'I don't go as far as that. Because he's threatened you, he's a worried man and worried men don't think straight. That information in itself has to be useful.' He was back to staring at the lights and wondering if Sickert possessed for himself an extremely conscientious guardian daemon.

'I'm guessing,' he admitted, 'but I feel that this evening wasn't the first time he'd phoned you recently. Wasn't he the somebody who told you, or warned you, that Stephanakis had been killed?'

'Yes, he was,' she answered calmly. 'I don't know why because we'd had no previous communication, though I thought at the time that he meant the news to hurt me.' She made a noise in her throat that could be taken for an inner laugh. 'He was that kind of a man. I suppose that's something else I should have told you, but frankly it didn't matter much and it could have led you to ask me all sorts of questions.'

'When I told you that Stephanakis kept under cover the papers relating to your separation and maintenance, you virtually excommunicated me on the spot,' he said, facing her again so that he could take in her reaction. 'I'd be interested to know why.'

'Hadn't you wondered why I'd never divorced him?' she demanded. 'God knows I had reason enough with his swinish behaviour. Haven't you considered that I would have done so hadn't I been forced not to? When I told him to get out and go wherever he wanted to with Stuchley, who he'd been sleeping with for ages anyway, he went quite happily. Or so I thought. It must have occurred to him later what I was about to do, for a few days afterwards he called and warned me that a divorce wasn't on.' She sounded introspective, her voice sad and tinged with bitterness. 'He knew I was in a position to expose him and his filthy pushing and he made it quite clear that as his wife – God Almighty. It sickens me just to say that word in connection with him – that as his wife nobody could make me give evidence of any sort against him. When I told him that that was his problem and not mine, he hit me in the face and pointed out that, being divorced, I'd be a very poor insurance risk. Those were his actual words and if ever I had wanted to kill anybody it would have been then.' She grimaced whatever it was she felt about that. 'He said it was no good me thinking he'd do it himself – he'd be somewhere else – but another man would who I'd never know. Then he said something about watching it and left me. Late the next night, like a fool, I was out walking my little dog when I heard a man behind me say "Remember this, doll", and I felt a frightful bang on the back of my head with something that must have been wrapped up because it didn't make me bleed. One of my neighbours found me and helped me indoors. I told her that I'd tripped and fallen over so that there would be no bother with the police and more trouble. Thank God nothing had happened to Gertrude or I might have.' Seeing his brief look of incomprehension, she said, 'My little dog who I love very much. For all that, I was frightened, as he knew I would be, so I agreed not to take any action other than to apply for a separation order through my solicitor. He left me with the house he'd rented and a financial settlement that I'm ashamed to admit I accepted, for I would have been in a terrible position without it. He knew that – he would – and had no scruples at all about using it.' She lapsed into silence, her gaze uncomfortably still on him, keeping him on edge in case she should distract him from digging what he could from her willingness to talk.

'Did Stephanakis use the stuff himself?' he asked her. 'On top of everything else he's done?' Without doubt, the man had been a conscienceless bastard and, for Rogers, there were times when the sum and nature of a man's villainies lessened his professional hostility to whoever had taken it into his hands to destroy him. There was a time for dying and its appropriateness had bestowed on whoever had loosed the crossbow bolt at Stephanakis some of the characteristics of a public benefactor.

'No,' she told him promptly. 'He only made certain that other people did, that they finished up well and truly hooked on to his wallet. He'd give out what he called tasters free of charge to do that.'

He stared at the pale oval of her face, recalling her telling remark about insects starting to bite, having heard something in her voice that needed his pursuing of it. 'Scream at me if you feel the need to,' he said gently, 'but were you one of them?' Though he had opened his sidewindow an inch or two for fresh air, he still felt saturated in her scent that filled the interior of the car with its sensuous and aphrodisiacal fragrance. It made a dispassionate questioning difficult.

She turned her head away from him to look broodingly through the windscreen, keeping him waiting. That would have been a sufficient answer for him but, turning back to him, she said quite without malice or resentment, 'I keep forgetting that you're not just someone I happen to like and who's here to help me, but a policeman who's probably trying to find out everything about me and to do me no good at all. You could be as bad as one of those nosy priests who say they want to save you from mortal sin but are only interested in finding out about the dirty bits to hit you with.'

'So you *were* one of them.' He nodded his head, making it a fact beyond question. 'Could I tell you that we aren't particularly interested in prosecuting users of dangerous drugs, that I'm personally only interested in their use when they relate to Sickert and to the death of Stephanakis. He supplied them to you, did he?'

'Yes, I was going to tell you in my own time.' She had resumed her staring through the windscreen. 'But he didn't start me on it. A friend gave me some at a party – twice – and then it seemed an exciting thing to do. She passed me on to pig, who was her pusher, and from then on it was all downhill. Not that it was much of a big deal leading to my marrying him, it just happened that he caught me at the tail-end of a rather painful affair. None of it's to my credit and I don't intend excusing it. Ages back, after I'd left the pig, I decided I wanted release from the habit as well. I did it by joining a drugs advice and support group and fighting my absolute need for it.' She turned to him, her green eyes a glistening black in the half-light. 'I expect you realize that it's important to me that you know I'm cured. If you want it, I'll give you my solemn word that I haven't touched cocaine or any other kind of drug for more than a year. Will you believe me?'

'I believe you,' he assured her. And he did, for self-denigration was seldom couched in lies. It left him with the administering of what he felt to be a sensible and diplomatic rebuff. 'You'll be pleased to know that if matters remain as they are then it's unlikely we shall be getting into each other's hair after tonight.' He felt a slight chagrin at the impassivity with which she heard that. 'There's just one last thing,' he said. 'You referred to Miss Stuchley earlier this evening as if you knew she wasn't an only child. Wasn't she?'

She frowned per perplexity. 'Did I? I must have, I suppose, because I've always thought of her as having a brother or a sister. I can't remember how I know, but she must have mentioned it to me, or somebody else did.' She hesitated, then said, 'You haven't mentioned anything about me going away. Aren't you concerned about that?'

'I am, of course.' Dammit, he'd forgotten. 'I think you should go as long as you tell me where. Not abroad, but some place where I can have you contacted if necessary. I'd like to put a guard on you here, but I'm afraid the threat isn't nearly specific enough for us to justify it.'

He turned the key in the ignition, starting the engine. 'Now,' he said briskly, 'I'll take you home.' His instincts were telling him to run for it. Not from her, but from a situation to which he knew his weaker flesh could submit.

'Surely not already.' She rested a restraining hand on his, appearing to have put the darker aspect of herself to one side and being back to her jauntiness of manner. 'There's more we can talk about.'

He could guess what was coming, was in several minds about wanting to hear it, but released his hand from a warm pressure nudging at his libido to switch off the engine. 'About Sickert?' he asked with self-acknowledged banality.

'About us.' She turned in her seat, exposing him fully to the headiness of her scent and the warmth of her body. 'Did you give any thought to what I said about you and me?'

'A little,' he admitted. 'But probably not altogether what you'd expect.'

'You thought I wanted you to go to bedders with me, didn't you?' Although said with a smile, it sounded dangerously challenging.

This was serious stuff and what he needed to oppose her, however amiably. 'That certainly did cross my mind,' he said drily. 'As you intended it to. Have you changed yours?'

She was studying his features in the little light there was, reading them like a text-sheet on masculine ambiguity, her own an unsettling few inches away and near enough for him to feel the soft exhalation of her breathing. 'Do you mind dreadfully if I say I haven't. I mean about wanting to be your lover. I know I wouldn't mind you wanting to be mine.'

Never in the business of affronting a woman's dignity by refusing what was a sexual invitation, he knew he had reached quandary time. What his reckless inner alter ego wanted was to grab her and, his overcoat and her raincoat notwithstanding, make violent love to her then and there in his erotically scented car; much, he remembered, as was the less than elegant custom in his own hot-blooded and impatient adolescence. Metaphorically putting on running shoes, his cautious, somewhat buttoned-down and professionally repressed sexuality made him say, 'What I might wish to do and what it might not be possible to do in the middle of a murder investigation are two different things. In either event, I don't know why you bother with me. You'd find I'm nearly always too busy or too tired, or more likely both together.' It was, despite his intent, a half-admission of his feelings.

She shook her head at him. 'I can see what you're thinking,' she said, not appearing to be put down at all, 'and it isn't true.

This isn't just about today. You are rather a public figure, you know, and I've seen you often in the bar of the Minster Hotel. The pig pointed you out to me simply ages ago and told me to keep out of your way because you were dangerous. That made me interested; well, it would, wouldn't it? He knew all about you. *And* about your affair with that woman doctor. I'm sorry if I seem pushy, but it used to worry me later in case you'd get really interested in her before I had the chance of getting to know you.'

'You're not serious; you can't be,' he muttered. 'I don't recall ever seeing you or him in the Minster.' He wondered how anybody, least of all Stephanakis, could have known about him and the departed Bridget Hunter. Not that there would have been anything in it for the smeary sod to use, but the thought of it would always irritate him.

'You didn't. Not him. He'd never go there. I said *I* saw you there. He pointed you out to me in the town. It probably made him feel more comfortable to know who you were.' Her teeth glistened white as she smiled at him. 'He said in his own sweet way that you were a hard bastard who'd arrest your own grandmother, that is if you had one, for a couple of drinks.'

He didn't tell her, but that was acceptable as a black commendation when given by a villain. 'There you are,' he said, seeing a sort of escape opening for him. 'Even with policemen you don't really know who you're getting involved with.'

He turned on the engine, suddenly all detective superintendent. 'I'm taking you back. I'll follow you to your door and I hope that you'll be sensible and bolt and bar yourself in. Don't open the door to anyone you don't know and dial the emergency number if you feel that you're being threatened in any way.' Switching on the headlights and reversing away from the parapet, he heard her say with jaunty confidence, 'You mayn't know it but you'll want me, I know you will,' and that wasn't anything for which he had an answer either.

Dropping her in the lane where he had picked her up, he followed her along the street and down into Potters Row where, pausing momentarily at her door, the moonlight blanching her as pale as the chrysanthemums at her side, she opened it and entered. Despite his age and experience, he had not yet come wholly to terms with female capriciousness and he was perversely disappointed that though she knew him to be watching her, she closed the door behind her without a backward glance.

22

Rogers was red-eyed with tiredness, bone-weary, disgruntled, hungry and self-admittedly not firing on all his cylinders. He tried to think of what he was not, and couldn't. Back in his office with nothing on his desk that demanded his immediate attention, he told himself he'd be damned if he was going to wait any longer for Lingard's return from Thurnholme Bay, deciding instead to book off duty.

Having been forced by the imagined shortage of time between his present impairment and approaching insensibility to buy a Tandoori take-away meal en route, he entered the street in which he thought he only occasionally lived and parked his car at its entrance. This, rather than parking outside his flat and advertising unwillingly his arrival to a Nanoushka possibly waiting in ambush. Cracks of light showing between the curtains of her windows justified his caution as he unlocked the communal door and crept furtively past her flat to climb the stairs to his own. He felt it to be shabby treatment of a lonely and nice woman who, unfortunately for herself, cared for him, but knew anyway that in his present condition he was in no fit mood even for talking to himself.

Outside his own door, his key held ready to unlock it, he heard his telephone bell ringing from inside. On any other occasion he might have gone in posthaste to answer it as if it were the possible bearer of financial good news. Now he waited, staring at the mahogany blankness of his door and hoping that it would stop; willing it to stop and to leave him in peace to eat his cooling supper and drink some coffee with enough whisky in it to expedite the coming of a night's unconsciousness.

It didn't stop and he unlocked his door at a deliberate snail's pace to answer it, knowing that such blind persistence in ringing could only foreshadow bad news for him. It did. His caller was the duty chief inspector, informing him that as he had driven away from his office an incoherent emergency call made by an agitated and anonymous female had been received. It was, he said, to the effect that an unknown man was believed to be dead in the car park at the rear of Lysle Street with an arrow in his back. The chief inspector had sent the uniformed Inspector Orriss, the only immediately available CID man, DPC Knowler, and three beat PCs to the scene, but had not yet heard anything back. Before he could leave the telephone and the logistical problems he was unloading thankfully on to Rogers, he was instructed more coldly than he perhaps deserved to refer to Standing Orders and notify those needing to know and those required to do something about it by attending on Rogers at the scene.

Replacing the receiver with a bang, Rogers, for probably the first time in his service, felt rebellious, thinking out aloud that whoever it was up there in the moonlit empyrean was making a bloody pig's breakfast of ordering the affairs of his over-exerted but still quite humble subject. Violent death was, he had to admit, primarily his business, though if he had ever considered its randomness of choice in his bailiwick, it was to be thankful that, so far, it seemed only to be happening to other people. Not yet caring to be definite in putting a name to the dead man awaiting him, he yet carried in a recess of his mind – wishful thinking, he reproved himself – a visualization of a grossly fat body lying in darkness with its now unneeded black-framed spectacles lying in a pool of blood.

Knowing that the murdered dead would always wait on his arrival, he thought he might snatch a few minutes eating time; then, hesitating briefly over the container of Tandoori chicken he still held, changed his mind. Not considering it to be either much to his taste or a tax deductible item, he tossed it untouched into the kitchen bin. After swallowing three paracetamol tablets to get rid of his newly-acquired headache, splashing cold water over his face and essaying a mind over fatigued matter revival, he left the flat, managing to pass Nanoushka's door without being waylaid. It did cross his mind outside that it was doubtful that there was that intention, for he had to accept that she must have been aware of his return, heard his feet thumping about above her head.

Driving back into the town's centre, he decided that while he would be considerably less than astonished to find the waiting corpse to be that of Sickert's, it would nevertheless alter drastically his couple of lightly-held theories of a motive for Stephana-kis's killing. Some murderous sod, he grumbled at his reflection in the windscreen glass, was playing silly buggers with the logic of his thinking.

Braking his car to a halt short of the entrance to the asphalted parking lot and a uniformed PC apparently there to keep lawful ratepayers out, he remained in his seat to take in what he could see of the locus of the killing. It was not a large area and was bounded on its left and right sides by the blank brick walls of high buildings. The cheek by jowl backs of the business premises of Lysle Street formed its rear, forty feet or so across from the access street of terraced houses from which Rogers was viewing it. The muddy saffron lighting of the street lamps barely reached the far side of the parking area, its deeply shadowed darkness relieved only by a cone of white light over the ticket issuing machine and the inner light of the telephone kiosk next to it. There were close to twenty cars scattered about, their rooftops misted silver under a bright moon. In the rear right-hand corner of the park and outside the back entrance to the Barbizan Club, two police patrol cars stood in close attendance on a brilliantly white Jaguar, recog-nizably Sickert's. Three PCs were maintaining a cordon sanitaire between the pressures of a small gathering of interested people and the three cars. Over their heads, Rogers could see Inspector Orriss, obviously waiting for somebody more senior to arrive and start issuing orders. Distant though Rogers was, he could already sense the disquieting atmosphere met in the presence of death. Feeling like an elderly zombie and leaving his car, he acknowl-edged the guarding PC's salute and put on the wholly false attitude of a well-slept man striding forward to meet a new dawn as he went to view the latest commitment to a dodgy justice that death had laid on him.

Orriss, an ex-army staff sergeant and a man of few words unless in answer to direct questions, said, 'Identified now, sir, and I've notified Control. He's Sickert . . .' – he jerked his head in the direction of the club – ' . . . the boss of that place there.'

What Rogers saw on the ground near the open door of the Jaguar, poorly illuminated by its interior light, was a tartan car rug covering the shape of a large body, the two ends of trousered legs and black shoes sticking out from beneath it. There was in it the unmistakable and absolute stillness of death. He crouched, lifting the rug and passing it to Orriss, studying the body revealed as a man might a page of rare postage stamps. Lying on his side with the moonlight washing ashen-grey those parts of his face not hidden behind beard and moustache, it was clearly a quite dead Sickert. His spectacles were still in position, magnifying the half-shut eyes, his expression suggesting a sudden anger with his mouth open as though stopped part way through a word by his death. A word, Rogers guessed, that would have been characteristically foul. He was coatless and wore a dinner suit with a pleated shirt and a bow tie. Protruding an inch or two from the fatness below where his left shoulderblade would terminate was the yellow-feathered butt of a crossbow bolt. A small patch of dark wetness around the butt gleamed in the moonlight.

Rogers stifled his repugnance against touching dead flesh and pressed his fingers on Sickert's neck, feeling it to be still warm though with no movement discernible beneath the skin. He resented his dying, his present unwitting slipperiness in escaping the snapping on of the law's handcuffs. Now, instead of working against the gambler, his death, apart from demolishing a couple of the detective's theories, would require him to work on his behalf in finding his killer.

He straightened his legs, grunting at the twingeing ache in his seized-up calf muscles. 'Put the rug back on him, Mr Orriss,' he said, retrieving his pipe from a pocket and stuffing tobacco into it. 'Then tell me what you've found out about all this.' While the inspector was laying the rug back over what had been Sickert, Rogers, putting a match to his pipe, noticed the silhouetted head and shoulders of an unidentifiable figure seated in one of the patrol cars. Somebody, he thought, the inspector was keeping up his sleeve, but he found it difficult to be terribly interested.

Orriss, having finished the covering of Sickert, said, 'From what I've been told, Mr Sickert, accompanied by a young woman who's now in the club with detective Knowler, arrived here at roughly twenty-two thirty hours to go to work. He regularly parks his car here – the white Jag's his, of course – and he was shot with that arrow business while him and the woman were getting out. Her name's Bowler, by the way, and when I saw her she was more than a bit hysterical. I don't know what Knowler's got out of her yet, but being with her boss when he bought it she must have seen something of what was going on. Seeing there was no argument about him being dead when I got here, and me knowing a goner when I see one, I didn't send for an ambulance as I knew you'd want the pathologist johnny to examine him as found.' He lowered his voice. 'We've an elderly lady in our car who's been wanting to go home and keeps on asking when you're going to get here. She's a Miss Froud-Bailey and, if you ask me, a bit of a Tartar. She heard the hullaballoo and saw Mr Sickert on the ground and dialled for us from the kiosk. I've only had a few words with her, but she says she thinks she saw who did it driving away from near where you parked your car.'

That hadn't been a bad effort and Rogers felt that he might make a profitable start on it. 'Thank God we've got a witness who's actually seen something,' he growled, keeping it slow and deliberate in case he slurred his words. 'I was beginning to believe we were living in the country of the blind. While I'm with her, would you get on the radio to Control and check that Dr Twite's on his way, that we have the prospect of some lighting and screens before daylight tomorrow . . . ' – he was being heavily sardonic – ' . . . and see that I get as many of my troops here as we can find. And Mr Lingard. He's probably at the Thurnholme Bay hospital so get him located and back here at full throttle whatever he might otherwise be doing.'

Opening the door of the occupied patrol car, Rogers said, 'Good evening, madam. I'm the detective superintendent you've been waiting for and I regret that I've been delayed.' Having done what he thought to be his mollifying of female impatience, he sat himself carefully in the driver's seat next to her and switched on the interior light.

Lean and cadaverously leather-skinned, Miss Froud-Bailey wore a sheepskin coat short enough to show a hairy tweed skirt over heavily stockinged legs. A deerstalker hat had been set uncompromisingly square on iron-grey hair. Apparently in her middle sixties, she looked as though she could still play a bruising eighteen holes of golf from the men's tees. She held a thick knobbed walking-stick in one hand; probably, Rogers thought, for use against anyone having the rare courage to accost her during the hours of darkness.

'Young man,' she said severely, 'had it not been for that nice inspector persuading me otherwise, I would not have waited for you at all. I only did what I considered to be my duty and now will you kindly hurry up with your questions as I wish to be taken home.'

Rogers liked her at first sight. She smelled familiarly of Parma violets and talcum powder and reminded him of his mother; and, in doing so, making him feel about fifteen years of age with pimples. 'As short as possible,' he told her, not too far from being deferential and hoping she couldn't smell tobacco smoke on his clothing, or suspect that he went with women. 'Could I ask you to tell me how you came to make the emergency call?'

She bowed her head. 'You may,' she said. 'I spent this evening at bridge with my friends Miss Hepplethwaite and Mrs Mottle at Mrs Mottle's home just along the road from here. I left there a minute or so before ten o'clock to return to my own home which is two hundred yards or so from Mrs Mottle's. When I was about to pass the car park, I heard a most peculiar slapping noise which quite startled me and which I could not then locate, although I am certain it came from inside the park. This was followed at once by . . . ' She faltered, her features twisting from an inner anguish, tears brimming her eyes as she suddenly looked very feminine and vulnerable. 'The poor, poor man. I saw him then, his arm reaching to his back . . . such a dreadful sound he was making as if his poor heart was being torn out of his body . . . and the girl with him screaming.' She swallowed and dabbed a handkerchief at her eyes, getting control of herself. 'I went over to them then – I was a first-aider as a girl and thought I could help, you understand – but I could see that he was certainly dead with that dreadful arrow thing in his back. The wretched girl had lost her head and was hysterical, so as there were other people there by this time I used the call box to telephone for the police.'

'I understand from the inspector that you saw the man who did it,' Rogers prompted her gently. He still liked her, but wished that she would get on with it.

'You understand correctly, young man; not, I fear, that it will be of use to you. The sound of that poor man dying diverted my attention from where the arrow was fired, but I saw – or I should say it is in my recollection that I saw – a man moving away from behind that van left near the wall . . . ' – she turned in her seat and pointed – ' . . . and then getting into a car that was parked in the street. That was odd,' she mused, 'because you don't have to pay for parking after six o'clock. Anyway, I must have heard the engine switched on because it moved away much too fast for the street and without its lights being on.'

'Was he carrying anything?' he asked. He looked again at the van she had pointed out. Anyone choosing not to use a crossbow from his own car would find cover from it and quite near to where Sickert had climbed from his Jaguar. O God! If he could close his eyes, lean back and think about it instead of having to do something.

She thought about that. 'I'm sure not. At least I don't recall seeing anything.'

'Could you describe the man?' The sound of a heavy engine and the dazzling bars of light that passed through the windows of the car signalled, he was sure, the arrival of the portable lighting and screens.

'Had I been able to I would have done so before now,' she rebuked him. 'He was never more than a shadow and for most of the short time I saw him he was moving behind his car to get into it. When he did that I was never then able to see more of him than about this.' She placed her hand horizontally at the level of her collarbones. 'The only certainty is that he wore no hat.'

'Don't think that I'm questioning your recollection,' he said cautiously, 'but in view of its being dark and your seeing the figure only peripherally so to speak, could it possibly have been a woman?'

She appeared about to send a cold blast in his direction, but then hesitated and said, 'Were I to have to swear on oath that it was a man, I would refuse to do so. But my opinion given to you is that I am certain it was.'

'And the description of the car?' he put to her; a forlorn hope and last resort stuff.

She sniffed, a superior sniff, as though to imply that he was being rather stupid. 'It wasn't a large car, or a small one either. And if you don't already know, all cats are grey at night and so are cars.' Then, surprising him, she said, 'It would be a witness to my personal philosophy were you able to assure me that there was some logic or justice in that poor man's death. It would concern me were there not.'

Rogers took refuge from disclosing Sickert's villainy in an absurd equivocation he thought possibly acceptable to her age and outlook. 'I don't know,' he said sententiously. 'Aren't we all a sort of greenfly cluttering up God's garden? And who knows why any particular one of us dies among so many?'

It wasn't acceptable, for she said sharply, 'Young man, you are quite definitely a fool.'

'I know,' he replied feeling chastened and opening the door to leave. 'But I do try. And I'm grateful for your help. I'll get the inspector to have you taken home.'

Taking the car's official issue handlamp with him, he walked over to the van she had pointed at and stood behind it. With an unobstructed view of the open driver's door of Sickert's Jaguar, he estimated it to be something like twenty-five feet away. Near enough, he considered, for even a man with an excessive miopia to hit Sickert's bulk. Using the handlamp, he scanned with no great expectations the asphalt for any marks or dropped debris where the killer had lain in ambush. On his knees and shining the beam beneath the van, his pessimism now proving misplaced, he saw a crossbow lying where it had obviously been thrown in discarding it. What appeared to be a yellow-feathered bolt lay against its stock.

It wasn't anything to get overexcited about. Not unless there was found on it the owner's name or an identifiable fingerprint, neither of which he was expecting nor putting any hope in. Deciding not to retrieve them until after they had been photographed *in situ*, he rose heavily from his kneeling – even that had been an effort – and called over the nearest PC. Showing him the crossbow and bolt, he detailed him to guard them closely, allowing nobody to touch them or to move the van without his express authority to do so.

Returning to Orriss, he found that he had finished his urging along of the essential services needed, telling the detective that the scenes-of-crime lights and screens had just arrived and were being unloaded. Most of the others were on their way, including Lingard who, having returned from Thurnholme Bay, had been in his office.

'Stay here and put him in the picture when he arrives,' Rogers told him. 'Then, as soon as they get here, I want the troops to start on a search of the area for anything we feel wouldn't normally be here. God knows what, but we might get lucky. Apart from having Miss Froud-Bailey taken home – she doesn't help much, by the way – see that nobody touches Sickert's body until Dr

Twite arrives.' He smiled at Orriss. 'I shouldn't be long, but on your head be it while I'm seeing what Knowler's got from Sickert's girlfriend.'

Before leaving the inspector to it, he lifted the rug from Sickert's body and took from his pockets a lizardskin wallet and a small leather folder containing what were obviously desk and safe keys. Orriss had eyed Rogers curiously while he was doing it and asked him if he was feeling all right, being rather testily assured that of course he was and having then to apologize for his shortness. He knew already with an all too familiar sinking feeling that whatever he would be able to put into motion at the scene was unlikely to reveal anything contributing further to the identification of a crossbowman with an apparent murderous distaste for a gambler and his dealer. Almost certainly not at the street from which, if Miss Froud-Baily was right about gender and involvement, he had fled nameless and nondescript into the darkness of the town. It needed, he knew, the godsend of a free and unweary half an hour or so of deep thinking without any external interference, or anybody else getting himself or herself killed or kidnapped, to piece together and to analyse what might have been hitherto regarded as unimportant items of information to make a sort of logical premise.

As if again to confound his pessimism, it was as he pushed at the door marked PRIVATE NO ENTRY to enter the club that the thought surfaced in his mind. By no means anything brilliant enough to make him more light-headed than he was already, it was, nevertheless, evidence enough to suggest that somewhere in the basement of his brain there had been an industrious subconscious working for him while the attic part with its fallible theories had been taking time off in lusting with its tongue hanging out after the forbidden flesh of Allegra Ascroft. Coincident with his opening the door he heard the deep throbbing of Lingard's Bentley and saw its distinctive dinner plate-sized headlights swinging into the car park. It was a moment when, as a tired shell of a man, he realized gratefully the sudden inestimable worth of a good untiring second-in-command. He closed the door he was about to enter and went to meet him.

23

Rogers had sent Orriss to the club to take over Sickert's office with a special responsibility to deny anybody not a police officer access to the desk or safe, and to send Knowler down to report, when Lingard, having dismounted from his Bentley, approached him. 'You've been banging my knocker, George,' he greeted him. 'I'm told you've serious problems with friend Sickert.' He said it with the demeanour of a man who had surmounted any that he might have had himself. He had taken his ordered visit to Thurnholme Bay as an opportunity and excuse for changing his noisome clothing and, dark as it was, he again appeared his customary elegant and attar of roses-smelling self.

'*We've* problems, David,' Rogers corrected him. Bending, he lifted the rug on the dead Sickert to one side. He felt that Lingard's apparent, though possibly skindeep only freshness made less onerous that which he intended imposing on his five years' younger second-in-command, and including with it the easing of his conscience. 'I've to return to my office and do things, so you're to take over the nuts and bolts part. Dwell on Sickert's deadness while I put you in the picture.'

It didn't take long and during it Rogers had handed Sickert's wallet and keys to Lingard and moved away with him to allow a scenes of crime crew to organize the lighting. 'You've caught up with Deborah's blond brother?' he asked. 'Or wasn't he our man?'

Lingard, charging his sinuses with the honey-coloured snuff, said between his sniffing, 'You were right, he is her brother. He was working a late shift or however they do it and I had to catch up with him at the hospital. As it happened, he was not only doing nothing but sitting down doing it with a rather attractive nurse. When she'd gone I sprang it on him who I was, so nobody else should know. He reacted to that as much as if I were about to clap the bracelets on him. Though there was something, I don't think on reflection that it was his anticipating getting bad news about his sister because he told me afterwards that his father had been in touch about the letter she's supposed to have written. And he said he was convinced she was all right wherever she happened to be. Which was his father's view as well, so he said.

For all that, I don't think he was particularly happy about it or about my being there. He was definitely twitchy and making a damned poor job of hiding it.'

'He visited his sister at least on the occasions we know about?' Rogers actually regretted that he had proved to be her brother, that he had lost him as a likely suspect.

'Yes, and more of course.' Lingard was more flippant than Rogers thought he should be. 'Though he started by doing a weakish bit of protesting that she was nothing short of being saintly convent material – and good for him that he did – he had to admit after I'd reminded him of the hard words they'd been heard to exchange that she could indeed be regarded as not only tetchy, but also as slightly blemished. Then he opened up. Trying to dig her out from beneath her current boyfriend and worrying his guts out because he suspected that she was on a drugs binge was what he seems to have been doing despite the whips and scorpions she was handing out to him. It wasn't in me to tell him, although he possibly already suspects it, that she was doing some of her fornicating on a commercial basis; or asking him how he'd have taken it if he'd wandered in on that other soft number Sleath while she was working on him for Stephanakis's benefit.'

'What was his reaction to Stephanakis's murder?' Rogers asked. 'I mean, he must have known she was living with him.'

'A stiff face and lots of decision-making going on behind his eyebrows. As if, I thought at the time, he believed I was suspecting her of doing it. Which I wasn't; well, not then and only keeping the book open. He said, "Am I supposed to be sorry that somebody had the decency to rid the world of him?" I told him probably not, but the question wasn't about the morality of it but about how his sister might be connected with it in some way.' The elegant detective pulled a face. 'My, my,' he murmured mock ruefully. 'I barged into a hornet's nest there. For somebody who's certainly a wet fish he was uncommonly sharp with me for even remotely thinking it. She wasn't that kind of a girl, he told me. She was fundamentally gentle and compassionate despite my sneering insinuations that I'd obviously gathered from people who were no friends of hers at all; that it was perfectly plain to anyone that having left the house long before he was killed that she couldn't have had anything to do with it. Which gave me an opening for asking had he any explanation why she should be abducted anyway and, if abducted, why she should be sending a don't worry I'm with a friend note the following day. That could have been the twitch-making factor with him, for he said that he had thought of it, but it wasn't anything that cut across the fact that she was obviously alive and unharmed.'

'And the last time he saw her?' said an unimpressed Rogers. He could see Knowler waiting to report to him. Detectives were beginning to arrive in twos and threes and they too were waiting, outside the cave of light in which Sickert's body was growing cold, for somebody to organize their activities.

'He says about six or seven months ago, and that was when he began to look on the sad side, ready to blub all over his white coat. He wouldn't tell me why not since and avoided what I kept asking him by saying, "That's the way it happened; I just gave up," and went on to ask me if his parents had been questioned about him seeing her. He was definitely nervous about that, though God knows it wouldn't, or shouldn't, have been such a crime. I told him I wouldn't have thought so, and why? He chewed on his back teeth and became very interested in his fingernails for a while and then said that him seeing his sister who had caused some fair old family upsets in her time would not have been approved at all. I read into it that she had been shown the door, cut off without a penny piece to her name and so on. I wonder why he bothered, she having been such a poisonous wench to them and him. If she'd been strangled and dumped in the canal it'd be no more than she's been asking for.' Lingard was suffering one of his occasional attacks of prudery.

'We won't get very fat out of that, will we?' Rogers could be philosophical about wasting time on a groundless line of enquiry, but he did prefer it to be recounted as concise as possible and painlessly. 'There's nothing else?'

Lingard hesitated. 'What I've given you so far is the truth as he gave it to me and relating to what I asked him about his sister. It's probably all we need to scrub him clean, though I can't make myself believe it's the reality, in fact it could be much less than the whole truth.' He dabbed finger and thumb into his snuff-box, his nostrils sniffing in the grains of tobacco while Rogers waited stoically on tiring legs for what he anticipated must certainly be anticlimactic even to the unimportance of what he had already heard. It wasn't a mood in which he would normally be and he knew that later he would have to make it up to Lingard in some way. 'You recall we'd more or less settled on our then unknown blond character being an outcast lover until we decided that he could be a well-disposed brother trying to help her?'

'It's what you've been telling me for the past fifteen minutes,' Rogers said drily. 'You've changed your mind and he isn't?'

'No, I'd bet on his having been both. Second thoughts omitted and all that tosh, I had a strong feeling the whole time I was chatting him up that he was holding back on his emotional relationship with her. It wouldn't be the first time by many thousands that an incestuous itch has had its way with siblings.'

'It wouldn't be,' Rogers conceded, 'and they used to tie them up in a sack and throw them in the Tiber or the Thames or some-where. Those I've had the misfortune to have dealt with here haven't made me feel that it's any mortal sin. So?'

'With somebody, with anybody, having if off with his sister there'd be jealousy wouldn't there? A special sharp-edged kind that would have a man grabbing for a thick stick or similar. It'd be enough to give him a motive, at least for putting down Stephana-kis. Very possibly, in theory, for putting down Sickert as well.' He shook his head and looked down his narrow nose as if disgusted. 'That was my fancy a half-an-hour back until chummy spoiled it by getting himself killed tonight. Still, one never knows . . . '

'Not one without the other, and that's a fact,' Rogers growled. 'You shouldn't be giving a likely suspect an alibi just when he's supposed to be out killing his second selection.' He became brusquely dismissive. 'And so far as your feeling about what acts of incest may or may not have been committed is concerned, I'd prefer we put that to one side. My own feeling is that incest between rational and consenting adult siblings is no more the law's concern than is adultery.' He smiled his rejection of any importance attaching to it. 'If you've no more, David, I'm seeing Knowler who I'm sure is going to tell me that Miss Bowler never saw a damned thing tonight. Then I'm off, so contact me only if you find anything likely to be earth-moving.'

Before beckoning the DPC over to him, he returned to the now brilliantly illuminated body of Sickert, already started by its stag-nating blood on the process of decomposition. Looking down at the dead face that now seemed to contain in it the terror of the last moments of his life, and seeing where blood and saliva had dribbled from his mouth into his beard, he thought about Miss Froud-Bailey's need for logic to justify the circumstances of his death. It was a need of his also, which, owning to a deep hatred for the killers of the innocent, led him often into examining for flaws the apparently innocent to discover whether or not the guardian angels, so-called, were exerting themselves sufficiently in their obligation to keep a benevolent watch on the good and the blameless. For Sickert, equally with Stephanakis, Rogers had every reason to suppose that he had earned his violent end, and his own approach to the problem of whom he now suspected to be his murderer was not to be affected by any unlikely lamentations over his sudden dying.

24

Having again doused his head in the ACC's private wash handbasin and sat himself at his desk, isolated in the deserted administrative wing of Headquarters, Rogers took from a drawer the collected papers of his investigation. The head dousing had not done much in the way of reviving him, but enough for him to stay awake and for it to underpin his amour propre, for any mental or physical impairment gave him in varying degrees a feeling of having been born substandard.

Before he started to read the papers he re-ran the memory reel of his visit to the scene of what could be accepted as Sickert's execution. No further information had been obtained from Knowler, who had stated his satisfaction with the truth of the account given of Sickert's death by the girl Susan Bowler. A sardonic Rogers had thought him dazzled in his naïveté by her bare shoulders and her breasts only just concealed beneath the white dress the DPC had been led into describing. She, he had said, had obviously been fooled into living with Sickert at the Kinnisdale Grange by his duplicity and a promise of marriage. Returning with him to the club, she had been halfway out of her seat in the Jaguar when she heard Sickert, who had preceded her from the car, give out a peculiar grunting sound as he reached behind his back and bend slowly to a kneeling position as he tried to support himself on the open door, then giving out his dying yell before falling sideways. She had rushed round to him, seen what she described as an arrow sticking out from his back and had completely lost her head, screaming and crying and, she thought, calling out for somebody to help him. She had seen nothing and heard nothing and Knowler, appearing now to be taking a jaundiced view of the dead man, was positive that what she said could be relied on. Because Knowler was young and not half cynical enough for a CID man, Rogers chose not to openly disagree with him. He had, anyway, anticipated such a result. As a precaution, however, he had asked Lingard, seasoned against bare shoulders and the like, to speak to her and check. It hadn't been the only chore he had unloaded on to him. When he had a man to spare, he was to send him to Potters Row, wake Mrs Allegra Ascroft, who would presumably be in bed, and inform her of Sickert's death. That and no more.

When he had re-read the papers, Rogers shut out as much of his external world as he could and did his deep thinking about attitudes and reactions to events. Where the physical facts attached to the death failed to spell out clearly a name, it was that at which his logic pointed that formed his new-born hypothesis. Of this, he was as certain of its substance as he was of his ability to flap his arms and become airborne. The frail and corrupt Deborah Stuchley was, as she had been throughout his investigation, the centrepoint of his thinking. With the Sickert killing a carbon copy of Stephanakis's, Deborah's abduction made even less sense, needing a further look at the implications he had earlier drawn from it. Those were that had she been taken by someone who could be called non-hostile in intent, her cocaine and much else might not have been left behind. The paradox there was that photographs of her and her parents had been taken. That is if they had, for they could have been removed or disposed of after Janet Whicher had been shown them. Had Deborah been taken by someone with an urge to kill Stephanakis then that made no sense either, unless shooting him down in the street outside could be thought preferable to waiting in his apartment after her forcible removal from it and killing him there without the risk of its being witnessed. Unless. And that 'unless' encouraged him to go a step further.

Odd that, he thought, breaking off and grimacing. Something pretty bad had happened to his palate, the tobacco he had just finished smoking in his pipe tasting indescribably foul. He laid it aside on his desk with the feeling that his body was becoming toxic, that he had better finish his thinking before it reached what was left of his brain.

Accepting that the note delivered the following day was genuine as vouched for by her parents, the question was, why had it been written? What was behind it? For a stop to be put on any police search for her? If so, why should it be assumed that the police had read into her being missing that she had been abducted, as distinct from being absent from the apartment for quite different reasons? True, she might reasonably be suspected of collusion in Stephanakis's death, but that wouldn't suggest to anybody that she had been abducted. Certainly what Janet Whicher had chanced to witness had not been broadcast. So the note was never, surely, sent just to stop her parents worrying about her being missing from an address of which they had been ignorant; and how in any case would she have been aware of their knowing of her being abducted at all?

Without thinking, Rogers reached out his hand to take up his pipe – usually, he had always maintained, his aid to a clear analysis of problems – then hesitated with a change of mind and decided to wait until he felt less ravaged. Instead, he opened the window behind his desk and breathed in lungfuls of cold air and the remaining traces of carbon monoxide from the empty late-night street below him.

Scratching at the facts of Deborah's abduction or her taking away, he accepted that, had it been effected by Webber and Gogarty, it was highly unlikely that Sickert would have done anything so foolish as to send the thick-witted Webber back to Disraeli Street to make what would have been a useless check on Stephanakis's whereabouts. In deciding that Webber and Gogarty need not be considered so far as any taking away of Deborah was concerned, he had also to scrub as unlikely any designs to that purpose by Sickert. Webber's later bungling attempt at breaking into the apartment was almost certainly done with an intent to retrieve the money in Stephanakis's possession, possibly together with anything kept by him that could suggest a drugs connection with Sickert. It left him still with a choice of deciding between her being jockeyed to the car with hard fingers circling her arm, or helped to it as might be done were she being taken away in a drugged stupor.

Then again, he recognized how the fat shadow of Geoffrey Sickert had reached long over everything and everybody that he had been investigating. Uninformative in life, it was unsurprising that in his death he was equally so, leaving little or nothing to connect him with the firer of the lethal bolt that had killed him. That brought the crossbow into relief. The abandoning of it would never, he was sure, be done in a panic to get away from the scene. It had been the instrument of a cold and murderous purpose that had been achieved, its discarding a mute admission of an end to the killings. The only support that it gave to his thinking was that it did not in any way conflict with the only solution to which his imagination could give room.

And that, Rogers now considered so far as any impairment in his thinking allowed, was that; the most he could squeeze out of what he knew. With no admissible evidence on which to base a decent interview, it was now a case of 'could be' rather than 'positively it had to be'. The only possible alternative to an interview with his suspect was for him to wait for Deborah to surface – if she ever did – and to find her in a mood of co-operative gabbiness. None of it was anything on which a sensible man would chance his arm, his rank and possibly his career as a crown servant. Should he not be fast enough with his footwork he might be unable to dodge justified accusations of malicious slander and unwarranted overzealousness to the *Police Complaints Authority* and from there to the office of the *Director of Public Prosecutions* for some inevitably bruising action.

And yet, he knew unhappily, he was bloody fool enough to be going to do it. Like a punched-out boxer able to find an extra burst of energy because he was no longer constrained by a clear-thinking reality, Rogers's mental processes were now becoming more inspirational than logical. Too, he seemed to have lost most of the caution that was so much a part of his professional persona. It would be a leap into the largely dark, though he would be careful, showing nothing behind an official impassivity, and sure enough of his uncertainty to leave himself room to backtrack if faced with contemptuous and right-sounding denials. Those, he comforted himself with his shaky belief in the decency inherent in the kind of person he was seeing, would be out of character.

Locking the papers away in his desk and putting back on his overcoat he left the office, not exactly smiling about what he had to do and dragging each step as if wading through the clinging mud of a bog.

25

Having parked his car well away from the house, Rogers walked soundlessly on grass and through a wrought iron gate into the garden at its rear. Standing out of the moonlight beneath a tree where the autumnal smell of dying foliage was strong, he took in what he hoped the shadowed back of the building would tell him in its sleeping quietness. The ground floor windows were in darkness, as had been those at the front. There were three latticed windows on the upper floor, two wide ones with a narrow one between. The window on his right was partly open with its curtains drawn back and, barely visible, a soft blue luminescence glimmered on the ceiling of the room. Rogers guessed it to come from a clock. It wasn't much, but something to show it to be a bedroom and presumably occupied. The window on his left had its curtains close drawn, its outward aspect dark and blank. That, he considered, was how it would be.

Moving to the front of the house and no longer needing to conceal his presence, he stood in the porch and rapped on the door with its brass knocker. He did it again before the pleasantly modulated voice he recognized as Dr Stuchley's came from a microphone grille unnoticed by him in the door stile. 'Yes?' it asked. 'Who is it?' It sounded the voice of a man not unused to being hauled out of bed at night.

Rogers bent his back to put his mouth near the grille and spoke. 'Detective Superintendent Rogers here, doctor. I'd like to have a word with you if you'd please come down.'

There was a long silence, then the voice said quietly, 'I see. Would you wait at the surgery, please. I'll be down immediately.'

Rogers noted that he had queried nothing about the lateness of his calling, the apparent urgency of his need for an interview or anything about his daughter whose situation should have been foremost in his mind. It added muscle to his confidence and he said firmly, 'I'm obviously not here for any medical advice and I'd prefer to speak to you in your house.' He heard the microphone click and go dead, and he waited.

Standing there in the darkness, he was well aware of the fear or uneasiness he would be causing in going through the routine of seeking an interview at night. A knock on the door at near enough midnight, his dark figure outside a possible omen of coming disaster or being the nemesis of a bad dream brought to reality by his knocking, could all be psychologically unnerving.

When the light in the roof of the porch was switched on, the door opened against a safety chain and Rogers was examined through its gap by Stuchley. Unhooking the chain he pulled the door fully open and let the detective enter the illuminated hall. Stuchley's face was held expressionless and there was no formality of a greeting. Wearing a wine-coloured quilted dressing gown with pale-blue pyjamas and leather slippers, his hair was not too ruffled or his eyes puffy from aroused sleep. As he led Rogers along the hall and past a stairway, the detective heard a door being closed on the floor above.

Stuchley, entering a door to a sitting-room, switched on a standard lamp and gestured Rogers to be seated, then sat himself to one side of him. Having only the one lamp lit it was a shadowed room, as much as he could see looking well lived-in, with pink rose-patterned chintzy furnishings, fox-hunting prints on the walls, lots of brass about the place and a small library of books in open mahogany cases.

Rogers, sitting in a softly-stuffed chair much too comfortable for his present condition and deciding not to commit himself too deeply for the moment and to skirt the real issue, said, 'I'm calling now, doctor, because I'm not at all happy about your daughter. In your position as her father, I feel you should be the first to know. The fact is, I now believe her to be involved in the death of her lover Solon Stephanakis.'

Stuchley blinked, his face tightening, a man patently on the immediate defensive. He said, 'I can assure you that she is not and never would be.' He sat stiffly, his usual florid complexion pale and drawn, his hands gripping the arms of his chair.

'Oh?' Rogers frowned, his eyes on Stuchley as disbelieving as he could make them. 'So, she happens to have told you why she went missing just before he was killed? And you're satisfied?' He shook his head. 'I'm not, and she'll have to come up with something more than a simple denial to satisfy me she's not an accessory to murder.'

'I know she wouldn't do such a thing.' The words came out haltingly, Stuchley staring back at Rogers as if pleading for the consideration of his asking no more.

'Your daughter seems not to have been abducted in the criminal sense,' Rogers continued as though Stuchley had said nothing. 'In fact, for various reasons and despite the evidence of the two men putting her in the car, we can rule out her being taken forcibly at all. There remain alternatives.' He paused, watching for Stuchley's reaction and, significant in itself, getting none that was perceptible, before carrying on. 'One is that she left the apartment freely of her own accord; in which case Deborah, being a known drugs addict, would certainly have taken her supply of cocaine with her – which she did not. But, say that she did leave voluntarily and overlooked the cocaine because of a coming event pressing itself upon her; then, unless she has an extrasensory perception of the future, wouldn't she have some serious explaining to do with her lover having been killed so soon afterwards?'

He raised his eyebrows as if expecting a reply, and Stuchley, though remaining silent, showed his inner turmoil by the restless rubbing together of his fingers. But at least – and Rogers was oddly grateful for it – the blue eyes showed no hostility to him for what he was saying.

'Another alternative and the only plausible one,' Rogers said, hoping to God he wasn't about to find himself ankle-deep in the manure of being wholly wrong, 'is that Deborah was taken away by someone who was dead against the way she lived and who cared deeply for her well-being. Cared enough to take her away forcibly or otherwise from a degrading situation and to make certain that she took no drugs with her. There were, apparently, no such objections to some family photographs, and it was obvious that it didn't matter what else of hers was left behind because he or they would no doubt think quite justifiably that it'd be tainted by its association with Stephanakis anyway.'

Stuchley's fingers had frozen to a waiting stillness at that and he had bitten momentarily at his lower lip. In the silence that was apparently the doctor's defence against the traducing of his daughter, Rogers thought he could hear the soft scraping of fabric against the closed door of the room they were in. It could, he knew, be only a listening Mrs Stuchley.

Lowering his voice, Rogers continued. 'That would have explained the ambiguous and rather unnecessary note you said you'd received from Deborah, wouldn't it? It did seem to me to be rather jumping the gun on information about her being abducted that had never been made public. If all that's so and she supports it, then I don't think I'd be far wrong in accepting that she'd been escorted from the apartment with the best of intentions, though for her part not necessarily willingly.'

Rogers stopped. The silence was now oppressive and full, he fancifully imagined, of the noiseless cries of a held-back guilt. With nothing further from Stuchley about Deborah, he knew that he was only a few words away from the truth. He leaned foward in his chair, not releasing him from the hard penetration of his eyes. 'From what I've told you,' he said, 'you must know that I have to interview Deborah to see whether or not she is able to confirm the facts supporting her innocence, or to admit her involvement in her lover's death. Even as her father you'd not be allowed to stop me from doing that.' It was a bleak and bitter choice he had presented him with, for Stuchley, unless blinded by his love for his daughter, must know an admission of what had been demanded of him would lead inevitably to his own ruin.

'You know, don't you?' he said finally, his words only just audible.

'That she's here? That she's been here since you took her away from Disraeli Street? Yes, I know.' He had taken the irrevocable step, step that held in itself so much trouble were he to be proved wrong. Now that it was done he didn't feel he could give a damn. Worse, he liked this man and putting him on the rack hadn't been anything in which he took satisfaction.

Stuchley made a gesture of resignation with his hands, his attitude that of a man with only trouble to look forward to. 'She's here. I had to do something about the degradation she was living in and I didn't believe it unlawful to kidnap

178

one's own daughter, if that's what you say it amounts to.'

Rogers rose from his chair. What Stuchley had said was true; there was no criminal abduction in the manner of her taking. But it made Stuchley's reaction to his questions about it a confirmation of the greater culpability with which he had burdened himself. 'I'd like to see her now,' he told him. He needed to stand on his feet in any case, for he was in the interrogation mode and that, for him, called for something other than the soft, almost feminine embrace of an easy chair.

Stuchley stood also. 'She's in no condition to be questioned,' he said dully. 'She really is a sick girl.'

'I shan't be speaking to her,' he told him. 'All I need is confirmation that she is here.' It was impossible that he should be put off and he was firm, needing to override his sympathy for this decent and likeable man.

Stuchley, a curiously diminished figure in his dressing gown, turned and left the room for the hall; then, with Rogers summoning up enough strength to lift his legs and stay close behind him, climbed the stairs.

Mrs Stuchley, wearing a floral bath robe over a nightdress, stood grim-faced and resolute on the dimly-lit landing, which appeared overfilled with white-painted doors. The one before which she stood was fitted unusually with two large bolts. She glanced from Stuchley to Rogers – brown unfriendliness in the eyes presented to the detective – then back to her husband, flicking her ash-coloured hair as if to indicate contempt. She was undoubtedly the dominant one of the pair. 'No,' she said harshly. 'She's my daughter as well.'

Stuchley, halted in front of her and looked more troubled than he had been with Rogers, was gentle with her. 'It's all right, my dear. She isn't going to be taken away. Mr Rogers only wishes to make certain she is with us. Please, my dear, I have his word.'

She searched for something in her husband's face that Rogers knew wives were prone to do, then said in a low voice, 'If you say so. I think she's still asleep, so don't make a noise and wake her.' She turned and reached, sliding back the bolts soundlessly and slowly opening the door to its twilit interior.

It was small room, Rogers saw from over her shoulder, that was fully carpeted though bare of all furniture but a single bed

179

and a small table on which rested a plastic bottle of mineral water, a plastic tumbler, a few paperbacks and a newspaper, a box of tissues and a portable radio. A small blue carton lay on the carpet with chocolates strewn around it. Heavyweight white metal mesh had been secured over the closed curtains and that, with the bolts on the door, made the room something of a cell. The pale-gold hair he could see tousled on the pillow moved and the woman in the bed, pushing back the sheet and coverlet from her face, struggled into a half-sitting position. Even in its dimness the light was not kind to her. Compared against the photograph he had seen, she was wretchedly emaciated, her blue eyes sunken in her lustreless doll-like face, her unpainted mouth set in an expression of utter loathing. For all her twenty-one years she looked like a badly corrupted schoolgirl, the fitting originator of the unpleasant fleshy smell that came from her occupation of a closed-in room.

Rogers clearly attracted none of her interest and he need not have existed. Staring at her father, she spat out viciously, 'What do you want now, you bloody meddling bastard! Are you trying to kill me!' then throwing a thin arm sideways and sweeping the bottle of water and the box of tissues to the floor.

As if she had hit him, Stuchley had drawn in his breath with a hissing sound. His wife, anger in her expression, said sharply, 'Now will you both please go,' and moved quickly into the room, closing the door against the two men already backing away from it.

'I'm sorry about that,' Stuchley apologized miserably to Rogers as they descended the stairs. 'She doesn't mean it. She's not herself at all and she does hallucinate occasionally. She probably sees me as somebody else.'

Rogers could hear Deborah's voice raised angrily in the closed room. 'That sort of outburst,' he said, 'is why, I'm sure, I was led to your surgery through the garden this morning. She's also acting very much less co-operatively than has the writer of that note you identified as coming from her. It does lead me to suggest that your wife wrote it.'

Stuchley, not answering immediately, held the detective's gaze with defeated eyes. 'Yes, but on my insistence. We didn't wish to deceive you, but it was necessary were I to have the time to get her back to what she had been. That,' he said earnestly, 'was the only reason I brought her home.'

They were back in the sitting-room and while Stuchley returned to his chair to brood on the patch of carpeting on which his slippered feet rested, Rogers remained standing to resume his questioning: his act of looming with intent, as he chose to call it. He said, 'The man with you when you took Deborah from the apartment – he was your son, of course?'

'He told me that one of your men had been to see him this evening.' Stuchley had mumbled that, not looking up and maintaining what Rogers saw as the introspection that followed lost causes.

'That didn't answer my question, doctor.' Though muffled almost to inaudibility, Rogers could just hear Deborah giving out the high-pitched wailing of desolation; an unnerving sound.

Her father had to have heard it too, though nothing of it showed in his expression. He said, 'No, it doesn't, but he must answer that for himself if he wishes to.'

There had been a finality about that, a definite refusal that could signal a mind now settled into an unwillingness to admit anything further. For a moment, Rogers felt the inner chill of failure, the frustration of being about to meet the immovable. He had no significant facts to throw at him; in effect, no ammunition other than perhaps a belief in a decent man's built-in need to clear his conscience, together with his ignorance of how much the detective knew and could prove.

About to throw a reaction-provoking Deborah at him again, Rogers said, 'This evening, Geoffrey Sickert, the former employer of your daughter, was shot to death with a crossbow bolt in the car park behind the Barbizan Club. The man shooting him was seen getting into his car which he'd left in the street near it and driving away.' He waited for any comment from Stuchley, who was now watching his fingers twisting on his lap like tortured worms. There was nothing, no surprise expressed in words or in his expression. Rogers said sternly, 'It does seem to me, doctor, that there's a strong possibility that Deborah supplied that man with details of the regular movements of both Sickert and Stephanakis for his purpose in locating them and killing them. If that's so, it means that she could, in the absence of any evidence to the contrary, be held to be as culpable of causing their deaths as the man himself.'

That was something else Stuchley hadn't foreseen and his face tightened. 'I don't wish to fight you, Mr Rogers,' he eventually said, 'but I cannot have you attack my daughter. What I did, I did without her knowledge or that of my wife and son. I did it through love of her and to save her from the degradation into which she'd been forced. No matter what she has done in the past or how badly she has behaved, she remains our daughter.' His voice broke and he blinked rapidly, seeming close to weeping. 'You've seen how she is. How could anybody remain indifferent to the dreadful things that were being done to her? When I saw her in the town, saw how pitiful her appearance was, what a travesty she was of what she had been, I knew that I had to do something. I'd be deceiving myself if I believed there was any real hope of her leading a normal and decent life, but what little there is determined us to try.' He breathed in unsteadily and blinked his eyelids again. 'She's the mental and physical result of what those men did to her, how they used her for their own filthy purposes. Do you blame me for how I feel?'

'It would be difficult to,' Rogers agreed. 'So we come to the point do we where you decided that the situation demanded more than just taking Deborah away?' He realized that though Stuchley had unmistakably implied it, he had been short of actually admitting killing the two men.

Stuchley breathed in deeply and held Rogers's gaze. 'Now that you obviously know, I've no intention of running away from it. I knew from the beginning that were I suspected it would be useless for me to deny it. I can't lie and I've no intention of trying to.' Though he was saying brave words, there was a pallor around his mouth reflecting the depth of the apprehension of what he was to suffer. 'May I make an analogy? When a physician meets with a disease-carrying virus he kills it. Or tries to. They were both dangerous filth and I did what I knew was necessary. I am not, I know, a cruel man and, in a sense, I gave them the mercy of a release from the vileness and corruption of their lives.' He shook his head. 'Don't think that I've any regrets for what I did, I haven't. I'll make no trouble, Mr Rogers, just so long as my wife and daughter are left in the peace they'll so badly need after you've taken me away.'

A sombre Rogers had been searching Stuchley's face for the truth of the confession and it was all there, though he found no satisfaction in it. With the non-professional part of his mind – as deathly tired as the part still on duty – he was wishing that he could tell him that though he had taken a sometimes flabby and ineffective law into his own hands, he couldn't find it in himself to wholly condemn him. Not for ridding society of a couple of conscienceless bastards who, by the very nature of their villainies, must have been responsible for the plunging of so many into despair, disease and, too often, a squalid and premature death.

Instead, he said tritely and unemotionally to a man manifestly willing himself to a courageous and dignified acceptance of retaliatory justice, 'I'm going to take you into custody, doctor, and to caution you that you are not obliged to say anything further unless you wish to do so, but that anything you do say will be taken down in writing and may be given in evidence.'

What he had said were the preliminaries to what would be the catastrophic disasters to his professional and domestic life that Stuchley must have feared, and Rogers hoped that for whatever later peace of mind he might find, it would never occur to him to doubt whether his daughter had ever been worth it.

26

Rogers, seated at his kitchen table at four o'clock in the afternoon, picked half-heartedly at a convenience meal he supposed should be called his breakfast. His eleven hours of mostly daylight sleep, though sodden and heavy from the toxicity of his stale blood, had definitely brought him back into the land of the fully conscious, though with a strong reluctance against breaking into happy smiles.

On his return to Headquarters the previous night, he had been kept on his feet for a further five hours conferring with Lingard and seeing Stuchley through the stultifying intricacies of prisoner reception laid down by the *Police and Criminal Evidence Act*. Stuchley, not waiting to be advised by a solicitor to either say nothing or to retract anything he might have said, had insisted on making a statement fully admitting his guilt, being then charged and placed in a cell.

He had said that he, in company with an unnamed assistant, had taken Deborah, too narcotized to offer any objection or to know what was happening, from her apartment in the absence of Stephanakis whose movements he had, on previous evenings, followed. He was then aware – how, he had refused to say, though Rogers believed almost certainly through his son – that his daughter had become a drug addict as a result of her earlier association with Sickert, being later dependent on Stephanakis for her supplies. With Deborah at his home and with the other man gone, he had told his wife that he was to do a late call on a patient, a not unusual happening, and had driven to Disraeli Street. There he had waited in his car for Stephanakis to arrive at what he knew to be his usual time. The crossbow, an elderly model, he had owned and used at university and had since stored in the attics and roof spaces of his different homes with other artefacts of the past, retrieving it then for it to be taken up in what he called its destined hour of redressing inflicted wrongs. He had difficulty in explaining the nature of his feelings at the time, other than that the dominant one was that this evil man had been, for the most part, responsible for the moral death of the daughter he still loved dearly despite the present drug-induced abnormality of her attitude towards him. When he had misjudged his aim and hit Stephanakis in the neck, he had been too long a doctor not to go to him where he lay on the steps. With infrequent passersby in the thick mist there had been little danger of either he or the man he had shot being seen. Stephanakis, he saw, was clearly within minutes of death and he left him, though not saying – probably because Rogers hadn't asked him – what he would have done had the wounding not been manifestly fatal. Returning to his car, he had driven home to begin the task of reconciling his daughter to the treatment he had devised for her detoxification. His killing of Sickert had been in much the same pattern as had Stephanakis's, his intent the more firm because he knew him to have been the initiator of Deborah's drug dependence. His statement suggested strongly that his feelings about killing Sickert had the emotionless determination of an intent already settled, for its nonexecution would have been, in his view, an injustice to Stephanakis who had already suffered. He hadn't been happy about the unclouded moonlight, but had relied on how few vehicles he knew would be in the car park in the late evening. He had shot Sickert from a close enough range to be able to assure himself that this time his aim had been accurate. Hearing the woman with Sickert screaming and realizing that another woman was walking towards his car left in the street adjacent to the park, he had had to rid himself of the crossbow – which he had intended disposing of at a different place – and then to get back to his car before she arrived. Until Detective Superintendent Rogers had called on him late that night, he believed that the woman had not seen him and that the rightness or not of what he had done would have been left to the judgment of his Maker; of which, he insisted, he had few fears.

Rogers had thought it an honest statement, but not one likely to elicit much sympathy or understanding from his earthly trial judge. Considering it, he had been able to convince himself – primarily, he admitted, because he wanted to – that neither a distraught Mrs Stuchley nor her son had had any hand in or knowledge of Stuchley's putting down of the two men.

Sandwiched somewhere between Rogers's dealings with him and Lingard's account of his coping with the fall-out from Sickert's death, there had been a telephone call from a divisional headquarters of the Merseyside Police. They, it appeared, had in custody on a drunk and disorderly charge a badly stammering man by the name of Daniel Gogarty. On being searched and found in possession of £955 in apparently stolen notes, he had been protesting to an uncomprehending Charge Sergeant his never queried innocence in what seemed to be the beating of a man to death with a golfing iron at Abbotsburn.

Lingard, having taken possession of the contents of the dead Sickert's safe and desk, had passed to the Drug Squad office the few papers possibly referring to his trafficking in drugs. In passing, Lingard had mentioned the finding of a large album containing coloured photographs of Sickert, usually wearing only his spectacles and gold wrist bracelets, on a bed and engaged in what Lingard called sexual congress of a sort with a variety of women. When told that the photographs had patently been taken by a concealed camera and almost certainly unknown to the women so grotesquely pictured, Rogers had told him to take the album to the basement boiler room and, without making any effort to identify the women concerned, to burn it. Though his doubt was minimal and it shamed him to own to it, his action had been partly a backing away from the possible disheartening discovery that Allegra Ascroft, despite her denials of any sexual involvement with Sickert, had been one of the women.

Done in more fragrant and civilized circumstances, he had heard it called a celebration of life and, when he had come out from under the vast amounts of paperwork consequent on the arrest of a man charged with a double murder, he anticipated that he might well be in high enough fettle to be able to do his own celebrating. That there could be two women with whom this could theoretically and happily be done demanded a possibly uncomfortable choice – if the choice was really his – and a measure of damage limitation.

With Nanoushka apparently keeping her distance from him, he had yet to find out if his credit with her was still good. If it was, there could be an expectation of gentleness, elegance and a lonely woman's affection. It was a pleasing prospect, though only mildly blood-stirring. In contrast, despite what he thought of the dangerously predatory Allegra Ascroft's previous misdemeanours and her suspect morality, she was potently attractive and definitely blood-stirring. Enough, in fact, to threaten the entrapment of any man's emotional freedom, and that was a danger he would do much to avoid. Naturally, favouring the one he had in mind didn't necessarily mean . . .

His telephone bell rang, cutting short his thinking. Regarding it with justification as the now implacable destroyer of his sleep and his social life, he rose from the table to answer it, already guessing that some ill-fated victim had lost blood enough to justify his being called out and to hell with whatever matter of non-importance it was he had been going to do for himself.